To Love Again

A Second Chance Nordic Romance

The Anderssons
Book 2

Helena Halme

Praise for Helena Halme

This is a sensational novel with some exciting twists.
5* NetGalley Review on The Island Affair

Another excellent first-in-series from Helena who has again created a raft of flawed yet lovable characters.
Reader 5* Review on To Melt a Frozen Heart

I usually try to avoid romance novels where possible, but Helena's stories seem to have something about them that draw me in and hold my attention throughout.
Reader 5* Review on To Melt a Frozen Heart

Cover @ Helena Frise
E-book ISBN: 978-1-7394723-4-4
Paperback ISBN: 978-1-7394723-5-1

HELENA HALME

The Anderssons Book 2

TO LOVE AGAIN

A Second-Chance Romance

Chapter One

Lapland, Now

The hotel shuttle bus hummed through the afternoon gloom, its headlights cutting through the swirling snow as Elsa Berg pressed her face to the frosted window. Each kilometre north from Kittilä Airport felt like travelling backwards through time, away from her constructed Stockholm life and towards something she'd spent ten years trying to forget.

Elsa noticed the other passengers chatting in various languages, their voices creating a gentle hum that should have been soothing. Instead, Elsa gripped her phone tighter, scrolling through Tobias's irritated messages without reading them.

'Spectacular, isn't it?' said the elderly woman beside her, nodding towards the blur of snow-laden pines through the window. 'This is my first time in Lapland. Are you here for the skiing?'

'Not exactly,' Elsa replied, grateful for the distraction. 'Just visiting friends.'

'How lovely. I'm hoping to see the Northern Lights while I'm here. Although the weather doesn't look promising,' The woman eyed the grey sky.

Elsa murmured agreement, though her mind was elsewhere. Somewhere ahead, in the warm lights of the hotel that were just beginning to appear through the trees, Victor Andersson was waiting. Not waiting for her, of course. He didn't even know she was coming. However, she knew that tomorrow she would have to confront him, the first time since Helsinki. Since the events that shattered her world.

The Hotel Äkäslompolo materialised through the swirling snow like something from a fairy tale, a welcome beacon against the brief Arctic afternoon. As the bus pulled up to the entrance, Elsa's hands trembled, though whether from the temperature or nerves, she couldn't say.

'Elsa!' A familiar voice called out as she stepped into the hotel lobby, and she turned to see Mikael Andersson approaching with arms outstretched. He looked relaxed, happy, the lines around his eyes speaking of laughter rather than stress.

'Mikael.' She accepted his embrace, breathing in the scent of his cologne. 'You look wonderful. Marriage suits you.'

'Happiness suits me,' he corrected with a grin. 'I can't believe you're here. After all these years of Christmas cards and promises to visit –'

'I know, I know. Life got complicated.' She gestured, encompassing her Stockholm existence, her legal career, everything that had kept her away from Finland – and from the memories this place held.

'And your boyfriend? Tobias?' Mikael's eyes moved past her shoulder, searching the small group of guests still collecting their luggage.

'He's coming. Work crisis.' The lie came easily. She found explaining the truth, that she'd needed those few hours alone to prepare herself for what was coming, too complicated.

Mikael's expression grew more serious. 'Elsa, I should mention –'

'Victor will be here.' She cut him off, surprised by how steady her voice sounded. 'I assumed he would be. He's your brother, after all.'

'He's my best man.' Mikael observed her for a moment. 'I wasn't sure if you knew. I'm sorry if that's a problem –'

'It's not a problem.' Another lie, but what was the alternative? She'd already made the journey, already disrupted her life to be here for one of her oldest friends. 'It was a long time ago, Mikael. We're both adults now.'

Relief flooded his features. 'Good. That's – good. Because I was worried –' He paused, then seemed to decide. 'Oh, and Kat and I are having a small pre-wedding dinner this evening. Nothing formal, just close friends and family. We'd love for you and Tobias to join us, if he makes it in time.'

Elsa felt her stomach drop. A pre-wedding dinner meant hours of proximity to Victor, forced conversation, and the pretense of normality. 'That sounds lovely,' she managed to say.

'I hope Tobias will make it,' Mikael continued, though there was something in his tone that suggested he wasn't sure about her boyfriend. 'These work emergencies – they have a way of dragging on, don't they?'

'He'll be here,' Elsa said with more confidence than she felt. 'He promised he wouldn't miss the wedding.'

'Of course. Well, I should let you get settled.' He was already walking towards the reception desk but then paused. 'Elsa? I'm glad you're here. Whatever happened between you and Victor – I'm glad it didn't stop you from coming.'

As the lift doors closed behind her, Elsa caught her reflection in the polished metal – pale, apprehensive, but determined. In just a few hours, she might see Victor Andersson again. Tonight, she might discover whether the feelings she'd buried were dead, or whether some ghosts were too powerful to stay buried.

The thought terrified her.

It also, she admitted, thrilled her.

Chapter Two

While Elsa prepared herself for the surprise dinner, she thought about seeing Victor again and her tummy flipped. She wasn't ready to meet him yet. She needed more time and a good night's sleep. The day had been a long one; a busy morning at work, trying to ensure her brief absence wouldn't be noticed, followed by the journey. Luckily, while she was in the cab on the way to the airport in Stockholm, a text from her assistant, Emma, had reassured her.

'Lindqvist meeting confirmed for Monday am. Hope the wedding is lovely!'

Elsa had smiled at Emma's efficiency – after five years, her assistant knew exactly how to keep her life organised even from a distance.

But the rush to the airport and a long bus journey to the Ylläs resort, and then Tobias's arrival, had left her exhausted. Perhaps she should make an excuse and cancel?

Tobias was even more negative about the dinner than the wedding itself.

'Do we really have to go to some pre-wedding social gathering too?' he'd complained, adjusting his tie in the mirror. 'Isn't suffering through the ceremony and reception enough?'

'It's just dinner, Tobias. Mikael is one of my oldest friends.'

'A friend you hadn't spoken to in years until you bumped into him at that tech thing,' Tobias had countered, his tone dismissive. 'And now suddenly, we've flown to the middle of nowhere for his wedding to some English girl we've never met.'

Elsa had felt her jaw tighten, but she'd forced herself to stay calm. 'Her name is Kat, and I've told you why this matters to me.'

But she hadn't told him everything. She couldn't tell him about Victor.

Tobias's reaction made up her mind. If she could handle difficult clients like the unpredictable Finnish tech entrepreneur, she could meet an old flame. Perhaps he too had moved on and was here with a long-standing partner? Mikael hadn't mentioned a girlfriend earlier, but that was hardly unusual. Even when Elsa and Victor had been together, Mikael had avoided talking about Victor. The brothers had never seen eye to eye, which is why Elsa was surprised to hear he was Mikael's best man.

Elsa decided to forget about Victor and concentrate on her old friend and his happy forthcoming nuptials. She'd hastily reapplied her make-up, giving her a renewed glow and going some way to hide the dark circles under her eyes. She snapped closed the powder compact and smoothed the satin skirt over her hips. She'd teamed the ice-blue skirt with a soft baby-blue mohair jumper, tucked into the waistband to further show off her figure. Knee-length black suede boots with block heels completed the look. The effect, she hoped, was sexy, yet not obviously so. She didn't want to look as though she'd tried too hard, after all.

The dinner was held in a traditional building with a steepled roof made of thick logs, seemingly in the middle of nowhere. A large sign and lights illuminating the contours of the building marked it out as a restaurant. Stepping inside, she was met with a rush of warmth and a rumble of noise coming from an opening at the far end of the room.

A woman in a black dress directed her to a room beyond the restaurant where a few tables were filled with diners. Elsa breathed with relief when she saw there was no sign of Victor.

Tobias's mood hadn't improved during the short taxi ride from their hotel. He'd spent most of the journey checking his phone. When he spoke, he'd made disparaging comments about the 'authentic Finnish wilderness experience'. When they arrived at the log restaurant, he looked as though he was attending a funeral rather than a celebration.

'How charmingly rustic,' he muttered under his breath as they were directed to their table, loud enough for the hostess to hear.

Elsa wanted to disappear into the floor.

But the atmosphere around them was joyous. Kat was warm and bubbly, immediately putting Elsa at ease with her infectious enthusiasm and genuine interest in hearing about Stockholm and Elsa's work. Mikael looked happier than Elsa had ever seen him, his usual quiet demeanour brightened by an obvious contentment that shone out whenever he looked at his bride-to-be.

The other guests were a delightful mix of Kat's London friends and family, including her mother Simona, brother Daniel, and sister Lily, and some of Mikael's new friends from Lapland, though she couldn't see his brother or parents. Elsa was particularly charmed by Pat and Reg, an older London couple who were investors in Mikael's ski school venture. Their silver hair and warm handshakes reminded her of her beloved grandparents.

'Where's the best man then?' Daniel, a rather good-looking male version of Kat asked, glancing around the table with a grin. 'Shouldn't he be here making embarrassing speeches about the groom?'

Mikael's expression tightened almost imperceptibly. 'Victor's flight was delayed. He'll be here first thing in the morning,' he said.

'Cutting it rather fine, isn't he?' Kat's mother, Simona, observed with raised eyebrows.

'He'll be there,' Mikael said, though Elsa caught the note of uncertainty in his voice. 'Our parents are on the same flight, actually. They're staying at the family chalet rather than the hotel.'

There was something in his tone – a careful neutrality – that suggested this arrangement wasn't entirely his choice.

'How lovely that they're all coming together,' Kat said brightly, but Elsa noticed the quick glance she exchanged with her fiancé.

'Yes,' Mikael replied simply, reaching for his wine glass. 'Lovely.'

The brief silence that followed spoke volumes about family dynamics. Elsa found herself wondering what tensions lay beneath Mikael's diplomatic response. She couldn't pretend she wasn't relived, though. She would get another few hours' reprieve before having to confront Victor. Her solace was short-lived, however, because Tobias seemed determined to spoil the evening for her.

When Kat enthusiastically explained their plans for sustainable tourism and Mikael's environmental activism against the proposed mine, Tobias interrupted with a dismissive snort.

'Sustainable tourism in Lapland?' he said, cutting across Kat mid-sentence. 'That's quite the oxymoron, isn't it? Flying people from around the world to see untouched wilderness rather defeats the purpose.'

The table fell into an uncomfortable silence. Kat's

bright smile faltered slightly, and Elsa saw Mikael's jaw tighten again.

'We're very conscious of our carbon footprint,' Kat replied carefully. 'We encourage guests to stay longer to make their journey worthwhile, and we offset all flights through verified reforestation programmes.'

'How wonderfully naive,' Tobias responded, reaching for his wine glass. 'I'm sure the environment will thank you for that.'

'Tobias,' Elsa hissed under her breath, but he either didn't hear her or chose to ignore the warning.

The situation deteriorated from then on. When the conversation turned to local Sami culture and traditions – something clearly close to Mikael and Kat's hearts – Tobias made a comment about 'playing dress-up for tourists' that left several people at the table visibly offended.

Kat's younger brother Daniel tried to rescue the conversation by asking Tobias about his work, but even that backfired when Tobias launched into a monologue about criminal law that managed to be both boring and condescending.

'The problem with idealistic environmental ventures,' he declared while cutting into his reluctantly chosen vegan main course, 'is that they rarely survive contact with economic reality. Good intentions don't pay the bills.'

'Actually,' Pat said mildly, 'we've found Mikael's business model to be quite sound. The numbers are very encouraging.'

Tobias gave the older woman a patronising smile.

'Of course, early investor optimism is common. The real test comes when you need to scale.'

Elsa spent most of the dinner apologising with her eyes to everyone at the table, while also trying to deflect or soften Tobias's increasingly inappropriate comments. She watched Mikael's expression grow more strained as the evening progressed, and she caught Kat shooting concerned glances at her fiancé.

The final straw came during dessert when Kat mentioned how excited she was about their small, intimate wedding ceremony.

'We wanted something authentic and meaningful,' she said, her eyes sparkling. 'No fuss, just the people who really matter to us in a place that's become so special.'

'How refreshingly anti-establishment,' Tobias replied dryly. 'Though I suppose it will have been a lot cheaper too.'

The silence that followed was deafening. Elsa felt her cheeks burn with humiliation as she saw the hurt flash across Kat's face and sheer anger tighten Mikael's features.

'Actually,' Mikael said quietly, his voice carefully controlled, 'we could afford any kind of wedding we wanted. We chose this because it reflects who we are.'

Tobias shrugged, apparently oblivious to the tension he'd created.

It was Reg who finally saved the evening. He changed the subject to ask about local wildlife, engaging Mikael in a conversation about the area's ecosystem. But the damage had been done. The warm, celebratory atmosphere was replaced by polite but strained conversation, and Elsa spent the rest of the evening waiting for the moment they could gracefully leave.

When they finally returned to their hotel room, Elsa was too furious and embarrassed to speak.

Tobias, seemingly unaware of his behaviour, complained about the food and the 'pretentious environmental messaging', at which point she locked herself in the bathroom to avoid saying something she'd regret.

Chapter Three

Victor Andersson sat in the front row of the aircraft alone, gazing down at the snowy landscape. They were just about to land at Kittilä airport. He'd made this journey more times than he could remember, but this time was different. This time he'd been dragged more or less against his will to attend his wayward brother's wedding.

Victor glanced across the aisle, where his father, Erik, and mother, Ulla, sat. Ulla had her eyes closed, but her rigid posture suggested she wasn't asleep. She'd been tense throughout the flight, her usual composure strained by what lay ahead. Erik, on the other hand, was engrossed in something on his large iPad – probably reviewing the final environmental impact assessments for the Northern project. With his reading glasses perched at the end of his nose, he could be mistaken for a well-meaning grandfather. Victor knew he was anything but. Erik Andersson was a man who expected results, and life was considerably easier when Victor delivered them.

The sun was just at the top of the clouds, a red and orange glow that briefly blinded Victor, before the plane descended through the cloud cover and the runway came into view. Victor glanced at his watch. 6.55 am. They were punctual at least. He'd have time to do what his father had asked before he was needed at the church.

The wedding itself would be tedious, Victor knew. His mother had insisted he accept Mikael's invitation to be best man, and Victor had learned not to disappoint her when she truly wanted something. It was easier to comply than to endure the guilt and emotional manipulation that would follow a refusal. Besides, someone had to represent the family properly at this spectacle.

Outside the airport, Victor and his parents said a brief goodbye. The family dynamics were complicated enough without spending the entire weekend together. Victor would be staying at the hotel with the other guests, while Ulla and Erik had chosen to overnight at the family's luxurious villa.

Victor was pleased to see the usual man at the wheel of the car he had booked. Matti would know where to take him, and he wasn't chatty. Today, Victor needed to focus on the task Erik had given him – a final site assessment before next week's board meeting. Nothing complicated, just ensuring he was fully briefed on the current status.

Take me to the site, please,' Victor told the driver

after putting his bag in the boot and getting into the back seat of the large black Mercedes.

As they turned away from the airport, Victor noticed the protest banners hanging from shop windows throughout Kittilä. 'NO MINES IN LAPLAND' in both Finnish and English. Some displayed photographs of reindeer and traditional Sami clothing. Victor felt the familiar weary resignation that came with his family name – always someone protesting something, always complications that made simple business more difficult than it needed to be.

'They've been busy,' Matti, the driver, observed, following Victor's gaze.

'The protesters?'

'Your brother's new wife and her friends. They've got people worked up.' Matti's tone was carefully neutral. 'Creates a lot of noise, anyway.'

Victor nodded absently. Erik had briefed him on the opposition, of course. It was always the same – emotional appeals, carefully selected photographs, people who didn't understand the complexities of modern industrial development. His father would handle the politics; Victor just needed to be informed enough to answer any technical questions that might arise.

As they drove through the town, Victor mentally catalogued what he saw – the seasonal businesses, the quiet streets, the general sense of a community that could benefit from year-round employment. Not that it was his job to make those judgements. Erik would decide the strategy; Victor would implement whatever was required.

Twenty minutes later, they reached the site. Victor had Matti wait while he walked to the edge of the proposed excavation area. The morning air was bitingly cold, but he forced himself to spend the time to make a proper assessment.

Standing there, Victor mentally reviewed the geological surveys he'd studied. The data was solid – substantial copper deposits, manageable extraction challenges, standard environmental mitigation procedures. Nothing in the reports suggested any significant problems, which meant the board meeting should proceed smoothly.

He pulled out his phone and took several photographs from different angles, then made notes about the current site conditions. Erik expected thorough preparation, and Victor had learned that attention to detail prevented uncomfortable questions later.

His phone buzzed with a text from his father: *Board meeting moved to Monday. Need your site assessment by tomorrow evening.*

Victor typed back a quick confirmation. The timeline was tight, but manageable. He'd already all but finished the report, and just needed to amend it in a few places. He'd complete his observations before the wedding and send Erik a comprehensive report.

Walking back to the car, Victor felt the familiar satisfaction of a task nearly completed. He wasn't passionate about mining the way his father was, but he understood his role in the family enterprise. Do the work competently, avoid unnecessary complications, support Erik's decisions – it was a straightforward arrangement that had served him well.

'Seen enough?' Matti asked as Victor settled back into the Mercedes.

'For now,' Victor replied, already thinking about his report structure. Technical assessment, environmental considerations, logistical factors – Erik would want comprehensive coverage but nothing that raised unnecessary concerns.

The hotel appeared in the distance, and Victor prepared himself for the social performance that lay ahead. Check in, greet the appropriate people, play the role of supportive older brother and dutiful company representative. It wasn't particularly challenging, just another aspect of his responsibilities.

In his room, Victor laid out his suit and reviewed his report. It took less time than he'd imagined, so he had a few moments to close his eyes and lay down on the bed.

An hour later, dressed and ready for his role as best man, Victor caught sight of himself in the full-length mirror. He looked exactly what he was – a competent mining executive doing his job, supporting his family's interests, taking the path that required the least effort and created the fewest problems.

Today was about getting through Mikael's wedding without incident and maintaining the family's reputation. Simple, manageable objectives that didn't require passion or deep conviction – just professional competence and social awareness.

Standing at the window, looking out at the snow-covered landscape, Victor felt neither satisfaction nor regret. This was simply what was expected of him, and he'd learned long ago that meeting expectations was the most efficient way to live.

Chapter Four

'For God's sake, Elsa, it's freezing!'

Elsa heard Tobias's sharp curse as he stepped carefully from the other side of the taxi, his expensive leather shoes evidently sinking into the pristine snow. She emerged more cautiously, her hands trembling – though whether from cold or nerves, she couldn't say. The Ylläs Chapel rose before them like something from a fairy tale, its red wooden walls and white-capped spire standing proud against the endless expanse of snow-laden pines. It should have been breathtaking. Instead, all she could feel was the growing knot of dread in her stomach.

She watched Tobias pull his coat tighter around himself, his breath forming clouds in the frigid morning light as he struggled to find purchase on the icy ground.

'It's beautiful,' she murmured, more to herself than to Tobias, who was already paying the driver with visible impatience.

'It's bloody in the middle of nowhere is what it is,' Tobias replied, banging the car door shut with unnecessary force. 'Remind me again why we couldn't have just sent a gift and stayed in Stockholm? I've got the Akerman case next week, and I should be preparing –'

'Because Mikael is one of my oldest friends,' Elsa interrupted, her voice sharper than intended. They'd had this argument three times in Stockholm, and she was exhausted by it. 'I told you that.'

Tobias's pale blue eyes fixed on her with the same expression he wore when cross-examining a hostile witness. 'One of your oldest friends whom you haven't seen in years. One conversation in a Helsinki bar doesn't exactly constitute a close relationship, Elsa.'

The taxi pulled away, leaving them standing in the chapel's small car park surrounded by other arriving guests. Elsa watched families emerge from sleek cars, children squealing with delight at the snow, couples laughing as they helped each other navigate the icy path. Everyone seemed to belong here except them.

Except her.

'You didn't have to come,' Elsa said quietly, adjusting her coat – a fitted fake fur – and trying to project a confidence she didn't feel. 'I told you I was perfectly capable of travelling alone.'

'Oh yes, I'm sure you would have loved that,' Tobias's tone was dry, professional.

The accusation stung because it held a grain of truth. She had been relieved when Tobias initially said he couldn't attend, claiming work commitments. It was only at the last minute that he'd changed his mind. Something about not wanting her to travel alone to 'the middle of nowhere to see people she barely knew.'

But that wasn't the real reason for his change of heart, and they both knew it.

'Tobias – ' she began, but he was already walking towards the chapel entrance, his long stride forcing her to hurry to keep up.

'Let's just get this over with,' he said without looking back. 'Smile, eat whatever plant-based nightmare they're serving, then get back to civilisation tomorrow morning.'

Elsa felt her cheeks burn with embarrassment as several other guests turned to look at them. Tobias's voice carried in the crisp air, his dismissive tone impossible to miss even if he was speaking Swedish. She wanted to apologise to these strangers, to explain that he wasn't usually this rude, but the words stuck in her throat.

Because lately, this was exactly how Tobias usually was.

As they approached the chapel doors, Elsa caught sight of her reflection in the antique glass panels. The collar of the ice-blue wrap dress she'd chosen, just visible under her coat, made her eyes look almost emerald, and the beautiful coat emphasised her slim figure. She'd taken more care with her appearance this morning than she had in months, telling herself it was simply because it was a special occasion.

But her heart knew better.

'Deep breaths,' she whispered to herself, the same words she'd been repeating since waking at 4am, staring at the ceiling while Tobias slept peacefully beside her.

The chapel doors opened, releasing a wave of warm air scented with pine and melting candle wax. The gentle murmur of conversation drifted out, punctuated by occasional laughter. It sounded welcoming, intimate – everything Tobias would hate.

'Elsa!' A warm voice called from inside, and she looked up to see Ulla Andersson, Mikael's mother, now almost an old woman, in a dove-grey outfit.

Despite her nerves, Elsa felt herself genuinely smiling for the first time that morning. 'Congratulations. You must be very proud.'

Ulla lit up with happiness, her greying hair reflecting her outfit. 'Thank you for travelling so far. It means the world to have Mikael's oldest friends here.' Her gaze shifted to Tobias with polite curiosity. 'And you must be – ?'

'Tobias Lundgren,' he replied, extending his hand with the practised charm he reserved for networking events. 'Elsa's partner. Beautiful ceremony venue. Very – authentic.'

The slight pause before 'authentic' wasn't lost on anyone. Ulla's smile remained fixed, but Elsa caught the flicker of something less welcoming in her eyes.

'Well, please, come in and get warm,' Ulla said graciously. 'Elsa, Mikael is up at the altar already. You'll be seated with us, the family. As the mother of the groom I insist.'

Elsa's stomach dropped, but she forced a smile, 'Thank you.'

'The front pew. Erik should be here soon –'

Mikael's mother glanced through the multi-coloured glass to the car park and the snow-covered road. 'I can't imagine what's keeping him. Never mind, we'll go in. Victor is with Mikael until the bride arrives and the ceremony starts, but he'll be sitting with us too, of course.'

The world seemed to tilt slightly. After all these years of wondering, all the sleepless nights and unanswered questions, Elsa was about to see him again. Victor Andersson. The man who had once held her heart in his hands and then inexplicably let it shatter.

'Elsa?' Tobias's voice seemed to come from very far away. 'Are you alright? You look like you've seen a ghost.'

She forced herself to breathe, to smile, to appear normal. 'I'm fine. Just – it's warm in here after the cold outside.'

But as they followed Ulla into the chapel proper, past the rows of wooden pews decorated with white flowers and pine boughs, Elsa's eyes were drawn inexorably towards the altar. There, standing beside Mikael in a perfectly tailored dark suit, was the man who had haunted her dreams for ten years.

Victor Andersson had always been tall, but he seemed even more imposing now, his shoulders broader, his presence commanding the space around him. His dark hair was shorter than she remembered, more refined, and there were new lines around his eyes that spoke of maturity and perhaps sorrow. But when he laughed at something Mikael said, throwing his head back in that achingly familiar gesture, Elsa felt her carefully constructed walls begin to crumble.

He was still beautiful. Still magnetic. Still everything she had tried so hard to forget. If possible, the bloody man was even more handsome than he had been ten years ago. His face showed some signs of maturity, with slightly deeper lines around his lips and a few wrinkles in the corners of his eyes. He was two and a half years older than her, so would be thirty-four next birthday. Annoyingly, Elsa still remembered the date of his birthday, 15 April. A spring baby, while she was born just before Christmas, on 23 December.

He looked tanned, which made his blond hair look even lighter. He was wearing a dark blue suit and a dusty pink shirt with a flamboyant flower-patterned tie.

'Elsa?' Tobias's voice was sharp now, demanding attention. 'I asked you a question.'

She tore her gaze away from Victor, her heart hammering against her ribs. 'I'm sorry, what?'

Tobias's pale eyes narrowed as he followed her previous line of sight.

'I asked if that's the groom's brother up there. The one who's making you act so strange?'

His gaze lingered on Victor with undisguised suspicion.

'I'm not acting strange,' Elsa said quickly, too quickly. 'I just – I haven't seen any of them in years. It's emotional.'

But Tobias wasn't fooled. After two years together, he knew her tells – the way she touched her throat when she was nervous, the slight breathiness in her voice when she was hiding something. His expression grew colder, more calculating.

'Funny,' he said as they were directed toward the front of the chapel. 'You never mentioned knowing the best man. Just the groom. One would think that if you'd known the whole family, you might have mentioned it before.'

Elsa didn't trust herself to respond. How could she possibly explain? How could she tell Tobias that Victor Andersson had been her first love, her first heartbreak, the standard by which she had measured every relationship since? How could she admit that she had specifically avoided mentioning him because even saying his name aloud still had the power to make her chest ache with remembered pain?

When they reached the front pew, Ulla Andersson made her way in first, followed by Tobias and lastly Elsa.

'Mikael is so pleased you're here. Victor will be too, I'm sure.'

As if summoned by his name, Victor chose that moment to glance behind him, at the pews. His gaze went across the assembled guests in a casual sweep that stopped abruptly when it reached Elsa.

For a heartbeat that felt like an eternity, time seemed suspended. Victor's expression shifted through half a dozen emotions – surprise, recognition, something that might have been longing, and then carefully controlled neutrality. But his hands, Elsa noticed, trembled slightly as he adjusted his colourful tie.

She felt Tobias stiffen beside her, his lawyer's instincts picking up on the charged atmosphere, even if he didn't understand its source.

'Well,' Tobias said, his voice deceptively mild. 'This should be interesting.'

And as Victor's gaze finally slid away from hers, leaving her feeling both bereft and relieved, Elsa couldn't help but agree. The next few hours were going to test every defence she had spent ten years building.

She hoped they would be enough.

Just then, a loud sound filled the air. A golden band clattered over the stone floor of the church, the sound echoing through the silence like a gunshot. Elsa watched it tumble then come to a stop at her feet. Turning abruptly, Victor scrambled after it, his face flushed with embarrassment. As he bent to retrieve it, his eyes met hers.

Suddenly she was eighteen again, standing in the doorway of her university apartment, remembering another incident.

Chapter Five

Helsinki, Eleven Years Earlier

'Elsa, I can explain – '

Victor's voice had cracked the same way it did now, that telltale tremor that meant he'd been caught in something he couldn't easily untangle. But back then, it wasn't a wedding ring slipping from nervous fingers. It was her heart slipping from his careless hands.

She'd come home early from her summer internship at the law firm, excited to surprise him with news of a potential job offer in Stockholm. The apartment had been too quiet, Victor's usual music absent, and she'd found him in her bedroom.

Not with another woman – that would have been simpler, cleaner. Instead, she'd found him rifling through her desk drawer, her private letters scattered across her bed like autumn leaves and clearly read. Letters from her father, detailing their family's precarious financial situation. Letters she'd never shown

Victor because she'd been too proud, too afraid he'd see her differently.

'These are private,' she'd whispered, her hands shaking as she gathered the papers.

'Elsa, please. I wasn't – I didn't mean to – '

He'd reached for her then, his expensive watch catching the light. The watch his father had given him for his twenty-first birthday, worth more than her family made in six months.

'You didn't mean to what? Read my personal correspondence? Discover that my father's been working three jobs just to keep our flat in Töölö?'

Victor's face had crumpled, and for a moment she'd seen the boy beneath the privilege, lost and genuinely sorry.

'I was looking for your passport. Mum wanted to know if you could come to the summer house for – '

'Without asking me first?' The words had come out sharper than intended, but the violation felt complete. 'You went through my private things to check my availability for your mother?'

'It's not like that.'

But his protest had been weak, and they both knew it.

She'd stood there, clutching the letters that detailed her father's pride in her scholarship, his sacrifices to give her opportunities he'd never had, his quiet worry about making ends meet. Letters that revealed everything Victor's family would never understand – the weight of being the first in your family to attend university, the pressure of representing not just yourself but everyone who'd believed in you.

'Did you read them all?' she'd asked quietly.

Victor's silence had been answer enough.

'The one where Dad talks about selling his car to help with my textbooks? The one where he mentions taking extra shifts at the factory so I wouldn't have to get a job during term time?'

Her voice had grown steadier with each revelation, even as her heart had been breaking.

'Tell me, Victor, what did you think when you read about how my family scrimps and saves while yours debates whether to summer in Tuscany or the French Riviera?'

'Elsa, I love you. Your family's situation doesn't matter to me – '

'Doesn't matter?' The words had exploded from her. 'It's everything that matters! It's who I am, where I come from, why I work twice as hard as everyone else in my class!'

He'd stepped towards her then, his hands outstretched, and she'd noticed his manicured nails, his soft palms that had never known manual labour. Everything about him suddenly seemed to highlight the distance between their worlds.

'I want to help,' he'd said desperately. 'My family has money. We could – '

'What? Pay off my father's debts? Buy me a new family that fits better with yours?'

She'd shaken her head, tears finally coming.

'You don't understand. I gave you a key so that you can get in without having to constantly press the buzzer downstairs, not to violate my trust. Worse – you did it so casually. Like my privacy, my family's dignity, was just an inconvenience to work around.'

Chapter Six

Lapland, Now

'Sorry, sorry,' Victor muttered, finally grasping the ring and straightening up, his face red with mortification as the wedding guests shifted restlessly.

Elsa blinked, the church coming back into focus. Twenty-two years old or thirty-three, some things about Victor Andersson never changed. Still fumbling when it mattered most. Still that same helpless expression when he realized he'd messed up.

But this time, it wasn't her heart he'd dropped.

This time, she was just a guest at someone else's wedding, watching the man who'd once held her future in his hands struggle with a simple gold band.

The irony wasn't lost on her.

Elsa forced herself to chat quietly to Ulla and Tobias, ignoring Victor, who was now standing with his head bent next to Mikael at the altar. After the incident with the ring, the brothers had hardly exchanged a word.

Being in such close proximity to Victor stirred emotions in Elsa that she had long buried and didn't wish to relive. She was glad he had his back to her now, yet she found herself taking in his shape, the muscular arms visible through his dark suit. Images of them wrapped around her threatened to enter her mind, but she brushed such thoughts away.

Instead, she caught the eye of Mikael as he glanced back towards the entrance of the small church. She smiled at him, and he nodded a silent greeting.

Elsa couldn't be happier for her school friend. Five months ago, when they bumped into each other in a bar in Helsinki, she was amazed to find that Mikael lived up in Lapland. And that he was getting married to a girl from London!

Elsa had been waiting for a client, an owner of a start-up that had just been offered an eye-watering deal by the Stockholm-based gaming company she worked for. As usual for the young entrepreneur, he was late for the meeting. Elsa only had 48 hours in Helsinki. Apart from meeting her client, she'd been attending Slush, a venture capital show favoured by young techies. It had been Elsa's last night. She and Mikael had briefly exchanged news, mainly about his upcoming marriage and her life in Stockholm with her boyfriend, Tobias, a fellow lawyer.

Mikael had been in town to tie up some loose ends.

'I've sold all my shares in the family firm. It's all behind me now!' He'd said, beaming. Some wrinkles had appeared around his eyes and mouth, and his posture was slightly better. Otherwise, he looked exactly as he did in Maths class.

Chapter Seven

Kat had been surprised at the wedding rehearsal to find that, in Finland, the groom met the bride halfway down the aisle. Even though her mother, Simona, was Finnish, her father was from England, where she and her siblings had been born and raised. When her dad had abandoned the family, and gone to Dubai, Simona and the children had stayed on in London. Kat had never lived in Finland, and sometimes the traditions confused her. This one suited her very well, though, especially as she'd decided not to have bridesmaids. This way, she wouldn't have to walk the whole length of the aisle alone.

The husky ride to the church had been Mikael's idea. The owner of the dogs was a friend of his. In fact, Arto had let them use the sledge and dogs during Kat's first time in Ylläs.

The familiar rhythm of the sledge runners cutting

through the snow brought back memories of that first magical week in Ylläs, when everything had seemed impossibly white and clean after the messiness of her London life. Arto had been so patient with her then – a heartbroken Englishwoman who'd never seen proper snow, let alone travelled by husky sledge. Today, he'd greeted her with the same warm smile, as if she were already family.

Kat gazed out at the pine trees heavy with snow, their branches creating a winter wonderland that still took her breath away even after living here for over a year. How different her life had become since that first desperate escape to Finland. She'd found love, a new home, a sense of belonging she'd never experienced in London. Yet today, beneath her happiness, butterflies danced in her stomach. She was about to meet Mikael's parents properly for the first time, as their daughter-in-law, and she knew Erik Andersson's reputation for being – challenging. And then there was Victor, Mikael's complicated brother, whose presence at the wedding had been uncertain right up until yesterday. She'd heard so much about the family tensions, the business disagreements that had driven a wedge between the brothers. Today felt like more than just a wedding – it felt like a test to see whether this fractured family could come together, at least for one perfect day.

At the time of her first visit to Lapland, Kat had been heartbroken after finding out that her long-term boyfriend, a French celebrity chef, had been sleeping with her mum. Not long afterwards, a 'Me Too' campaign had finally caught up with Jacques and he'd been disgraced. Kat hadn't heard from him since seeing him in London about a year ago. He'd begged her to come back, but she knew it was in the hope he could join a popular food show she'd been working on. Her mum, too, whom Kat had nearly forgiven, had cut all ties to the man. Simona was desperately sorry about what had happened, even though she kept reminding her that Jacques had been more her age than Kat's. Kat hoped that Simona was telling the truth, but she really didn't care anymore.

Kat sighed and decided not to think about the rat, or about her mother's role in the breakup of her relationship. She was about to marry the most wonderful man, the honest, responsible, and very caring Mikael. The man who sent her pulse racing every time he came close.

Leaning back, she snuggled into her woollen blankets (strictly no animal fur!), then glanced at the snow-laden pine trees flashing by. She sighed contentedly and decided to stop worrying about anything. This was their day, hers and Mikael's. No one, including her mum, would spoil it for them.

Chapter Eight

At a few minutes to twelve, Mikael heard the sound of dogs, and together with Victor, turned to face the congregation. The heavy doors to the church opened, but instead of his new bride, Mikael saw his father enter the church. When Erik settled himself on the furthest pew from the altar, a rage rose inside Mikael. Erik Andersson didn't look at him, and had his head bent, his hands clasped together as if in prayer. The hypocrisy of the man! Mikael knew he didn't believe in God, or if he did, it wasn't in a kind and forgiving deity. But worse than his father's theatrical piety was the knowledge of what Erik had been doing while his son waited at the altar. Mikael was still on the company's Teams messaging system and had learned that the board meeting had been moved up to Monday. The Northern project permits would be fast-tracked while the family was distracted by wedding celebrations, and he and Kat would be on their honeymoon. His father had planned it perfectly.

Mikael's eyes moved to the front pew. To his surprise, he saw Elsa and her awful boyfriend sitting next to his mother, Ulla. His mother was whispering to Elsa, but she noticed her son looking and smiled at him. That must be awkward for Elsa, he thought, but he was glad his old friend had made the wedding. He hoped that Tobias, sitting with a bored look on his face, had just been tired from the journey last night. Surely, he couldn't be like that all the time? How could Elsa, who Mikael knew to be a kind-hearted person, live with him otherwise? He'd give the guy the benefit of the doubt.

Talking of unpleasant people, he hoped his father wouldn't be rude to Elsa during the reception, although Mikael knew he probably would. His father did what he wanted and never considered other people's feelings. He only hoped that his mother would be a good enough buffer between Elsa and Erik. Before turning away, Mikael saw his father stare right at him, his gaze as steely as it had been when Mikael announced he was leaving the family company. A local man sitting next to Erik said something to him, but Mikael's father didn't reply. Instead, he shook his head. That meant the end of the conversation. Mikael had seen that gesture from his father so many times, it made him feel sick to witness it here, at his own wedding.

Mikael was nervous. He tried to calm himself by staring at the intricate wooden ceiling. He glanced at his watch. It was ten minutes past twelve, the scheduled time for the wedding.

He tried to concentrate on his breathing just as the teacher of the weekly yoga class, which he was attending with Kat, had taught them, but it was no use. He couldn't stop fidgeting. He was glad he'd decided to follow his mother's wishes and ask Victor to be his best man. It was lonely at the front, with everyone's eyes on him, but his brother seemed miles away, deep in his own thoughts.

He turned to Victor.

'She's very late,' he whispered, but Victor didn't hear.

His head was turned sideways towards Elsa, but she was staring down at her hands. What was Victor doing? Mikael hoped there wouldn't be a scene at the wedding. He knew their relationship had ended badly, and Elsa had sworn never to talk to Victor again. Perhaps it had been a bad idea to invite Elsa to the wedding. But she'd been one of his closest friends, and ten years was surely long enough for the pair to have moved on. Elsa had Tobias, and Victor – well, Victor had a string of women, as always. Besides, Elsa and Victor had only been teenagers then. But the obvious charge between them told another story.

Mikael had tried so hard to warn Elsa about Victor, but she had fallen for him, nevertheless. And sadly, she must have found out too late that Mikael was right about his brother.

'What?' Victor replied, suddenly aware that his brother had spoken.

Mikael tapped his wristwatch, raising his eyebrows.

In an unusual gesture of friendliness, Victor placed his hand on Mikael's shoulder and smiled. 'I'm sure she's crazy about you, you're a catch. She'll be here, don't worry.'

Mikael took two deep breaths. He asked Victor if had the ring, and he replied, with a flash of anger in his eyes, 'Yes, I have it here.'

He put his hand inside the pocket of his suit jacket and pulled out the small object. Relief flooded through Mikael.

Suddenly, another thought crossed his mind. What if Kat had changed her mind? It wasn't unheard of. He thought of all the arguments and misunderstandings they'd had at the beginning of their relationship. What if she had begun to doubt his commitment to her and her passion for the environment again?

The time seemed to have stopped. Mikael glanced at his watch again. Kat was thirteen minutes late now. Only a minute had passed since he last looked at it. Hadn't he heard the dogs outside long ago? The dogs that were supposed to bring Kat to the wedding in a sledge. Perhaps it had been another pack pulling tourists around.

Chapter Nine

Victor was deeply embarrassed. How had he been so clumsy as to drop the bloody ring? He'd made a fool of himself in front of the one person who mattered the most. What must Elsa think of him now?

Victor had never wanted to be here. He had a love-hate relationship with weddings. While he saw smiling, happy people, he also knew many of their lives were miserable beneath the surface. He couldn't shake the thought of the number of weddings he'd attended that had ended in divorce two years later. Some couples stayed together, only to become resentful, taking every chance to bad mouth each other. He'd lost track of how many married people he knew who now fitted that mould.

His parents were a prime example. Erik and Ulla Andersson barely conversed anymore. Much of their rift was because of Mikael's actions, but Victor knew that his father had been unfaithful long before. His mother likely knew, or at least suspected. Victor couldn't recall the last time he'd seen them share any affection.

Divorce was out of the question. That would be too scandalous, threatening their mining firm's reputation, especially with the media frenzy over Mikael's refusal to join the family corporation – a situation caused solely by the woman now walking down the aisle in this dilapidated wooden church.

Victor sighed again and glanced at his watch. He'd usually be brunching with friends at Cafe Strindberg on the North Esplanade at this time on a Saturday. Unless he was treating his latest conquest to champagne breakfast at the nearby Hotel Kämp. Or perhaps he'd still be in bed, himself enjoying something delicious under the covers. Instead, he was in the frozen wastelands, witnessing a wedding that would likely end in divorce sooner or later.

If it hadn't been for his mother, Ulla, begging Victor to accept his brother's invitation to be his best man, he would be kilometres away. Victor sighed. As usual, he'd been forced to carry out his parents' wishes.

If sacrificing his weekend wasn't bad enough, the painful past he thought he'd buried long ago was sitting in the front pew. How long had it been since he'd set eyes on Elsa?

It was all Mikael's fault. If he hadn't fallen for a Greta Thunberg groupie, they would both be in Helsinki enjoying themselves now. Instead, Mikael had settled here in the middle of nowhere, pretending to be a plant-munching Lapp or Sami reindeer herder. Even if their mum had been born up here, Mikael couldn't pretend to have roots in Lapland. Ulla had left as soon as she could and was doing very nicely as the wife of the mining magnate Erik Andersson.

Victor's gaze shifted again to where Elsa sat in the front pew, and his chest tightened when he saw the man beside her. That must be her boyfriend.

From the altar, Victor could see only the man's profile and posture. Dark hair, well-dressed in what looked like an expensive suit. He appeared to be around Victor's age, perhaps a year or two older. There was something about the way he carried himself that suggested confidence, even arrogance, though Victor acknowledged that might be jealousy colouring his perception.

What struck Victor most was the space between them. Even sitting in the same pew, there seemed to be a distance between Elsa and the man. Their posture lacked the intimacy usually seen between couples at weddings. Victor analysed every detail he could observe, hating himself for caring so much.

This was the man Elsa had chosen. This was the person she'd built a life with since – since that awful day in Helsinki. He tried to imagine what their relationship was like, what drew Elsa to him, what made her happy. The not knowing was almost worse than if he'd been able to identify obvious flaws.

Victor remembered how protective he'd once felt

about Elsa, how he'd wanted to shield her from anything that might hurt her. Now someone else held that role – if the guy even understood how precious she was. From his limited vantage point, Victor couldn't tell if the guy appreciated what he had in Elsa, couldn't gauge whether he made her laugh the way she deserved to laugh, whether he saw all the brilliant, wonderful things about her that had once captivated Victor.

The organ music upped its volume, but Victor found his attention still divided. Part of him was present for his brother's wedding, but another part remained focused on the woman in the front pew and the stranger beside her who had somehow gained what Victor had lost.

As for his stubborn brother – Victor found Mikael's refusal to yield infuriating, a familiar frustration. Besides, why make life difficult for yourself? Obey Erik; mimic obedience; reap rewards. And when Erik was too old, assume control. He'd rather do it with Mikael, but he'd sold his shares, so that was that.

Erik had sworn never to set eyes on his youngest son again. Yet today he would do exactly that. But where was he? It wasn't like his father to be late for anything. Turning to see if he had joined Ulla and Elsa in the front pew, he spotted his father at the back of the church. Was that some kind of protest?

Victor shrugged. He'd never understand Erik Andersson's motives or actions. His thoughts turned to Elsa and his own actions. What a fool he'd made of himself grinning at her like a fool after he'd retrieved the ring.

He'd been so close to her long legs. And when her fur coat had parted, he'd noticed her dress, a wrap-type affair with a deep-cut cleavage. The vision had nearly made him lose his cool. Something in Victor's groin area had shifted, and he'd nearly choked on his breath as his eyes moved to her face. She wore her blonde hair down, with long curls falling around her lovely oval face. Her green eyes were even a deeper emerald than he remembered.

Their eyes had met, and Victor had realised that she'd been looking straight at him and smiling. He'd tried to return the gesture, but feared he'd given her a creepy grin instead.

Why was he here, standing next to Mikael, trying to support his wayward brother at the most important moment of his life, while his own thoughts were a messy mixture of elation and fear? He couldn't understand how he'd been cajoled into being Mikael's best man. They weren't close, but he couldn't face his mother's disappointment – or worse – tears. She was the reason he'd agreed to support his brother in this, his most foolish endeavour yet.

How Mikael had gone along with the plan was another mystery. He must have better friends than him, Victor. When they were younger, they'd been close, but something happened during their teenage years to put distance between them. Perhaps it was the different attitudes they took to the family firm and their father's bullying?

Victor was a pragmatist. In time, the firm would be theirs – or now his alone – so he just needed to keep his mouth shut and do as he was told until Erik Andersson died.

Mikael was soft, in Victor's opinion. He wanted 'happiness' – whatever that meant. Victor had tried it, but he hadn't been able to hold onto it. He'd outgrown believing in soppy love stories.

Yet here he was, standing in the open, sensing Elsa's eyes on him. Each time he dared to glance at her, he saw her calm half-smile, sitting like an ice princess in her ice-blue dress, her eyes vast lakes for him to sink into. Her hair caught the light filtering through the chapel windows, transporting him back to another afternoon when that same poise had attracted his attention.

Chapter Ten

Helsinki, Fourteen Years Earlier

Victor Andersson was having a spectacularly ordinary Tuesday when his life changed forever.

He had skipped his boring data analysis lecture, Professor Hakkarainen's lectures on database management being notoriously tedious. He knew the subject was an essential part of his geology degree, but today he couldn't concentrate. Instead, he'd wandered into the Helsinki Gymnasium, his old school.

The place still felt like home. More importantly, it was better than going home to Ullanlinna, where his so-called lack of academic excellence and ambition would be the cause of yet another lecture from his father.

At nineteen, Victor had grown accustomed to being a disappointment. Not academically – his grades were perfectly adequate – but in the indefinable way that seemed to matter most to Erik Andersson. He lacked what his father called 'killer instinct', the ruthless drive that had built the family mining empire. While other wealthy sons seemed naturally suited to boardroom politics and corporate warfare, Victor found himself more interested in the actual rocks than the profits they might yield.

Restless energy led him to the school, supposedly for paperwork, but actually to kill time before his seminars. The corridors were busy with the controlled chaos of a school day – students hurrying between classes, teachers looking harassed, the familiar smell of industrial disinfectant and adolescent anxiety.

He was passing the history corridor when he heard Mikael's distinctive laugh echoing from one of the classrooms. His younger brother had always been the more popular of the two siblings, despite – or perhaps because of – his studied indifference to their father's expectations. Where Victor felt crushed by the weight of being the heir apparent, Mikael seemed to float through life unburdened by legacy or obligation.

Victor paused outside the classroom door, not really intending to spy but curious about what could make his perpetually serious brother laugh with such abandon. Through the glass panel, he could see Mrs Nieminen's history class winding down, students already packing their bags in anticipation of the bell.

That's when he saw her.

She was sitting next to Mikael, her head bent over a notebook as she wrote something with quick, economical strokes. Her hair caught the afternoon light streaming through the tall windows – a shade that defied simple categorisation, somewhere between gold and brown. Straw, perhaps, though that seemed too mundane a word for something that seemed to contain sun-bleached grasses, caramel and summer afternoons all at once.

Victor found himself stepping closer to the door, drawn by an impulse he couldn't name. The girl – for she was clearly still a schoolgirl, probably sixteen or seventeen – looked up at something Mikael said, and Victor caught his first glimpse of her face.

She was beautiful, but not like the girls who usually caught his attention. This wasn't the polished, porcelain perfection of his social circle, where every feature had been enhanced and every expression carefully calculated. Her beauty was natural and captivating. Striking green eyes sparkled with intelligence and mischief; freckles dotted her nose; and her smile was genuine yet slightly sardonic.

But it was her expression that truly captivated him. A vibrant, almost electric energy emanated from her. This was someone who paid attention, who noticed things, who thought deeply about what she observed.

Victor had spent his entire life surrounded by people who wanted something from him – his name, his family's money, his future prospects. But this girl was looking at Mikael like he was simply – Mikael. Like his thoughts mattered more than his bank account, like his jokes were funny because they were clever rather than because laughing was politically expedient.

The bell rang, jolting Victor from his reverie.

Students began filing out of the classroom, and he realised he was standing rather obviously in the doorway, staring. He stepped back, trying to look casual, but it was too late.

Mikael emerged from the classroom and spotted him immediately, his expression shifting from surprise to wariness in the space of a heartbeat.

'Victor? What are you doing here?'

Before Victor could formulate an answer, the girl appeared beside Mikael, slinging a worn canvas bag over her shoulder. Up close, she was even more stunning – tall with an unconscious grace in the way she moved. Her clothes were impeccable but not fashionable. Home-made, even.

'Elsa,' Mikael said, his tone carrying a note of warning that Victor didn't quite understand, 'this is my brother Victor. Victor, this is Elsa Berg. We're in class together.'

Victor extended his hand automatically, his social training kicking in even as his brain seemed to have stuttered to a halt. 'Hello.'

When Elsa took his proffered hand, her grip was firm and confident, her skin warm despite the October chill. But it was her eyes that nearly undid him – intelligent, assessing, entirely unimpressed by his expensive clothes or practised charm.

'Victor Andersson,' she said, and there was something in her tone that suggested she'd heard of him. Not necessarily good things, if Mikael's expression was anything to judge by. 'Mikael's mentioned you.'

'Has he?' Victor found his voice, though it sounded strange to his own ears. 'All good things, I hope.'

Elsa's smile was enigmatic. 'He said you were studying geology at university. That must be fascinating – understanding how the earth was formed, how landscapes change over time.'

The response caught Victor off guard. Most people, when told about his studies, either glazed over with boredom or made some vapid comment about rocks being rocks. But Elsa spoke as if she genuinely found the subject interesting, as if she understood that geology was about reading the story written in stone and sediment.

'It is,' he said, and meant it for perhaps the first time. 'Though I suspect most people find it a bit dry.'

'Most people don't think deeply enough about the world around them,' Elsa replied with a slight shrug. 'They see a mountain and think "pretty view". They don't wonder about the forces that pushed those rocks skyward, or how many millions of years it took, or what stories are trapped in those layers of stone.'

Victor stared at her, momentarily speechless. In one casual observation, this seventeen-year-old girl had articulated something he'd never been able to explain to his friends, or even himself. She understood that his chosen field wasn't about rocks – it was about time, about process, about the epic patience required to build a world.

'Exactly,' he said, and his voice came out rougher

than intended. 'Most people don't think about deep time.'

'Deep time,' Elsa repeated, testing the phrase. 'I like that. Makes our little human dramas seem rather small in comparison, doesn't it?'

Mikael shifted uncomfortably beside them, clearly sensing undercurrents he didn't understand or approve of. 'We should probably get going, Elsa. Physics starts in ten minutes, and you know how Koskinen gets when we're late.'

'Of course,' Elsa said, but her gaze lingered on Victor for another moment. 'It was nice meeting you, Victor. I hope your studies in – deep time – continue to be rewarding.'

As she walked away with Mikael, Victor stood rooted to the spot, watching the sway of her blonde hair and the confident set of her shoulders. Other students flowed past him like water around a stone, but he barely noticed. His entire world had narrowed to the retreating figure of a girl who'd looked at him and seen something worth seeing, who'd understood his passion without needing explanation or justification.

He'd fallen in love before – or thought he had. Quick infatuations with suitable girls from suitable families, relationships that had felt more like auditions for the role of the future Mrs Victor Andersson than genuine connections. But this – this was something else entirely. This was recognition, as if he'd been waiting his entire life to meet someone who spoke his language.

'Victor?' A voice cut through his daze. He turned to

see one of his former classmates approaching, someone whose name he couldn't quite recall. 'Didn't expect to see you here. Fraternising with the juveniles?'

The casual condescension in the comment made Victor's jaw tighten. A week ago, he might have laughed it off, made some equally dismissive joke about his baby brother's friends. But now, having seen the intelligence and dignity in Elsa Berg's eyes, the comment felt like an insult not just to her but to something precious and newly discovered within himself.

'Just visiting Mikael,' he said coolly, then turned and walked away before he said something he'd regret.

As he made his way out of the school, Victor's mind was racing. He knew, with the certainty that sometimes accompanies life's turning points, that everything had just changed. Not just his afternoon, not just his week, but the entire trajectory of his existence.

He'd met the girl he was going to marry.

He should have been terrified. At nineteen, he relied on his father, lacked clear goals, and found the idea of corporate work stifling, even if geology held a certain fascination for him. But instead of fear, he felt an odd sense of relief, as if a question he hadn't known he was asking had finally been answered.

Walking through the crisp October air towards the tram, Victor found himself planning. Not the calculated strategic planning his father was always urging on him, but something entirely more organic and hopeful. He would find reasons to visit the school again. He would learn Elsa's interests, her dreams, her favourite books and foods and music. He would discover what made her laugh and what made her think and what made her look at the world with such keen, uncompromising intelligence.

Most importantly, he would convince her that beneath his privileged exterior lay someone worthy of her attention, someone who could match her passion and complement her fire.

It wouldn't be easy. Mikael's warning expression had made it clear that his brother had reservations about any relationship between them. And Elsa herself seemed far too perceptive to be easily impressed by wealth or status – if anything, those things might work against him. She would judge him by his character, his authenticity, his capacity for depth and growth.

The challenge thrilled him.

As Victor sat and watched Helsinki's streets pass by, he caught himself smiling at his reflection in the tram window. For the first time in months, possibly years, he felt genuinely excited about the future. Not because of expectations or obligations, but because of possibility.

A girl with sun in her hair and wisdom in her eyes lived somewhere in the city. He was determined to make her fall in love with him, no matter how impossible it seemed.

The thought should have been arrogant, presumptuous. After all, he'd exchanged perhaps fifty words with her, knew nothing about her background or her feelings or even whether she was involved with someone else. But Victor found that none of that mattered. A spark of recognition had passed between them. This recognition was more important than anything else, because it signified that they both understood who he truly was.

As he walked towards his family's imposing apartment block in Ullanlinna, Victor made himself a promise. Whatever it took, however long it required, he would find a way into Elsa Berg's life. Not as the Andersson heir or the charming university student, but as himself – complicated, uncertain, but absolutely sure that she was worth fighting for.

He had no idea that within six months, she would agree to go out with him. He couldn't have imagined that within a few months more, they would be desperately in love, planning a future that seemed limitless in its possibility.

Equally, he couldn't foresee his future at twenty-three, ruined by misunderstanding and his failure to fight for what mattered.

That October afternoon, Victor Andersson walked into his family's home, Elsa Berg's smile seared into his memory. He was just a young man, experiencing love at first sight.

Chapter Eleven

Lapland, Now

At seventeen minutes past twelve, more than quarter of an hour past the time given on the order of service, a hush spread through the church. Mikael and Victor stood straighter and taller.

Elsa also sat a little straighter, forcing herself to meet Victor's gaze as it moved from the doors to her. When their eyes met, the flutter in her tummy increased, and she had to concentrate on her breathing to calm her beating heart. She saw Victor's eyes skim her upper body for the briefest moment before looking away. Elsa lowered her head and clasped her hands together, hiding the smile that his obvious reaction had provoked. She had known the ensemble she'd chosen for the wedding was right. It was more daring than her usual style, but she knew it was important for her to look good today. After trawling the shops for days, she'd chosen an ice-blue Ralph Lauren wraparound dress she'd found in a tiny shop in Östermalm, the posh part of Stockholm. Elsa had looked at herself in the hotel room's full-length mirror earlier that morning and been pleased. The dress had a deep V-cut at the front, making the most of her – let's face it – ample chest. A matching belt emphasised her small waist. But the best part of the dress was the way it revealed her legs as she walked, as if by accident. Most men she had dated complimented her on her legs. That included Victor. Not that Elsa wanted Victor back.

No, no.

She just wanted him to appreciate what he was missing.

Mikael and Victor could not have been more different. Victor was quick-tempered and impulsive, while Mikael was calm and liked to plan his moves carefully. Even their looks were dissimilar. While Mikael was blond and blue-eyed, Victor had mid-brown hair with dark brown eyes. He took his colouring from his mother, Ulla, while Mikael was the spitting image of his father, Erik. It was strange that the father and his youngest son looked so alike, yet they'd never got on.

The organ began playing soft music, and the brothers gave each other a nod. Mikael began walking down the aisle to meet his bride.

Chapter Twelve

Tobias checked his watch for the third time in ten minutes. At last, it looked as though the ceremony was about to begin. He'd been calculating how much billable time he was losing sitting in this rustic chapel in the middle of nowhere. He'd made it clear to Elsa that attending her school friend's wedding was an inconvenience, but she'd insisted it was important to her.

What he hadn't expected was the way she'd tensed up the moment she'd seen the groom's brother at the altar. Or the way her breathing had changed when the same groomsman – tall, broad-shouldered, annoyingly confident – had dropped the ring and picked it up right by her feet.

Tobias had built his career on reading people, and right now, every instinct he possessed was telling him that something was wrong with this picture.

The man who'd dropped the ring was now

approaching their pew. Tobias, before Elsa, who was leaning across him to talk to the groom's mother, observed the man's casual, authoritative movements and his intensely focused gaze on Elsa, a sight that made Tobias clench his jaw. When their eyes met briefly, Tobias felt an immediate, visceral dislike. This stranger's demeanour held a predatory quality.

'It's nice to see you,' the man whispered, placing his hand on Elsa's shoulder and leaning far too close to her. Tobias noticed the intimacy of the gesture. This wasn't how someone greeted an old school acquaintance.

As Elsa turned, Tobias watched her reaction with growing unease. She seemed to forget he existed the moment this man appeared.

'Victor,' Elsa replied, her voice soft, becoming almost breathless, as she added, 'I couldn't miss my best friend's nuptials.'

'Tobias Lundgren,' Tobias said, extending his hand across his girlfriend with the crisp efficiency that had served him well in countless courtrooms. 'Elsa's partner. And you are?'

'Victor Andersson, Mikael's brother,' he replied, offering a rather firm handshake, while taking a seat at the end of the pew, next to Elsa.

Andersson. The groom's brother. Tobias's mind began cataloguing details. The expensive suit, the confident posture, the way he spoke to Elsa with such familiarity. More importantly, his introduction had made Elsa freeze, as if someone had caught her in a lie.

Tobias had spent years with other lawyers, judges,

and criminals, learning to identify threats, to recognise when someone was encroaching on his territory. Victor Andersson was doing exactly that, and worse, he was doing it with the casual arrogance of someone who believed he had every right to.

As the ceremony progressed, Tobias studied the interaction between Elsa and Victor rather than watching the bride and groom. The way Victor dismissed him after their introduction. The way Elsa seemed to mirror Victor's movements unconsciously. The way she responded to every whispered word he spoke as if it carried some deeper meaning.

Tobias had never been a jealous man. Jealousy was inefficient and unprofessional. But sitting in that pew, watching his partner of two years transform into someone he didn't recognise, he felt something cold and possessive unfurling in his chest.

The connection between them was unmistakable. This wasn't about old school friends or casual acquaintances. Unfinished business, unresolved history, and an undeniable chemistry – impossible to fake or forget – created their connection.

Whatever Elsa had told him about her reasons for coming to this wedding, she hadn't told him about Victor Andersson. And Tobias Lundgren didn't like being lied to.

Tobias made a mental note to find out what his partner had failed to say about her connections to the Andersson family. More importantly, he intended to make it very clear to Victor Andersson that Elsa was taken.

The ceremony continued, but Tobias, unable to understand Finnish in any case, remained fixed on the drama unfolding next to him in the front pew. He recognised the tension between Elsa and Victor as something he had recently experienced himself. He cast his mind back six months, to the sun-drenched days he'd spent in Provence.

Chapter Thirteen

Provence, Six Months Earlier

The lavender fields stretched endlessly under the Provençal moonlight, painting the world in shades of silver and deep violet. Elsa had fallen asleep in their hotel room, exhausted from the wedding festivities and perhaps one too many glasses of champagne. She looked peaceful, her dirty blonde hair spread across the white pillowcase, one hand tucked under her cheek like a child.

Tobias watched her for a moment, feeling nothing.

That should have been his first warning.

He slipped from their room and made his way down to the hotel bar, telling himself he needed air, needed space, needed anything but the suffocating predictability of his relationship with Elsa. She was lovely, of course. Intelligent, accomplished, everything his mother approved of in a potential daughter-in-law. But she was also safe, contained, careful in ways that had suddenly felt like a cage.

He found Annabel on the terrace, her fair hair catching the last rays of sunlight as she stood alone by the stone balustrade. She'd changed from her bridesmaid dress into something flowing and white that made her look like a goddess against the darkening sky.

'Not tired?' she asked without turning around.

'Elsa's asleep. I didn't want to disturb her.' The lie came easily.

Annabel turned then, and he saw she'd been crying. She had smudged makeup, and her usually composed facade was cracked.

'What's wrong?' he asked, stepping closer.

'Oh, you know. Weddings make me sentimental.' She laughed, but it sounded hollow. 'Watching Rufus promise to love someone forever – it makes you think about what you don't have.'

Tobias knew he should make polite conversation and then excuse himself so that he could return to Elsa. Instead, he moved closer, drawn by something he couldn't name.

'You're beautiful,' he mumbled. 'Any man would be lucky –'

'Don't.' Her voice was sharp. 'Don't say what you think I want to hear, Tobias. We've known each other too long for that.'

The rebuke should have stung. Instead, it excited him. When was the last time someone had challenged him? When was the last time someone had refused to be charmed by his practised words?

'Then what do you want me to say?'

She looked at him for a long moment, her blue eyes unreadable. 'Nothing. I want you to go back to your girlfriend and pretend this conversation never happened.'

But she didn't move away.

Neither did he.

'What if I don't want to?' The words surprised him even as he spoke them.

'Then you're an idiot.' But her voice was softer now, and when he reached out to brush a tear from her cheek, she didn't pull away.

'Probably,' he agreed, and kissed her.

It was nothing like kissing Elsa. There was nothing gentle or predictable about Annabel's response. She kissed him back with a hunger that matched his own, her hands fisting in his shirt as if she couldn't get close enough. They broke apart breathing hard, staring at each other in the gathering darkness.

'This is insane,' she whispered.

'Completely.'

'Elsa's my friend.'

'I know.'

'She's sleeping upstairs, trusting you.'

'I know.'

Annabel closed her eyes. 'I should tell you to leave.'

'But you won't.'

When she opened her eyes again, he saw his own recklessness reflected there. 'My room. Ten minutes.'

Chapter Fourteen

Lapland, Now

Lily, sitting inside the candle-lit church, was trying not to laugh. Her brother Daniel, only a year younger than her, was making jokes about Mikael's brother.

'Best man duties include: hold the rings, don't drop the rings, and definitely don't chase the rings around like you're in a comedy sketch.'

Dissolving in a fit of giggles was clearly inappropriate, but she and Daniel were terribly hungover. Last night, even after strong protests from her siblings, Kat had gone to bed straight after the welcome dinner, so she and Daniel had hit the après-ski bar. It had been Daniel's idea to do shots, something Lily was now bitterly regretting. Her head was pounding, not helped by the organ music swelling around the high-ceilinged chapel.

Growing up, it was always Daniel who got her into trouble. With just 15 months between them, they'd been like twins, though their fun would often lead to bitter arguments, and even physical fights.

Their mother, Simona, had called them 'The Boxing Twins'. But as they grew older, their relationship had changed. When Lily went to uni in Edinburgh, they'd chatted daily on WhatsApp. They'd started by sending each other funny links and then graduated to more personal messages.

When Daniel went to Birmingham university himself, Lily had been the first person he talked to about a girl named Natalie that he fancied. She was seeing someone else, and Daniel had asked Lily's advice on what he should do.

'Nothing,' had been her reply.

Last night, when quite drunk, Daniel had told Lily he thought he was in love with Natalie. 'But I'm in the friendship zone now,' he'd sighed and downed another liquorice vodka shot.

Glancing up at her brother now, Lily couldn't understand how this Natalie person could resist Daniel. Tall and lean, with muscular arms and a mischievous grin, Daniel had a charm that was hard to resist. Lily couldn't help but smile as she watched him try to stifle a laugh when the best man got up from the front pew to hand over the ring – without dropping it this time – to the Pastor. Lily nudged Daniel, to remind him of the solemnity of the occasion, though she didn't want to ruin his upbeat mood. She knew that beneath his carefree facade, her brother had a sensitive side that yearned for love and connection.

Despite their differences, Lily and Daniel had each other's backs, no matter what. Their shared pew seemed to symbolise their connection. Daniel may have been the instigator of many of their misadventures, but he was also the one who stood by her through thick and thin. He'd always defended her from bullies at school. He knew how to make her laugh.

As the Pastor blessed the bridal couple and Kat and Mikael kissed, radiating joy and love, Lily felt a pang of longing for that kind of deep connection. She glanced at Daniel, who was now watching the ceremony with a mixture of awe and amusement.

In that moment, Lily made a silent vow to always be there for her brother, just as he had always been there for her. She knew that no matter what challenges or heartaches life threw their way, they would face them side by side.

Chapter Fifteen

Elsa sat rigidly in the front pew, acutely aware of the two men flanking her. She felt like a wishbone about to snap, caught between two opposing forces that threatened to tear her apart.

The irony wasn't lost on her. Here she was, feeling more conflicted than she had in years, witnessing the most joyous moment of Mikael and Kat's lives. She felt a profound sense of not belonging. The comfortable life she'd built was at odds with the intoxicating pull of the man who could still captivate her with just a look.

As the ceremony continued, she couldn't help but steal glances at Victor. He looked devastatingly handsome in his formal wear, though she noticed his hands trembling slightly as he adjusted his tie. The sight of his nervousness sent an unexpected pang through her chest. She knew that tremor – it was the same one that had betrayed him before his university presentations, the same vulnerability that had made her fall for him in the first place.

Stop it, she commanded herself, forcing her attention back to the happy couple.

Watching Mikael and Kat was almost more painful than looking at Victor. The love radiating between them was so pure, so uncomplicated. When was the last time she had felt that kind of certainty? That unwavering joy? Kat looked absolutely stunning in her vintage dress, every inch the unconventional bride. While Mikael gazed at her, as if she was the answer to every prayer he'd ever whispered.

Elsa touched her throat nervously, a gesture that didn't go unnoticed by Tobias. She could feel his lawyer's instincts dissecting every micro-expression, every glance, every breath. His pale eyes were calculating and suspicious, and his demeanour had been questioning since they'd been seated. She'd tried to act normal, but Tobias was too smart to be fooled for long.

The weight of her deception pressed down on her like a stone. She'd told Tobias that Mikael was just an old university friend. She'd conveniently omitted the part about his devastatingly attractive brother, who had once been the centre of her universe. How could she explain that Victor Andersson represented everything she'd been running from for the past decade?

I'm being ridiculous, she told herself. *I'm here with Tobias. I have a good life in Stockholm. This is just nostalgia, nothing more.*

But was her life in Stockholm so perfect? Her mind went to what had happened just a week before they were due to fly to this wedding.

Chapter Sixteen

Stockholm, A Week Earlier

Elsa had promised to accompany Tobias to a prestigious networking event. This was her way of trying to persuade him to attend Kat and Mikael's wedding. It would be the perfect opportunity to show Tobias how much he meant to her. She hoped it would allow them to finally get back their relationship back on track. The event would be a dazzling affair, with glittering lights and the buzz of excited conversations filling the air. On the evening of the event, however, Tobias cancelled at the last minute. He said an urgent legal case required his attention. Elsa was already in the cab on the way to the hotel where the event was due take place, so she decided to attend alone.

As she mingled among the crowd, she bumped into Tobias's older colleague, a man whom Tobias disliked intensely. The two were always in competition with each other, and Tobias had accused Hugo of poaching his clients. He was certain that the older man had tried to steal a high-profile case from him last year.

'I know he's jealous of me. His career is nearly over and I, more than ten years his junior, have already won more noteworthy cases,' Tobias had told Elsa.

At parties, Hugo would be over-attentive to her, handing her drinks and touching her back. Elsa hated it, and Tobias said it was a trick to make him jealous.

'It's not going to work,' he'd laugh, but he would always come to her rescue.

Tonight, Tobias wasn't here. As soon as Elsa spotted Hugo, she tried to ignore him, but the crowd pushed them together and she had no choice but to greet him.

'Tobias is not with you tonight? If I were him, I'd never let you out of my sight.'

Elsa allowed the smarmy man to give her a kiss on her cheek.

'No, he is busy with a case.'

'His loss, my win,' Hugo grinned. 'I must say that dress is very flattering. The colour really brings out your eyes.'

Elsa brushed down her emerald-green dress. She now wished she'd worn something loose instead of the figure-hugging number. She shivered watching Hugo cast his eyes up and down her body.

'Nice to see you, Hugo, but I really must mingle.' Elsa tried to bring a smile to her lips.

'Not so fast, my little lady!' Hugo put his sweaty

palm on Elsa's bare arm. 'I have some information that might interest you.'

Elsa sighed. 'Oh yes.' She knew this was a trick but she couldn't be rude. She scanned the crowd for a friendly face, someone who could come and rescue her from the clutches of this unpleasant man.

'Do you know Annabel Thorn?'

Elsa nodded. There was an unpleasant glee in Hugo's eyes.

'You guys went to that big wedding, didn't you, down in Provence? Where she was a bridesmaid? I heard all about it. Apparently, she was the spitting image of that sister of England's Princess Kate. You know the one with the curvy backside? She and Tobias went to university together or something like that?'

'Yes, yes, what is this all about?' Elsa was getting impatient. An announcement had just been made that they should be seated for dinner, and she wanted to reach her table before the speeches began.

Hugo moved even closer and, speaking to her collarbone, said in a low voice, 'I think she might be playing away.'

'What?'

'With your Tobias, no less.'

Hugo was smiling at her, his eyes gleaming.

The room started spinning. All Elsa could see was a blurred outline of the nasty man in front of her. He'd seen Tobias, her Tobias, dining with Annabel – the very same captivating woman who'd been the bridesmaid at a wedding they'd attended in Provence.

Everyone had talked about how stunning she'd looked in her tight-fitting satin dress. Elsa had immediately disliked her but had tried not to show it. The woman was a university friend of Tobias, after all. But to upstage the bride like that was in Elsa's book unforgiveable.

Hugo was now telling Elsa how Tobias and Annabel had been sitting in a half-obscured banquette in a French restaurant just off Biblioteksgatan. Elsa knew the place Hugo meant. She knew it well. It was where Tobias had taken her on their first date. It was all white tablecloths, private little nooks, and intimate lighting. The food was sublime.

Their heads had been touching, and Hugo was certain, he'd even seen them kiss.

'Have a good evening, Elsa,' Hugo said when Elsa didn't react to his salacious revelation. He bent down to give her a parting peck on her cheek, but Elsa took a step back just as his lips were about to touch her skin.

As she watched Hugo make his way to another lone woman and lift his lips into a smarmy smile, her insides began to churn. She felt physically sick. She immediately regretted the salmon canapé she'd eaten, as well as the half glass of champagne.

She was stunned by Hugo's words. Initially, she tried to tell herself that it was merely an innocent work dinner. What the horrible Hugo said was just another attempt to sabotage Tobias's life. Yet, deep within her, a sense of unease began to stir. She was rooted to the spot and people milled around her, some giving her curious looks.

Elsa walked out of the networking event in a daze, her mind swirling with conflicting thoughts and emotions. The night that was supposed to showcase her commitment to Tobias had turned into a whirlwind of doubts and suspicions. As she stepped out into the cool night air, the city lights blurred before her eyes, mirroring the confusion in her heart.

The image of Tobias sitting at an intimate dinner with Annabel haunted her, each detail etching itself into her mind. She tried to shake off the sinking feeling in her chest, but the ache of betrayal gnawed at her insides. Was it possible that Tobias could be involved with Annabel? The mere thought sent shivers down her spine. A mix of anger, hurt, and disbelief clouded her thoughts.

Elsa hailed a cab and gave her address to the driver. The journey back home was a blur of passing streetlights and distant honking horns, the city whizzing by in a haze. Elsa's mind raced with questions, doubts, and a jumble of emotions that threatened to consume her. She couldn't shake off the image of Tobias and Annabel together. A scene of their heads bent close in an intimate conversation played on repeat in her mind like a haunting melody.

The cab pulled up to their apartment building, and Elsa stepped out onto the quiet street, the night enveloping her like a shroud. She fumbled for her keys, her hands trembling with a mixture of fear and anger.

With each step up the stairs to her apartment, the weight of the evening bore down on her shoulders, a burden she couldn't shake off.

Unlocking the door, Elsa walked into the dimly lit apartment. The silence echoed in her ears like a mocking reminder of her solitude. She kicked off her heels and sank onto the couch, the events of the night replaying in her mind with brutal clarity. The soft glow of the lamp cast long shadows across the room, adding to the eerie atmosphere. Elsa leaned her head back against the cushions, closing her eyes as she tried to make sense of emotions swirling within her.

What was it about her that made men look elsewhere? First Victor, and now Tobias.

In a sudden burst of frustration, Elsa grabbed a nearby cushion and flung it across the room. Tears welled up in her eyes, blurring her vision as she struggled to contain the anguish threatening to overwhelm her. The realisation that both Victor and now Tobias had strayed tore at her heart, leaving her feeling raw and exposed. Elsa had always prided herself on her independence and strength, but in that moment, she felt utterly vulnerable and lost.

She had trusted Tobias, believed in their love despite the scars of her past, only to have those tender feelings shattered by the spectre of another woman.

As the tears streamed down her cheeks, Elsa's mind raced with questions and doubts. Was she not enough for Tobias? Had she failed to fulfil some unspoken need or desire? Was this why Tobias had so often been cold and not wanted sex with her? Blaming the pressures at work when he was really pining for someone else? Elsa's mind drifted back to the sun-drenched vineyards of Provence. Annabel had been the belle of the ball at her friend's marriage to the Englishman, Rufus. She tried to remember if Annabel had had any kind of effect on Tobias, something she certainly would have noticed in her usually dispassionate boyfriend.

She recalled Tobias seeming distant, lost in his own thoughts as they celebrated his friends' union. That was nothing unusual. Often, a past or future case preoccupied him.

But now, with Hugo's insidious words echoing in her ears, every interaction, every shared moment between Tobias and Annabel took on a new, sinister light.

She remembered how Tobias had excused himself from their table during the reception, claiming he needed some fresh air. Elsa had thought nothing of it, caught up in the joyous atmosphere of the event. Tonight, as she sat alone in the dimly lit apartment, the pieces clicked into place with painful clarity. The way Tobias's eyes had lingered on Annabel as she danced with the other bridesmaids and the bride, a wistful look in his gaze. The shared laughter that Elsa had dismissed as friendly banter. The subtle touches and smiles that now felt like a cruel mockery of her trust. Elsa's heart ached with a mixture of betrayal and hurt. The weight of suspicion and doubt cast a cloud over the safe life she thought she had with Tobias.

Chapter Seventeen

Tobias came into the room and lit a lamp by the sofa. Elsa watched him move about their familiar space as if nothing had changed, as if her world hadn't shifted on its axis tonight. Part of her wanted to scream, to demand answers immediately. But another part, the part that had been hurt before by Victor, urged caution. She needed to be smart about this, not let her emotions cloud her judgement like they had ten years ago.

'What's going on?' He picked up the cushion Elsa had thrown on the floor. He sounded like a parent coming home to chaos, his voice, tired.

'It's only a cushion.'

Tobias placed it back on the sofa and stood in front of Elsa.

'Why are you sitting here with your party dress on in near darkness? Aren't you going to get out of that and ready for bed?'

Again, the thought of a man talking to a child came into Elsa's mind, fuelling the anger inside her. She lifted her head and looked directly into Tobias's eyes.

'Are you upset about tonight? I told you I needed to review the case.'

'No, that's not it.' Elsa said.

'Well, then, let's forget all about it.' Tobias yawned demonstrably.

'No,' Elsa said. Her insides were churning, and she felt faint. She realised she hadn't eaten anything at all that evening, and lunch had been a hurried packet of raw almonds. After Hugo's revelation. She had no idea how long she'd waited in the darkened apartment for Tobias to get back.

Tobias remained silent, his eyes locked with Elsa's as if searching for something within their depths. The tension in the room grew palpable, the air heavy with unspoken words and unresolved emotions. Elsa felt as though she was teetering on the edge of a cliff, waiting for a gust of wind to push her over. She took a deep breath. 'I spoke with Hugo at tonight's event.'

'Oh, how unlucky for you.'

'He told me something very interesting.'

'Well, that's something. Usually he's boring as hell.'

'He saw you with Annabel.'

Elsa could see the effect of her words. His face registered surprise, but he soon gathered himself.

'Annabel and I are old friends, Elsa. Just like you and this Mikael, whose wedding you want to attend.

Which reminds me, if I am to take a whole weekend off, I need to get to bed. I've got a lot to do.'

Elsa got up and hugged herself with her arms. 'If you're too busy, you don't have to come.'

Tobias came over and put his arms around Elsa. At first, she froze, but his familiarity made her relax into his embrace. It was unusual for him to be so physically demonstrative. Besides, it was late, and she, too, was tired.

'Not everything is a big deal. I want to come with you to Lapland. I'm sure the wilderness will do me some good.'

His words, tinged with a sarcastic edge, struck a nerve. The mention of Lapland was deliberate.

'I told you, it's my home country, and if you don't want to go, please say so! It's probably for the best; the time away will give me a chance to think things through.' Elsa pulled herself away from him.

His face was neutral and his voice calm when he said, 'Nonsense. I told you, there's nothing going on between me and Annabel. We will go to your friend's wedding, and when we come back, we'll discuss this some more. OK? Now, let's go to bed.'

Elsa realised he was deflecting, trying to use the lateness of the hour and his work – always his work – as an excuse not to talk about Annabel. A troubling thought crossed her mind: how long had it been going on? From Tobias's reaction – not getting angry but trying to top the conversation, made her certain he was guilty. A sense of déjà vu fluttered over her heart.

Questions about Tobias's sincerity and her own predisposition for betrayal lingered, heavy and unsettling.

Before dawn the next morning, after a restless few hours lying next to the sleeping Tobias, listening to his steady breathing and wondering how he could be so unaffected by their late-night argument, Elsa tiptoed out of bed and into the kitchen to make coffee. Yesterday felt unreal; a bad dream. Tobias had refused to accept that there was anything between him and Annabel.

'I'm totally within my rights to see an old friend for dinner. You see your friends all the time.'

He uttered these words in bed after Elsa had insisted he tell her the truth about his relationship with Annabel. There was a coldness in his voice Elsa hadn't heard before. It was as if he was arguing for the defence, rather than talking to her.

Elsa sat on the small kitchen bar and noticed that Tobias had left his mobile on the counter.

With a quick glance over her shoulder, she listened for any sounds coming from the bedroom to make sure Tobias was still asleep and reached for the phone. She hesitated for a moment, her fingers hovering over the screen, before unlocking it with a shaky breath. She couldn't believe that Tobias hadn't changed his passcode and felt guilty for snooping. But she had to know if there was any truth in Hugo's claims.

Her heart sank with each word she read. The joking tone, the familiarity in their conversations – it all felt like a punch to the gut.

Elsa's hands trembled as she set the phone back down, feeling a mix of anger and betrayal swirling inside her.

Her mind raced, trying to make sense of it all. Why would he lie about something so innocent? Was there more to their relationship than he was letting on? Elsa clenched her fists, feeling a surge of determination wash over her. She couldn't let this go, couldn't ignore the truth staring her in the face.

Retrieving her own phone, she located Annabel's Instagram account. It was typical for the woman that her account wasn't private. She found herself scrolling through Annabel's perfectly curated feed of glamorous parties and exotic vacations. She'd never been interested in following Tobias's friends, but now saw many of them, including her busy criminal lawyer boyfriend, featured on Annabel's posts. The pictures mocked Elsa, a harsh reminder of Tobias and his other woman.

A knot formed in Elsa's stomach as she clicked on a photo of Annabel and Tobias, arms linked and smiling at some event she hadn't been invited to. The caption read, 'Date night with my favourite man', and Elsa felt bile rise in her throat.

Just then, a soft groan came from the bedroom, and Elsa's heart skipped a beat. She quickly closed the Instagram app and placed the phone back on the counter, her mind racing with thoughts of what to do next. Tobias emerged from the bedroom, rubbing his eyes sleepily as he made his way to the kitchen.

'Morning, Elsa,' he greeted her with a yawn, oblivious to the storm raging inside her. He put a coffee pod into their Nespresso machine and sat down opposite her, reaching for his phone as if this was just another normal day. The machine gurgled, masking the strained silence between them. Outside, a weak light across the water and over Stockholm signalled the start of a new day. Elsa felt as if she too had woken up from a slumber that she'd been in for two years.

They hadn't made up last night, so how could Tobias act as if nothing had happened?

Elsa couldn't take it anymore.

'Is it a good morning, Tobias?'

Elsa's voice was laced with a mixture of hurt and anger. She locked eyes with him. Tobias paused mid-yawn, his expression shifting from groggy to puzzled as he lifted his gaze from his phone and took in the intensity of her expression.

'What do you mean?' Tobias asked, his brows furrowing in confusion. Elsa could see the innocence in his eyes, or at least what seemed like innocence. She felt a surge of frustration at how effortlessly he could play the part of the oblivious partner.

Elsa stood up abruptly, her hands clenched into fists at her sides.

'Don't even try,' she snapped, her voice trembling with emotion. 'I've seen your cosy chats with Annabel, and her pictures of you two. Apparently, you are her 'favourite man'. What Hugo told me last night rings rather truer this morning than it did last night!'

Tobias's eyes widened in surprise, and for a moment, a flicker of guilt crossed his features before he quickly masked it.

'I can't believe you've gone snooping in my phone!'

Tobias's accusatory tone only increased Elsa's anger. She refused to back down, her fiery spirit coming to the forefront as she stood her ground.

'You're deflecting, Tobias. This isn't about me checking your phone, it's about the lies and deceit.' Elsa's voice shook with a mixture of hurt and frustration. She had buried her trust issues deep within herself after being hurt before, and now they'd resurfaced with a vengeance.

Tobias's expression hardened, his jaw tensing as he tried to come up with a response. But Elsa could see through his facade now, the cracks in his armour revealing the truth she had been denying.

'You need to explain yourself, Tobias. I deserve the truth.' Though she projected strength, Elsa's request for the truth masked a deep-seated fear of what she might uncover.

Tobias took a step closer, his eyes searching hers as if trying to evade the impending confrontation. But Elsa held her ground, her green eyes blazing with intensity.

As they sat at the table in strained silence, Elsa's resolve solidified. She couldn't continue like this, pretending everything was fine when it clearly wasn't.

Finally, Tobias spoke up.

'I can't be the boyfriend who's constantly reassuring you. I require a partner who comprehends my profession, not one seeking amusement.'

Elsa was stunned into silence. She had been trying to be understanding. She had sacrificed so much to accommodate him. And yet, here he was, making her feel like the problem.

'And Annabel, does she feel the same?'

Tobias took a deep sigh. He looked down at his hands.

'We're over. I chose you over her.'

Elsa stared at him.

He lifted his eyes and Elsa saw sincerity in them.

'I'll come with you to the Lapland wedding. Is that enough of a sign of my commitment for you?'

Chapter Eighteen

Lapland, Now

The ancient words of the Finnish wedding ceremony washed over the congregation like a blessing. Elsa found herself comparing her current relationship to what she was witnessing. When had she last looked at Tobias the way Kat was looking at Mikael? When had she last felt that breathless excitement, that sense of coming home?

The truth was uncomfortable: she never had. Not with Tobias.

Tobias was safe, predictable, and successful. He provided stability and security. Or so she had thought. She'd convinced herself that this was what she wanted. But sitting here, watching true love unfold before her eyes, she couldn't ignore the hollow feeling in her chest.

She was piggy in the middle, caught between two worlds. Between two men, two versions of herself. There was the woman she'd become – controlled, professional, safely ensconced in her relationship with

Tobias. And then there was the woman she'd once been – passionate, spontaneous, madly in love with Victor Andersson.

She glanced sideways at Tobias, studying his sharp profile. He was handsome in his own way. A conventionally attractive man with perfectly styled blond hair and an expensive suit. But there was something remote about him, something that had always kept her at a distance even in their most intimate moments. With Tobias, she felt like she was performing the role of the perfect girlfriend rather than being herself.

During the ring exchange, Mikael whispered something in Kat's ear, and her laughter suddenly filled the chapel. The sound was pure joy, uninhibited and genuine. Elsa felt tears prick her eyes, though she wasn't sure if they were from happiness for the couple or grief for what she'd lost.

What am I doing here? She wondered desperately. *What am I doing with my life?*

The ceremony was drawing to a close, and with it, her brief respite from the inevitable confrontation with Victor. She could feel his eyes on her several times during the proceedings, each glance sending shivers down her spine. And Tobias – Tobias was watching her watch Victor, his expression growing more suspicious by the minute.

As the pastor pronounced Mikael and Kat husband and wife, and the couple shared their first kiss as a married couple, Elsa felt something crack inside her chest. It was the sound of her carefully constructed defences beginning to crumble, the walls she'd built around her heart starting to show their first fissures.

The congregation erupted in applause, but Elsa barely heard it. She was suddenly transported back to another time, another place, where she'd been young and foolish and so completely in love that she'd believed it would last forever. Back to when Victor's smile could light up her entire world, and his touch could make her forget everything else that mattered.

The memory hit her like a physical blow. It was so vivid she could almost smell the old books that had perfumed the classroom. She'd been seventeen, convinced that she was going to conquer the world. How naïve she'd been. How utterly, heartbreakingly naïve.

As the newlyweds walked back down the aisle, Elsa closed her eyes and let herself remember what it had felt like to be young and in love, before everything had gone so terribly wrong.

Chapter Nineteen

Helsinki, Fourteen Years Earlier

The October afternoon light streamed through the tall windows of Mrs Nieminen's history classroom, casting long rectangles across the worn wooden floor. Elsa bent over her notebook, writing quick notes about the lesson's main points while half-listening to Mikael's whispered commentary about their teacher's particularly uninspiring delivery today.

'I swear she could make the French Revolution sound boring,' Mikael muttered, earning a small smile from Elsa despite her attempt to stay focused.

She was just finishing her summary when Mikael said something that made her look up with genuine amusement – how Mrs Nieminen's lecture style could probably end wars through sheer tedium. The laugh that escaped her was quiet but spontaneous, and she caught Mikael grinning at his success in breaking through her studious concentration.

The bell rang, and immediately the controlled

chaos of the end-of-class began. Students started packing their bags, the scraping of chairs and rustle of papers filling the room. Elsa took her time, reorganising her meticulous notes while Mikael stuffed his crumpled papers into his bag.

'Coming to Stefan's party Friday?' Mikael asked, slinging his bag over his shoulder.

'I have a physics test on Monday,' Elsa replied, tucking a strand of fair hair behind her ear.

'All work and no play makes Elsa a dull girl,' Mikael teased. 'Come on, Elsa. Even top students need to have fun sometimes.'

Elsa hesitated. She wasn't like Mikael, she couldn't afford to coast on her family's name or wealth. Her father worked endless hours to keep a roof over their heads, determined his only child would have opportunities he'd never had. Every grade, every test was a step towards the grades she needed for university. She wanted to make her father proud and to do well for herself.

'I'll think about it,' she conceded, knowing she wouldn't go.

'OK. Maths next?' Mikael asked, smiling at her.

'In ten minutes. Old Man Koskinen will have our heads if we're late again.'

They were among the last to file out of the classroom, and Elsa was still adjusting the strap of her bag when she noticed someone standing near the doorway. Her first impression was of expensive clothes and confident posture – someone who clearly didn't belong in the school corridor but seemed entirely at ease being there anyway.

Then she recognised him.

Victor Andersson looked exactly as she remembered and nothing like she recalled, all at once. She'd seen him around the school and heard enough about Mikael's older brother over the years to form an opinion of him: the golden boy, the charming disappointment, the heir who couldn't quite live up to expectations. But seeing him now in person was different. He was taller than before, with an intense quality to his dark brown eyes that seemed at odds with his reputation for casual indifference.

'Victor?' Mikael's voice carried a note of surprise, and something else – wariness, perhaps. 'What are you doing here?'

Elsa found herself studying Victor's face as he struggled to answer, curiosity overriding her usual reserve. There was something almost vulnerable in his expression before he recovered his composure. She'd been around Mikael long enough to recognise the Andersson family dynamics – the weight of expectations, the complex relationship with Erik Andersson's empire. But now she realised how those pressures might affect the older brother too.

The introduction was brief, perfunctory. Elsa watched Victor extend his hand with automatic politeness, but there was something else in his manner – a genuine attention that seemed different from the casual charm she'd heard so much about.

When she took his hand, his grip was firm and warm, but it was his eyes that held her attention. He was looking at her as if he was actually seeing her, not just going through the motions of a polite introduction. It was – unexpected.

Their conversation about his geology studies surprised her. When she mentioned finding landscapes and deep time fascinating, something lit up in his expression. She saw passion, and not the polished charm of someone working an angle. For a moment, she thought she glimpsed the person beneath the reputation.

But beside her, Mikael shifted uncomfortably, and Elsa became aware that something was happening in this conversation that went beyond polite small talk. The warning look Mikael was giving his brother wasn't lost on her, nor was the way Victor seemed completely absorbed in their brief exchange.

'We should probably get going, Elsa,' Mikael interrupted, his tone carrying an urgency that seemed disproportionate to their ten-minute deadline. 'We don't want to be late.'

She nodded, hearing the signal. Whatever was happening here, Mikael was clearly uncomfortable with it. And despite her curiosity about this unexpected side of Victor Andersson, she trusted Mikael's judgement.

As they walked away, Elsa could feel Victor's gaze following them. The sensation was unsettling. Not unpleasant, exactly, but charged with an intensity that made her hyperaware of every step.

'That was interesting,' she said once they were out of earshot.

Mikael's expression was grim. 'Was it?'

'He's not what I expected.' She glanced back despite herself, but Victor was no longer there. 'The way he talked about geology; he actually seemed passionate about it.'

'Victor's passionate about a lot of things,' Mikael said carefully. 'For about five minutes.'

There was a warning in his tone that Elsa didn't miss. She'd known Mikael long enough to read between the lines. Whatever Victor's reputation with girls was, his brother didn't want her becoming another casualty.

'I see,' she said quietly.

They walked in silence for a moment before Mikael spoke again, his voice softer but still concerned. 'Look, Elsa, I love my brother. But he's – complicated. He doesn't mean to hurt people, but he does anyway. He gets caught up in the idea of something, or some-one, and then when reality doesn't match the fantasy – '

He didn't finish the sentence, but he didn't need to. Elsa understood perfectly. Victor Andersson was the kind of person who collected experiences and people like interesting specimens, studying them intensely until something new caught his attention.

'Thank you for the warning,' she said, meaning it. 'But you don't need to worry. I'm not in the market for complicated right now.'

Mikael's relief was visible. 'Good. Because you deserve better than being someone's temporary fascination.'

'Is that what I am?' she asked, more curious than concerned. 'A temporary fascination?'

'I don't know,' Mikael admitted. 'But just be careful.'

As they entered the classroom, Elsa found herself thinking about Victor's eyes when he'd talked about deep time. His genuine enthusiasm, the sense that he understood that the world was bigger and more complex than most people realised. It was attractive, she had to admit. But Mikael was right to be worried.

She had too much at stake to let herself be distracted by someone like Victor Andersson, no matter how unexpectedly interesting he might be. Her future depended on focus, on making the grades she needed for university, on proving that a girl from her background could succeed on her own merits.

Still, as the teacher began explaining partial fractions, Elsa caught herself thinking about layers of stone and the stories they told, about the patience required to build a world. And despite her better judgement, she found herself wondering what other unexpected depths might lie beneath Victor Andersson's polished surface.

The thought was dangerous, and she pushed it firmly aside. Some curiosities, she told herself, were better left unexplored.

Chapter Twenty

Three days later, Elsa found herself at Stefan's party, anyway. The house was packed, music pulsing through the rooms as teenagers sprawled across expensive furniture with plastic cups in hand. Mikael had convinced her to come with promises that it would be low key and that she could leave early. Both promises had proved false. The party was anything but low-key, and Mikael had disappeared within minutes of their arrival, pulled away by his ice-hockey teammates.

Elsa stood in the corner of the living room, nursing a cup of lukewarm punch and wishing she'd stuck to her original plan of staying home to study. The atmosphere was a far cry from the quiet evenings she was used to, spent with her father watching old movies or reading in companionable silence.

'You look like you're plotting an escape,' a voice said beside her. Elsa turned to find Victor leaning against the wall, watching her with amusement dancing in his eyes. He looked different tonight – more relaxed in jeans and a simple button-down shirt, yet somehow even more handsome than in the school corridor.

'I'm considering my options,' she replied, trying to ignore the sudden flutter in her stomach. 'The bathroom window looks promising, but I'd have to climb through the blackthorn bushes.'

Victor laughed, the sound rich and genuine.

'A thorny situation indeed,' he said, his gaze meeting hers. 'Though I hope you'll stay a while longer.'

Elsa took a sip of her punch to hide her surprise. 'I thought university students had better things to do than crash high school parties.'

'Ordinarily, yes.' Victor stepped closer, closing the distance between them. She could smell his cologne – something expensive and subtle that made her think of winter forests. 'But Mikael mentioned you might be here tonight.'

The implication hung in the air between them, charged with possibility.

Elsa's pulse quickened, but she kept her expression neutral. 'Did he now? That's interesting, considering he abandoned me the moment we arrived.'

Victor glanced across the room to where Mikael was showing off to a group of giggling girls. 'My brother has many virtues but recognising what's right in front of him isn't one of them.'

He turned back to her, his look intent. 'I, on the

other hand, make it a point to notice exceptional things when they cross my path.'

'Is that what I am? A thing to be noticed?' Elsa challenged, raising an eyebrow.

Victor's smile faltered, genuine contrition replacing his practised charm. 'Poor choice of words. I apologise.' He ran a hand through his hair, suddenly looking less like the confident university student and more like a nervous boy. 'What I meant was – I'd like to get to know you, Elsa. Properly this time.'

The vulnerability of his admission caught her off guard.

'Why?' she asked simply.

Victor seemed taken aback by the direct question. He studied her for a moment, as if reassessing his approach. 'Because you're the first person who's made me stumble over my words in years,' he finally said, honesty replacing his earlier polish. 'Because you didn't seem impressed by me in the slightest, which is – refreshing. And because when I saw you standing alone in this corner, looking like you'd rather be anywhere else, I thought perhaps we might rescue each other from this tedious party.'

Elsa couldn't help the smile that tugged at her lips. 'That's quite a speech.'

'I'm quite serious,' Victor replied, holding her gaze. 'What do you say to getting out of here? Kappeli is still open. Better company, and definitely better drinks than whatever is in that cup.'

Elsa hesitated, caution warring with curiosity.

Everything she knew about Victor Andersson suggested this was a terrible idea. Mikael's warnings echoed in her mind – Victor's reputation for breaking hearts, his impulsive nature, his shallowness. And yet –.

'Just a coffee,' she said finally. 'And I need to let Mikael know I'm leaving.'

Victor's face lit up with genuine pleasure. 'Of course. Although – ' he added, glancing over at Mikael, who was now doing an impression of their history teacher to uproarious laughter, 'I think he's otherwise occupied.'

Elsa shook her head. 'I still need to tell him. He's my friend, and he'll worry.'

Something shifted in Victor's expression – respect, perhaps – and he nodded. 'I'll wait by the door.'

Twenty minutes later, they were seated in a quiet corner of Café Kappeli, steam rising from the cups of rich coffee between them. The ornate glass pavilion was almost empty at this hour, the few remaining patrons absorbed in their own conversations.

'So,' Victor said, watching her over the rim of his cup, 'tell me about Elsa Berg. Beyond being the only person who can tolerate my brother in history class.'

Elsa wrapped her hands around her mug, letting the warmth seep into her fingers. 'What do you want to know?'

'Everything,' he said simply. 'But we can start with why you looked so miserable at that party. Most girls your age would be thrilled to be there.'

'Most girls my age don't have to get up at 8 am on

Saturdays to go to a job,' Elsa replied, more sharply than she intended. 'Some of us can't afford to sleep in all weekend.'

Instead of being offended, Victor leaned forward, interest sharpening his gaze. 'No, I suppose they don't,' he agreed. 'So why were you at the party at all?'

Elsa sighed, stirring her coffee absently.

'Mikael can be very persuasive when he wants to be. He thought I needed to 'live a little' before exams consumed my life.' She glanced up at Victor. 'Why are you so interested, anyway? I'm sure there are plenty of university girls vying for your attention.'

'Yet here I am, with you,' Victor pointed out. His expression grew more serious. 'The truth? You're unlike anyone I've met before. You look at me and see a person, not the Andersson name or bank account.' He hesitated, then added quietly, 'It's a rare experience for me.'

The vulnerability of his admission caught her off guard. This wasn't the arrogant player Mikael had described. This was someone more complex, more interesting. 'I find that hard to believe,' Elsa said, but her tone had softened.

Victor shrugged, with a half-smile playing on his lips. 'Believe what you like. But I'm curious about you, Elsa Berg. The straight-A student who's friends with my troublemaker brother. The girl who speaks her mind regardless of who she's talking to. The beautiful blonde who'd rather be studying on a Friday night than at the biggest party of the term.'

'Beautiful?' Elsa echoed, a blush warming her cheeks.

'Is that the only part of that sentence you heard?' Victor asked, amusement in his eyes.

'It's the most suspicious part,' Elsa retorted, trying to ignore the flutter in her stomach. 'I've seen the girls who usually catch your eye, Victor. I'm not exactly in that category.'

Victor's expression grew serious. 'And what category would that be?'

'You know. Glamorous. Sophisticated. The kind who look like they've stepped out of a fashion magazine.'

Victor was quiet for a moment, studying her face. 'Can I tell you something about those girls, Elsa? Something honest?'

She nodded, curious despite herself.

'They're interchangeable,' he said flatly. 'They laugh at the right moments, say all the expected things, and never, ever challenge me. It's like talking to beautiful, well-dressed mirrors.' He leaned forward, his gaze intense. 'But you – you're a real person. You told me off within two minutes of meeting me. You told Mikael you were leaving the party instead of just disappearing with me. You're sitting here asking why I'm interested instead of trying to impress me.' His voice softened. 'Do you have any idea how rare that is?'

Elsa didn't know what to say. The earnestness in his voice, the intensity in his eyes – it all seemed so genuine, so at odds with everything she'd heard about him.

'Besides,' he added, a hint of his usual confidence returning, 'you *are* beautiful. Especially when you're not trying to be.'

Elsa looked down at her coffee, heat creeping up her neck. 'You're very good at this,' she murmured.

'At what?'

'Saying exactly the right thing to make a girl's heart flutter.'

Victor reached across the table, his fingers lightly brushing against hers. 'Maybe with you, I'm just being honest.'

Elsa should have pulled away. She should have remembered Mikael's warnings, should have guarded her heart against Victor Andersson's legendary charm. Instead, she found herself turning her hand over, letting his fingers intertwine with hers.

'I don't believe you,' she said softly. 'Not yet. But I'm willing to be convinced.'

Victor's smile, slow and genuine, reaching all the way to his eyes, made something shift inside her. It was the smile not of the notorious Victor Andersson, heir to a mining fortune and breaker of hearts, but of a boy who had just been given something unexpected and precious.

'I look forward to the challenge,' he said, squeezing her hand lightly.

Outside, cold sleet began to fall again, pattering against the glass ceiling of the cafe. But inside, in the warm glow of the lamps, Elsa felt as though she was standing on the edge of something new and exhilarating – something that might fly her to dizzying heights or send her crashing to the ground. Either way, sitting across from Victor Andersson, his hand warm around hers, she knew her life had just irrevocably changed.

Chapter Twenty-One

The photographer had finally finished arranging them for what felt like the hundredth family group shot when Mikael stepped forward, his arm around Kat's waist. Ulla smoothed down her dove-grey suit and watched her youngest son glow with happiness as he stood beside his new wife. The ceremony had been beautiful, despite Erik's last-minute arrival, and now the two families were gathered, waiting to proceed into the reception together.

Ulla should have felt nothing but joy in this moment. Instead, she found herself studying her husband's rigid posture and his slight distance from the group. The familiar irritation began to build in her chest.

'Mum, Dad, I'd like you to properly meet my wife, Katherine.'

Kat stepped forward, her wedding dress rustling

softly, and extended her hand to Ulla first. 'Mrs Andersson, it's lovely to finally meet you properly.'

Ulla smiled at her new daughter-in-law. 'Please, call me Ulla. And congratulations, my dear. You looked absolutely radiant during the ceremony.'

Erik stood slightly behind his wife, his posture still rigid. When Kat turned to him, he gave a perfunctory nod. 'Katherine. Welcome to the family.'

The words were correct but delivered with all the warmth of a business handshake. Ulla saw Mikael's jaw tense.

'Thank you,' Kat said, her voice steady despite the obvious chill. 'I'm honoured to be part of your family.'

Next, Mikael gestured to both families, 'more introductions are in order. Kat's family, I'd like you to meet my parents, Erik and Ulla Andersson, and my brother Victor.'

'Mrs Wootton, it's lovely to finally meet you properly,' Ulla said, shaking the other woman's hand.

'Please, call me Simona,' Kat's mother replied.

Erik moved forward with mechanical precision. 'Congratulations on raising such a – spirited daughter,' he said, and Ulla caught the slight pause before 'spirited', knowing he was thinking of Kat's environmental activism.

Victor stepped up next, extending his hand to Simona with his practised charm. 'A pleasure to meet you. And these must be Kat's siblings?'

'My daughter Lily, and my youngest, Daniel,' Simona said proudly.

'Ah, the ring bearer, or should I say catcher?' The young man's face carried more than a hint of mischief as he grinned at Victor.

Victor laughed, running a hand through his hair. 'Not my finest moment, I'll admit. Good reflexes, though.'

'Can you imagine if you hadn't caught it and we'd all had to dig around the chapel looking for it?' Daniel continued with a grin. 'Like we were mining for – ' The words died in his throat.

Erik's expression froze, and Victor shifted uncomfortably. Even young Daniel seemed to understand he'd put his foot in it.

'Well,' Erik said finally, his voice Arctic, 'I believe we ought to go in and get some drinks, Ulla?'

Without waiting for a response, he turned and walked towards the dining room. Ulla shot an apologetic look at Kat's family before hurrying after him. Victor, too, moved away, following his parents and leaving the Woottons to deal with the aftermath of Daniel's innocent but poorly timed mining joke.

Once they were standing with their glasses of champagne in the far corner of the dining room, away from the other guests, Erik pulled out his mobile. Ulla watched him with growing irritation.

'Put that away,' she said quietly, but firmly.

'It's just a quick check of emails – '

'Erik.' Her voice carried a warning. 'You were nearly late for your own son's wedding. You sat at the back of the church like a stranger. And now you're checking emails whilst we wait to celebrate with our son's guests?'

Erik's hand stilled on his phone. She placed her glass on a nearby table and twisted her wedding ring around her finger, a nervous habit she'd developed over the years, and allowed her mind to drift back to that morning at the family chalet.

The phone had rung just as they were preparing to leave for the chapel. Ulla had been adjusting her pearl necklace in the hallway mirror, ready to walk out the door together, when Erik's mobile began its insistent buzzing.

'Leave it,' she'd said, watching his face in the mirror. 'Erik, we need to go. The ceremony starts in thirty minutes.'

But he'd already answered, his voice shifting into the clipped, professional tone that had dominated their lives for decades. 'Andersson here. What's the situation?'

For ten minutes, she'd stood in the hallway of the chalet that held so many family memories, listening to her husband discuss mining permits and environmental assessments while their youngest son waited at the altar.

'You were late for your own son's wedding,' Ulla said quietly, her voice barely audible above the gentle chatter of the other guests settling around them.

Erik lowered his phone, his jaw tight with familiar defensiveness. 'I wasn't late. I was there well before the bride.'

'You arrived about thirty seconds before the bride. Less than a minute, Erik. I watched every person walk into that chapel, wondering when you were going to appear and making excuses for my absent husband.'

'The call was important. The environmental board —'

'I don't care about the environmental board.' The words came out sharper than Ulla had intended. She leaned closer to her husband, lowering her voice. 'I care about our son, who looked towards the back of the chapel during the ceremony to see if his father was actually there. I care about our daughter-in-law, who had to wonder if the groom's family couldn't even be bothered to arrive on time.'

For a moment, they stood in tense silence, watching the rest of the guests laughing and chatting with each other. Ulla watched Erik's face, noting the new lines around his eyes, the way his hair had gone almost completely silver in the past few years. When had they stopped being partners and become adversaries?

'Do you know what Mikael told me yesterday?' Ulla said finally. 'He said he wasn't sure you'd actually come. His own father, and he wasn't sure you'd show up for his wedding.'

Erik's head turned sharply towards her. 'He said that?'

'He did. And after this morning, I'm beginning to think he was right to worry.' Ulla's voice carried thirty-four years of accumulated frustration. 'When did the company become more important than our children,

Erik? When did quarterly profits become more significant than milestones in our sons' lives?'

'Everything I've built, everything I've worked for, has been for this family – '

'Has it?' Ulla challenged. 'Or has it been for your ego? For your need to control everything, to build an empire that will outlast you regardless of whether it destroys your relationships with the people who actually matter?'

Ulla tried to calm herself and concentrate on the wedding reception. She watched Kat and Mikael enter the room and felt a fierce pride for her youngest son mixed with an aching sadness. Mikael had become the kind of man who would never leave his wife sitting alone in church at their child's wedding. He'd never prioritise business calls over the people he loved.

Somehow, he'd learned to be everything his father had forgotten how to be.

The realisation should have been comforting. Instead, it only made Ulla more acutely aware of everything she and Erik had lost along the way.

Chapter Twenty-Two

The Hotel Äkäslompolo's dining room had been transformed into an elegant reception space, with round tables adorned with winter flowers and flickering candles arranged around the edges, leaving the centre open for mingling. Wait-staff moved quietly through the space, offering champagne and vegan canapés to the wedding guests, who were chatting and laughing in small groups.

Kat's heart still beat hard against her chest, but now it was with happiness rather than nerves. Her hand felt warm and steady in Mikael's as they moved through their guests, accepting congratulations and warm embraces. This informal drinks reception had been perfect – allowing everyone to mingle naturally before the formal dinner began.

'You look absolutely stunning, Kat,' Elsa said, stepping forward to embrace her. 'I love the colour of your dress. It's perfect on you.'

Kat smiled gratefully at Mikael's friend. 'Thank you. And likewise, your outfit is absolutely beautiful.'

The warmth of Elsa's compliment was a welcome contrast to the uncomfortable energy she'd been feeling from some of the wedding guests. Or the awkward introductions between the families earlier. Trust Daniel to put his foot in it! As for Tobias, Elsa's partner. He seemed to want to be anywhere but here, and his cutting remarks about the venue and the environmental message last night had been downright rude.

Across the room, she could see Erik and Ulla Andersson standing slightly apart. Erik was checking his phone while Ulla watched the mingling guests with tired eyes. At least they'd removed themselves from the general socialising.

'You've done so well!' Simona whispered into Kat's ear, appearing suddenly beside her with a glass of champagne in hand.

Here we go, Kat thought, her stomach tightening with familiar dread.

'First you snag a famous French chef and now the son of a filthy rich Finnish industrialist!'

'Shh,' Kat glanced at Mikael, who was deep in conversation with some of their Helsinki friends near the bar area.

If her new husband heard her mother reducing their love to some sort of get-rich-quick scheme – the thought made her feel sick. She'd married Mikael because she loved him deeply, not because of his family's money. Money that came from the very industry she was actively campaigning against.

'Oh, come now, darling,' Simona continued, her voice carrying despite Kat's attempts to quieten her. 'There's no shame in doing well for yourself. You always were a clever girl.'

Kat cringed as she noticed Tobias's pale eyes shift their way from where he stood near the canapé table. He'd clearly been listening to every word. His thin lips curved into what might have been a smile but looked more like a smirk.

'Mrs – ' Tobias stepped forward, abandoning his plate to extend his hand towards Simona, employing an oily charm that made Kat's skin crawl. 'I don't believe we've been properly introduced. I'm Tobias Lundgren, Elsa's partner.'

'Simona Wootton,' her mother replied, practically purring as she shook his hand. 'Kat's mother.'

Kat watched in horror as Tobias's gaze travelled slowly and deliberately over her mother's inappropriate outfit. She'd been mortified when she'd seen the tight Dior-style pink and cream checked suit, which was far too sexy for the mother of the bride.

'What an absolutely stunning ensemble,' Tobias said, his voice dropping to what he probably thought was a seductive tone. 'That colour is incredibly flattering on you. Very – sophisticated.'

Simona actually giggled – *giggled* – like a teenager.

'Oh, you're too kind,' she said, doing a little turn that made the already scandalously short skirt ride up even higher. 'I bought it especially for the occasion. One must make an effort on such a special day.'

Kat felt heat creep up her neck. The cream blouse was unbuttoned so low that the edges of her black bra were clearly visible when she moved. She'd been hoping no one would notice, but Tobias was certainly noticing. His eyes lingered on the exposed skin in a way that made Kat feel nauseated.

'The fit is – beautiful,' Tobias continued, completely oblivious to, or more likely, deliberately ignoring, the disgusted expression on Kat's face.

He's actually flirting with my mother. At my wedding. While his girlfriend stands three feet away.

Kat glanced at Elsa, who was staring at Tobias with a mixture of embarrassment and barely concealed horror. The poor woman looked like she wanted to disappear into the floor.

'Oh, you flatter me,' Simona said, touching Tobias's arm in a way that made Kat want to scream. 'I do love a man who appreciates good fashion. So many men these days have no sense of style.'

'I completely agree,' Tobias replied, moving closer to Simona. 'Though I must say, it's not just the outfit that I noticed. You have an incredible figure for – well, for someone with a daughter old enough to be married.'

That was it. Kat had reached her limit.

'Mum,' she said firmly, stepping between Tobias and Simona. 'Could I speak with you for a moment?'

'Of course, darling,' Simona said, but her eyes

remained fixed on Tobias. 'Though I was having such a lovely conversation with this charming gentleman.'

'I'm sure you were,' Kat said through gritted teeth. 'But I need to speak with you about the table arrangements.'

She practically dragged her mother away, before the situation became any more embarrassing.

'What are you doing?' Kat hissed in a low voice.

'I'm being friendly,' Simona replied innocently. 'He's rather handsome, isn't he? Very distinguished. The touch of silver at his temples gives him quite a sophisticated look.'

'He's Elsa's partner,' Kat said, glancing back at Elsa, who was now staring at her phone with obvious discomfort. 'And you're flirting with him. At my wedding.'

'Oh, don't be so sensitive,' Simona waved her hand dismissively. 'I'm just being polite. Besides, a little harmless flirtation never hurt anyone.'

Kat stared at her mother in disbelief. After everything that had happened with Jacques, after all the pain and betrayal, she was still playing the same games.

'Harmless?' Kat repeated. 'Mum, you're practically throwing yourself at him. And that outfit –'

'What's wrong with my outfit?' Simona looked down at herself, adjusting the neckline of her blouse in a way that somehow made it even more revealing. 'I look fabulous.'

'You look like you're going to a nightclub, not your daughter's wedding,' Kat said, her voice rising slightly before she caught herself and lowered it again. 'That skirt is so short I can see your underwear when you sit down, and your blouse is unbuttoned so low that –'

'Kat!' Simona's voice sharpened. 'I will not be reprimanded by my own daughter for looking good. Just because you chose to dress like a Victorian governess doesn't mean the rest of us have to.'

Kat looked down at her vintage-style wedding dress, a beautiful cream-coloured creation that she'd chosen specifically because it felt timeless and elegant. She'd loved it when she put it on this morning, but now her mother's words stung.

'It's my wedding day,' she said quietly. 'I should be able to dress how I want without being criticised by my own mother.'

'And I should be able to dress how I want without being criticised by my own daughter,' Simona shot back. 'Now, if you'll excuse me, I have a handsome man to return to.'

Kat watched helplessly as her mother sashayed back to Tobias, who was standing awkwardly near Elsa but clearly waiting for Simona's return. The whole situation was humiliating.

Kat took a deep breath, trying to shake off her embarrassment about her mother's behaviour, and rejoined the reception. She spotted a familiar figure approaching the canapé table – a young woman with distinctive bright pink hair wearing a traditional Sámi gákti, the deep blue wool decorated with intricate red and yellow ribbon work. The outfit stood out beautifully amongst the formal wedding attire.

'Tuija!' Kat exclaimed with genuine warmth. 'I'm so glad you could make it.'

Tuija Virtanen turned, her serious expression softening into a smile as she embraced Kat. She was in her late twenties, lean and angular with striking pink hair styled in a sleek bob. Her English carried the distinctive accent of someone from the northern regions.

'I wouldn't have missed it,' Tuija replied. 'It's not often one of my favourite people gets married in my own backyard.'

'How are your parents? Still running the reindeer farm?'

'Thriving, despite the tourists wanting selfies with every animal.' Tuija's smile was genuine. 'Mum sent along some cloudberry preserves for you – they're at the gift table.'

'That's so thoughtful.' Kat felt a warmth that had nothing to do with the room's temperature. This was what she'd hoped for tonight – connections with the people who'd made Lapland feel like home.

'The dress is beautiful, by the way,' Tuija said, admiring Kat's vintage-style gown. 'Very you – elegant but not showy.'

'Thank you, second-hand, obviously!' Kat replied, and the two women smiled at each other.

'Of course, I wouldn't expect anything else.'

'How's the new job at the tourist centre?' Kat asked, trying to keep her eyes and thoughts away from her mum and Tobias, who seemed to be standing even closer to one another.

'Busy. Everyone wants to see the real Lapland these days.' She picked up a canapé topped with wild mushrooms and lingonberry, examining it approvingly. 'At least until they discover it doesn't come with luxury heating.'

They both laughed, and Kat felt some of her earlier tension ease. Tuija was one of her people. The ones who understood why this place mattered, who'd become family over the past few years.

'I should let you get back to your new husband and guests,' Tuija said, glancing around at the mingling crowd. 'Congratulations again. You've found a special man there.' Tuija nodded at Mikael in the distance.

As she moved away, Kat watched her pink hair catch the light, a splash of colour amongst the more conventional wedding hair. It felt good to have locals here, people who truly understood what Lapland meant to her and Mikael.

Chapter Twenty-Three

'Everything alright?' Mikael appeared at Kat's side, his warm voice a welcome relief.

'Fine,' Kat said automatically, then looked up at her new husband's concerned face. 'Actually, no. Not fine. My mother is flirting with Elsa's boyfriend, and I'm worried she's going to cause a scene.'

Mikael glanced over at the group, where Tobias was complimenting Simona's shoes while Elsa stood to one side looking increasingly uncomfortable.

'Ah,' he said with understanding. 'Want me to go and extricate her?'

'Would you?' Kat asked gratefully. 'I don't know what's wrong with Tobias, but he's being incredibly inappropriate. And my mother is just eating it up.'

'On it.' Mikael pressed a quick kiss to her cheek. 'Don't worry, love. We promised each other that nothing would spoil our day, remember?'

Kat watched as her husband smoothly approached

the group, engaging Tobias in conversation about Finnish business law while deftly introducing Simona to a neighbouring circle of guests. Within minutes, he'd managed to separate Tobias from Simona without anyone losing face.

This is why I married him, Kat thought with a surge of love and gratitude. *He's not just kind and gorgeous – he's diplomatic and thoughtful and he always knows exactly what to do.*

'Can I have your attention everyone?' Reg's voice called over the chatter of the guests. 'Time to take your seats!'

Kat took a deep breath, pushing thoughts of her mother's inappropriate behaviour to the back of her mind. This was her wedding, hers and Mikael's. They'd worked so hard to get to this point, overcoming family disapproval, cultural differences, and their own fears about commitment. She wasn't going to let anyone or anything diminish the joy of this day.

She turned to Mikael with a brilliant smile. 'Let's go and sit down, husband.'

'Take my hand, Mrs Andersson,' he replied, and pressed a kiss to her knuckles.

Their table for two was set apart with understated elegance – white linen adorned with winter greenery, white roses, and flickering candles at varying heights. Kat's heart swelled when she noticed the small wooden hearts carved by one of Mikael's local friends nestled amongst the spruce boughs, and the handwritten place cards reading 'Mr Andersson' and 'Mrs Andersson' – the first time she'd seen her new name in writing.

As they made their way to the table, Kat caught sight of Tobias still hovering near her mother, despite Mikael's intervention. The man was practically salivating as he watched Simona adjust her skirt, and Kat felt a wave of pity for Elsa, who was trying so hard to pretend she didn't notice her partner's wandering attention.

But as she and Mikael sat down, the awkwardness and the bad behaviour of some of the wedding guests melted away. Glancing around the room, where many familiar, smiling faces greeted her, she was ready to celebrate their love with the people who mattered to them.

Let Tobias flirt with inappropriate women. Let her mother embarrass herself in her too-tight, too-short outfit. Kat had found her person, and nothing else mattered.

Chapter Twenty-Four

Elsa felt as though she was watching a car crash in slow motion. Each compliment Tobias paid to Simona, each lingering glance, each inappropriate touch, sent a fresh wave of humiliation washing over her. She stood frozen by the window, pretending to admire the view of the snow-covered mountains beyond the hotel while her partner of two years made an absolute fool of himself – and her – in front of everyone.

But what made it worse was the familiarity of it all. The way Tobias leaned in close to Simona, the way his eyes lingered on her exposed skin, the way he seemed to forget Elsa existed the moment another woman captured his attention. It was Victor and Café Strindberg all over again. It made Elsa feel invisible and inadequate.

Men, she thought bitterly. They were all the same in the end.

'Elsa?' Victor's voice was soft beside her, careful not to draw attention from the others. 'Are you all right?'

She turned to look at him, this man who had taught her not to trust, and felt her walls slam back into place. His dark eyes were filled with what looked like concern, but she'd learned not to trust that expression. She'd seen it before, right before he'd shattered her heart into a thousand pieces.

'I'm fine,' she said curtly, turning back to the window.

Victor moved closer, and she caught the scent of his familiar aftershave – the same citrus scent he'd worn all those years ago. It made her stomach clench with unwanted memories.

'No, you're not,' he said quietly. 'And I don't blame you. He's being a complete arse.'

Elsa almost laughed at the irony. Victor, of all people, criticising another man's behaviour. 'Rich coming from you,' she said, her voice sharper than she'd intended.

'What's that supposed to mean?'

She then looked at him properly, seeing the confusion in his eyes. Either he was a very good actor, or he'd genuinely forgotten how he'd treated her. 'Nothing,' she said. 'Just – men, aren't they? They're all the same.'

'Elsa, what's wrong? You're acting like – '

'Like what?' she interrupted. 'Like I don't trust you? Like I remember exactly what you're capable of?' The words tumbled out before she could stop them, ten years of hurt and anger finally finding their voice.

Victor's expression shifted, something like realisation dawning in his eyes. 'Is this about what happened between us? Because if it is, we need to talk properly –'

'Talk?' Elsa's voice rose slightly, then she caught herself and lowered it to a hiss. 'We had our chance to talk ten years ago, Victor. You chose to break my heart instead.'

'What? That's not what happened –'

'Isn't it?' She gestured towards Tobias, who had moved on to complimenting Simona's jewellery, his hand resting possessively on her arm. 'Because it looks exactly like what happened to me. Different woman, same betrayal.'

Victor followed her gaze, then looked back at her with something that might have been sympathy. 'Elsa, you can't compare what's going on there to what was between us. We were –'

'We were nothing,' she cut him off. 'Just like I was nothing to you when you were meeting your blonde friend at Café Strindberg. Just like I was nothing to you when you were all over Nina at that party.' Her voice cracked slightly on the last words, betraying the pain she thought she'd buried.

Victor's face went pale. 'Christ, Elsa. Is that what you think? That I was – that I chose them over you?'

'I don't think anything,' she said, fighting to keep her voice steady. 'I know. I saw you.'

'You saw me doing what, exactly?' His voice was urgent now, desperate. 'Because whatever you think you saw –'

'I saw enough.' She turned away from him, unable to bear the intensity of his gaze. 'And I'm seeing enough now to know that nothing's changed. Men like you, men like him – ' she nodded towards Tobias, 'you just can't help yourselves, can you? There's always another woman, always someone more interesting, more exciting.'

Victor moved closer, and she suddenly found herself backed against the window. The cold glass pressed against her, and for a moment she was transported back to their first trip to Lapland, when everything had been perfect between them.

'Come outside with me,' he said quietly. 'Please. Let me explain.'

Elsa looked at him suspiciously. 'Why? So you can feed me more lies? So you can try to charm your way back into my life?' She shook her head. 'I've heard it all before, Victor. You're very good at making women feel special, right up until you get bored and move on to the next one.'

'That's not – ' He stopped, running a hand through his hair in frustration. 'Fine. Think what you want about me. But don't let him destroy your self-worth because you think all men are the same.'

'Aren't you?' she asked. 'Prove to me that you're different. Prove to me that you didn't choose her over me.'

Victor's jaw tightened. 'I can't prove a negative, Elsa. But I can tell you the truth if you're willing to listen. Which clearly you're not.'

'The truth?' She laughed bitterly. 'The truth is that you were with another woman when you were supposed to be with me. The truth is that you made me feel like I was crazy for being hurt by it. The truth is that you never once tried to explain or fight for us – you just let me walk away.'

'You ran away!' Victor's voice was sharp with old pain. 'You disappeared without a word, without giving me a chance to explain. You just – vanished.'

'Because I knew what I'd see if I stayed,' she said, her voice breaking. 'I knew you'd look me in the eye and lie to me, the way you're probably lying to me now.'

She heard Reg's voice rising above the guests once again, urging those still milling about to find their tables and get seated. As she walked across the room to find Tobias, Elsa's mind betrayed her, drifting back to another time when she and Victor had travelled north together – when his promises had seemed unbreakable.

Chapter Twenty-Five

Lapland, Fourteen Years Earlier

'Are we there yet?' Elsa asked mischievously from the passenger seat of Victor's Range Rover, breaking the silence that had stretched between them for the past hour.

In the backseat, Mikael snorted. 'Didn't know we had a kid in the car,' he said, with a teasing tone.

'Oi, I'm a full three months older than you!' Elsa protested, reaching backwards to give Mikael's shoulder a playful slap.

'Wow, in that case, I'd be careful with quick movements. You might slip a disc or something,' Mikael retorted, tossing his glove at her.

The thick mitten missed Elsa and landed squarely in Victor's lap. He glanced at it with exaggerated disapproval, catching Elsa's eye before turning his gaze to the rearview mirror.

'Children, please,' he said, a smile playing at the

corners of his mouth. 'Let's stop in Jyväskylä for coffee. You infants obviously need a break.'

Elsa stuck her tongue out at him, earning a laugh that transformed Victor's face, softening the sharp angles and lighting up his eyes. It still caught her off guard sometimes how quickly he could shift from the brooding, intense man everyone else saw to the playful, warm person he was with her.

Three months into their relationship, and she was still discovering new facets of Victor Andersson.

After their coffee stop, the Range Rover ate up the kilometres of snowy road, its powerful engine purring, as Victor navigated the route north with the easy confidence he brought to everything. Behind them, Mikael had dozed off, his head lolling against the window and snoring softly.

'He always falls asleep in cars,' Victor commented, catching Elsa's gaze next to him again. 'Since he was a baby. Our mother used to drive him around Helsinki just to get him to nap.'

'I didn't know that,' Elsa said, surprised by the glimpse into their childhood. For all his charisma and charm, Victor rarely volunteered personal information, especially about his family.

'There's a lot you don't know about me as well,' Victor replied, his tone light but his eyes serious. 'I'm looking forward to changing that this week.'

Heat bloomed in Elsa's cheeks that had nothing to

do with the car's heater. Three months of dating Victor had been a whirlwind of stolen moments between his university schedule and her demanding final year at the gymnasium. Dinners at exclusive restaurants that Elsa had never entered before, weekends spent exploring hidden corners of Helsinki, long walks along the frozen harbour with their gloved hands intertwined. But always constrained by time, always with the shadow of his family's expectations hovering in the background.

This week in Lapland would be different. Seven uninterrupted days together in a luxury cabin with Victor's university friends. A chance to be just Elsa and Victor, away from the watchful eyes of Helsinki society and the whispers that followed them – the daughter of a factory worker and the Andersson heir.

'Are your friends already there?' Elsa asked, trying to ignore the flutter of nerves in her stomach. She'd met them briefly at a party, but spending a week in their company was different.

'They should arrive tonight,' Victor replied. 'Don't worry, they'll love you.' He paused, then added softly, 'How could they not?'

The simple sincerity in his voice made Elsa's heart skip. It was these moments – when the confident facade slipped, revealing glimpses of vulnerability – that had drawn her to him despite Mikael's warnings, despite her own misgivings about getting involved with someone from Victor's world.

As they continued north, the landscape trans-formed around them. The forests and lakes of central

Finland gave way to the stark beauty of Lapland – vast expanses of snow stretching to the horizon, broken only by the dark silhouettes of pine trees. The sky deepened to a rich indigo as the brief winter daylight faded, stars appearing like diamond chips scattered across velvet.

By the time they reached Ylläs, night had fully descended. Victor turned off the main road onto a narrow track that wound up the side of the fell, the Range Rover's headlights illuminating the swirling snow before them.

'Are you sure this is the right way?' Elsa asked, peering through the darkness.

'Trust me,' Victor replied, navigating a steep section with ease. 'I've been coming here since I was a kid.'

A few minutes later, they rounded a curve, and the cabin came into view. But 'cabin' was a gross under-statement. Standing before them was a grand, two-storey log structure with floor-to-ceiling windows aglow with warm light. A sleek deck wrapped around the exterior, complete with what appeared to be an outdoor hot tub overlooking the valley below.

'Welcome to Andersson Lodge,' Victor announced, pulling up to the front entrance.

Mikael stirred behind them, yawning as he blinked awake. 'Home sweet home,' he muttered, stretching. 'Better than last year at least. Remember when the pipes froze?'

'Don't remind me,' Victor groaned, turning off the engine. 'Father was livid about the repair bill.'

Elsa sat still in the front seat, taking in the scale of

the 'cabin'. She'd known the Anderssons were wealthy – their home in Ullanlinna was one of Helsinki's most prestigious addresses, and Victor's casual references to summer houses and ski trips had painted a picture of privilege way beyond Elsa's experience. But seeing this property, used just a few weeks each year, brought the disparity between their worlds into sharp focus.

'Elsa?' Victor's voice cut through her thoughts. He'd opened her door and was extending his hand to help her out. 'Everything okay?'

She nodded, accepting his hand and stepping out into the crisp night air. The cold hit her like a physical force, her breath immediately crystallising in front of her face.

'It's beautiful,' she managed, gazing up at the star-filled sky. 'I've never seen so many stars.'

Victor followed her gaze upward, his expression softening. 'Wait until you see the Northern Lights. They're incredible up here.' He squeezed her hand gently. 'Come on, let's get inside before you freeze.'

The interior of the lodge was even more impressive than its exterior. Soaring ceilings with exposed wooden beams, a massive stone fireplace dominating one wall, and tasteful furnishings that managed to be both luxurious and inviting. Floor-to-ceiling windows looked out over the valley, though in the darkness Elsa could see only their own reflections and the distant lights of the ski resort.

'Your room is upstairs, second door on the right,'

Victor told her, carrying her bag despite her protests. 'Mine's at the end of the hall. Mikael's across from you.'

Elsa followed him up the grand staircase, her feet silent against the polished wood. The second floor was just as elegant as the first, with a gallery overlooking the great room below and doors leading off to what she assumed were bedrooms.

Victor stopped at one, pushing it open with his shoulder. 'Here we are.'

The bedroom was larger than Elsa and her father's entire apartment in Helsinki, dominated by a king-sized bed with crisp white linens and a fur throw. A private en-suite bathroom gleamed with marble and glass, and another wall of windows promised stunning views come morning.

'This is – a lot,' Elsa said, unable to keep the awe from her voice.

Victor set her bag down, watching her reaction with an unreadable expression. 'Too much?'

Elsa hesitated, unsure how to articulate the swirl of emotions in her chest. Gratitude for his generosity, certainly. Excitement for the week ahead. But also a nagging discomfort, a feeling of being a tourist in a world where Victor was a permanent resident.

'It's wonderful,' she said finally, offering him a smile. 'Thank you for inviting me.'

Victor crossed the room in two strides, his hands coming to rest lightly on her hips. 'I've been looking forward to this week for ages,' he murmured, his voice dropping to a register that sent shivers down Elsa's spine. 'Just us, away from everything.'

His lips found hers in a gentle kiss that quickly deepened, his arms pulling her closer until she was pressed flush against him. Elsa felt herself melting into his embrace, the familiar heat building between them.

When they finally broke apart, both slightly breathless, Victor rested his forehead against hers. 'I should let you settle in,' he said reluctantly. 'The others will be here soon, and we'll have dinner downstairs.'

'Okay,' Elsa agreed, equally reluctant to let him go.

After he left, Elsa sank onto the edge of the bed, her fingers tracing the soft fur of the throw. The luxury surrounding her was so far removed from her daily reality that it felt almost like a dream. Her father's apartment in Helsinki, with its practical furnishings and walls lined with books, seemed a world away.

For a moment, doubt crept in. What was she doing here? Could she really bridge the gap between her world and Victor's? Or was she just delaying the inevitable realisation that they were too different, from places too far apart to ever truly meet in the middle?

But then she remembered the look in Victor's eyes when he'd kissed her just now, the way he seemed to see her – really see her – in a way no one else ever had. Not the girl from an ordinary working-class family, or the teacher's pet, but Elsa. Just Elsa.

With renewed determination, she stood and began to unpack. This week was their chance to see if what they had could be real, beyond the bubble of their Helsinki romance. She wouldn't waste it on doubts.

Chapter Twenty-Six

The evening passed in a blur of introductions and drinks as Victor's friends arrived, another couple, two single guys and another girl. They were all from prominent Helsinki families and all studying at the same university. They welcomed Elsa with curiosity and polite interest, though she could feel them assessing her, trying to place her in their social hierarchy.

'So, Elsa, how did you and Victor meet?' asked Linnea, a willowy blonde with perfect posture and an accent that suggested time spent at international schools.

'Through my friend Mikael, Victor's brother,' Elsa replied, taking a sip of the expensive champagne Victor had pressed into her hand. 'We've known each other for years.'

'Mikael? Really?' Linnea's perfectly shaped

eyebrows rose in surprise. 'I didn't realise you two were close.'

'Since we were eleven,' Elsa confirmed, feeling a flicker of defensiveness. 'We've been in the same class since middle school.'

'How nice,' Linnea murmured, her tone suggesting it was anything but. 'And what does your family do?'

Before Elsa could answer, Victor appeared at her side, his arm sliding around her waist. 'Elsa's father is a brilliant engineer,' he said, his voice carrying a subtle warning. 'And Elsa herself is heading to Helsinki University next year to study law.'

'How impressive,' Linnea replied, her smile not quite reaching her eyes. 'If you'll excuse me, I think Henrik is looking for me.'

As she walked away, Elsa leaned into Victor's side. 'Thanks for the rescue.'

'Ignore Linnea,' Victor said, pressing a kiss to her temple. 'She's just jealous because you're not only beautiful but also have a brain.'

Elsa laughed, some of the tension easing from her shoulders. 'Is that why you're with me? For my brain?'

Victor's eyes darkened as he gazed down at her. 'Among other things,' he murmured, his voice low and intimate despite the crowded room.

Elsa flushed, but before she could respond, Mikael appeared, looking slightly uncomfortable in the sleek surroundings.

'There's talk of a midnight sauna,' he informed

them, casting a wary glance at the gathering. 'I'm heading up to change.'

'Excellent idea,' Victor agreed, turning to the group. 'Sauna in twenty minutes!'

As they went off to change, Elsa felt a flutter of uncertainty. Sauna was a Finnish tradition, of course, but she'd never experienced it in a mixed-gender setting with near-strangers.

Victor seemed to sense her hesitation. 'You don't have to join if you're not comfortable,' he assured her. 'But it's really quite wonderful, especially in winter. The lodge has a traditional smoke sauna by the lake.'

'I'll try it,' Elsa decided, pushing aside her reservations. This week was about new experiences, after all.

Twenty minutes later, wrapped in a fluffy robe, carrying an additional towel to cover herself in the sauna, Elsa made her way down to the lake with the others. The night was crisp and clear, and filled with stars. The smoke sauna was a separate structure, rustic and authentically Finnish compared to the luxury of the main lodge.

Inside, it was darker than in a more modern sauna, with walls covered in soot. The heat enveloped her immediately, dry and intense. The other guests were already there, sitting on the wooden benches in varying states of undress. Victor patted the space beside him, and Elsa settled in, trying not to feel self-conscious in her towel.

'First time in a traditional smoke sauna?' Henrik

asked, pouring water over the hot stones with a hiss of steam.

Elsa nodded, feeling sweat begin to bead on her skin. 'It's – intense.'

'Best way to experience it fully is after a swim,' Victor said, his eyes gleaming in the dim light. 'After we're properly warmed up, we'll take a dip in the lake.'

'The frozen lake?' Elsa clarified, her eyes widening. She knew that some people got into the sea around Helsinki from the many public saunas, but they were mostly old – or young – health nuts, rather than well-to-do members of the Finnish upper class.

The group laughed, but it was good-natured rather than mocking.

'It's invigorating,' promised Sofia, one of the other girls. 'Terrifying at first, but then amazing.'

As the heat built, conversation flowed more freely. The initial awkwardness faded as they shared stories from university, plans for the skiing week ahead, and increasingly outrageous tales from previous winter breaks.

'Remember when Victor tried to take on that black diamond run after drinking half a bottle of vodka?' Henrik recalled, prompting howls of laughter.

'In my defense, it looked much easier from the bottom,' Victor retorted, grinning.

'You broke your arm in two places!' Mikael reminded him.

'And charmed the ski patrol woman into not telling

Father,' Victor added, winking at Elsa. 'One of my finer moments.'

Elsa laughed along with the others, feeling some of her earlier tension ease. They were just people, after all – privileged, certainly, but still young and seeking the same connections and experiences as anyone else.

When the heat became almost unbearable, Victor stood and extended his hand to Elsa. 'Ready for the lake?'

She hesitated only briefly before taking his hand. 'As I'll ever be.' Victor told her to grab a pair of swim shoes that she could wear into the water, as well as a pair of gloves.

'I don't want to be responsible for giving you frost-bite on your first go,' he said. Once again, his tenderness made her heart flip.

Outside, the cold air hit her heated skin like a physical blow. The lake stretched before them, a section near the shoreline cleared of snow to reveal the dark ice beneath. A long mat led to a large hole cut into the ice, steam rising from the water into the frigid night air.

'Ladies first,' Henrik suggested, gesturing towards the hole.

'Not a chance,' Linnea retorted, giving him a playful shove.

Before anyone else could volunteer, Victor stepped forward, shedding his robe in one fluid motion. Completely naked, he paused at the edge of the hole, glancing back at Elsa with a wicked grin.

She was glad of the darkness of the night because

her cheeks were burning red hot not only from the sauna but the sight of Victor's perfectly formed backside.

'See you on the other side,' he said, and then plunged into the water.

His head disappeared briefly before he resurfaced with a whoop, water streaming from his hair. 'Come on in!'

One by one, the others followed, their shrieks and laughter echoing across the frozen landscape. Elsa hung back, watching their antics with a mixture of amusement and trepidation.

'It's not as bad as it looks,' Mikael assured her, pausing beside her before his own turn. 'But no one will think less of you if you skip it.'

Elsa squared her shoulders. 'No, I want to try.'

She walked determinedly to the edge of the hole. Victor was still in the water, watching her with undisguised admiration in his eyes.

'The trick is to just go for it,' he advised. 'Don't hesitate.'

Taking a deep breath, Elsa quickly slipped off her towel, and ignoring the freezing assault on her body, closed her eyes and jumped.

The shock of the cold was indescribable – a thousand icy needles piercing her skin simultaneously, driving the air from her lungs. For a moment, panic seized her as she sank beneath the surface. Then strong hands caught her, pulling her up into the night air.

'Breathe,' Victor instructed, his arms supporting her as she gasped.

After the initial shock, the sensation transformed into something else entirely – a tingling, vibrant awareness that seemed to illuminate every nerve ending. Elsa laughed, the sound bubbling up from deep inside her.

'It's amazing!' she exclaimed, surprised by her own reaction.

Victor's answering smile was bright with pleasure and something else – pride, perhaps, or a deeper emotion she wasn't ready to name. 'You're amazing,' he replied, his voice low so that only she could hear. Their bodies were close to one another and in spite of the chill of the water, Elsa felt a heat rise inside her.

They stayed in the water for only half a minute before the cold became too intense. Climbing out, Elsa immediately wrapped herself in her towel, her body trembling with a mixture of adrenaline and decreasing body temperature.

'Back to the sauna to warm up,' Victor directed, leading the shivering group back to the wooden building.

The second round in the sauna was more fun than the first, the shared experience of the ice plunge having broken down remaining barriers. Elsa found herself chatting easily with Linnea about her university plans, while Victor talked skiing strategies with Henrik and the others.

It was past midnight when they finally returned to the main lodge, pleasantly exhausted from the sauna's heat and the night's socialising. In the grand living room, a fire still burned in the massive stone fireplace, casting a warm glow over the space.

'Nightcap?' Victor suggested, gesturing towards the well-stocked bar in the corner.

Some of the group agreed, settling onto the plush sofas, but Elsa shook her head. 'I think I'll head up,' she said, stifling a yawn. 'It's been a long day.'

'I'll walk you,' Victor offered immediately, setting down his glass.

They climbed the stairs in comfortable silence, Victor's hand resting lightly on the small of her back. At her door, he paused, reluctance clear in his expression.

'I had a good time tonight,' Elsa told him sincerely, despite her earlier reservations.

'Even the ice plunge?' Victor asked, smiling.

'Especially that,' Elsa admitted. 'It was exhilarating.'

Victor's gaze dropped to her mouth, his expression shifting to something more intense. 'You continue to surprise me, Elsa Berg,' he murmured, leaning in to brush his lips against hers.

The kiss deepened quickly, igniting the same spark that always flared between them. Elsa found herself pressed against her door, Victor's body warm against hers, his hands caressing her still-damp hair.

When they finally broke apart, both were breathing heavily. For a moment, Elsa considered inviting him in. They had been seeing each other for three months, dancing around the edge of intimacy without crossing the final threshold. Here, away from the constraints of Helsinki, it would be easy to take that step.

But something held her back – not reluctance, exactly, but a desire to be sure, to know that what they had was more than physical attraction or the thrill of knocking down social barriers.

'Goodnight, Victor,' she said softly, pressing one last kiss to his lips.

He sighed, resting his forehead against hers. 'Goodnight, Elsa. Sweet dreams.'

As he turned to go, Elsa couldn't help but admire the strong lines of his back, the grace with which he moved. Whatever doubts she had about bridging their different worlds, there was no denying the connection between them – a pull as inevitable as gravity.

'Victor,' she called impulsively, just before he reached his door.

He turned, eyebrows raised in question.

'I'm glad I came,' she said simply.

His answering smile was like the sun breaking through clouds. 'So am I,' he replied. 'More than you know.'

'Stay with me tonight,' she said softly, the words escaping before she could second-guess herself.

Victor's eyes widened, surprise giving way to something deeper, more intense. 'Are you sure?' he asked, his voice husky.

Elsa nodded, certain in a way she had never been before. 'I've never been more sure of anything.'

In the privacy of Elsa's room, illuminated only by

the soft glow of stars through the windows, they came together with a tenderness that brought tears to Elsa's eyes. Victor's touch was reverent, his whispered words counterpoint to the crescendo of emotion building between them.

When they finally lay entwined, breathless and sated, Elsa felt as though she had found a piece of herself she hadn't known was missing. The perfect contentment she had never felt before.

Chapter Twenty-Seven

The morning of their last day in Lapland dawned crisp and cloudless, the kind of Arctic morning that made every breath feel like drinking starlight. Elsa woke to find Victor already awake beside her, propped up on one elbow, watching the way the early light painted silver patterns across her face.

'Good morning, beautiful,' he murmured, pressing a soft kiss to her temple.

'Mmm,' she replied, stretching luxuriously beneath the thick duvet. 'What time is it?'

'Early. But look.' Victor nodded towards the floor-to-ceiling windows that dominated one wall of their bedroom.

Elsa sat up, pulling the sheet around herself, and gasped. Overnight, fresh snow had blanketed the land-scape in pristine white. The pine trees looked like something from a Christmas card, their branches heavy with powder that caught the morning light and threw it back in millions of tiny diamonds.

'It's incredible,' she breathed. 'How much fell?'

'At least thirty centimetres, maybe more. Perfect conditions for what I have planned today.' Victor's excitement was infectious. 'Have you ever been on a snowmobile?'

Elsa shook her head. She'd never been to Lapland before, so how could she have experienced snowmobiles? But she didn't want to break the mood by pointing out another difference between them.

'You'll love it,' Victor assured her, his eyes bright with excitement. 'It's the closest thing to flying whilst still on the ground.'

After breakfast, Victor led her to a sleek snowmobile waiting just outside the lodge. He spent a few minutes showing her the basics – how to start the engine, operate the throttle, steer effectively without overcompensating. Then he climbed on behind her, his chest pressed against her back as his hands covered hers on the handlebars.

'Ready?' he asked, his breath warm against her ear even through her helmet.

Elsa nodded, adrenaline already surging through her veins. With Victor guiding her movements, she started the engine and tentatively eased them forward. The snowmobile responded to the lightest touch, cutting through the fresh powder with surprising agility.

'You're a natural!' Victor called as they picked up

speed, following a groomed trail that wound through the forest.

The wind whipped away Elsa's laugh, but she felt a surge of pure joy as they raced across the frozen landscape. Victor was right – it was like flying, the boundaries between herself and the machine dissolving so that they moved as one entity through the winter wonderland.

They rode for over an hour, climbing higher into the fells until they reached a viewpoint overlooking the valley. Victor took over driving for the last stretch, navigating a steeper, more challenging section of the trail with practised ease.

At the summit, they killed the engine and removed their helmets, gazing out at the breathtaking panorama spread before them. The world was rendered in shades of blue and white, the sunlight sparkling on the untouched snow. In the distance, the frozen lake reflected the vast Arctic sky.

'It's the most beautiful thing I've ever seen,' Elsa breathed, her words forming clouds in the frigid air.

Victor wasn't looking at the view. 'I can think of something more beautiful,' he murmured, his eyes fixed on her face.

Elsa turned to him, about to brush off the compliment with her usual practicality, but something in his expression stopped her. There was an openness there, a vulnerability that stripped away her defences.

'Victor – ' she began, unsure what she wanted to say.

He stepped closer, until she could see the individual snowflakes caught in his eyelashes. 'I know we've only been together for a few months,' he said, his voice low and serious. 'But I've never felt this way about anyone before, Elsa. When I'm with you, I feel like – like myself. Not Victor Andersson, heir to Andersson Mining, or Erik's son, or the guy everyone expects to either fail spectacularly or succeed beyond measure. Just – me.'

Elsa's heart raced, not from adrenaline now but from the raw honesty in his voice. 'I feel that too,' she admitted. 'Like you see the real me.'

Victor's gloved hand came up to cup her cheek. 'I love you, Elsa Berg,' he said simply. 'I think I've loved you since that day in the school corridor when you looked at me like I was nothing special.'

Elsa's breath caught in her throat. They hadn't said those words yet, and it seemed too soon. But hearing them now, in this pristine wilderness with the entire world spread out below them, felt both terrifying and exactly right.

'I love you too,' she whispered, the words falling from her lips like a truth she had known all along.

Victor's kiss was gentle at first, then increasingly urgent, as if he could pour all his feelings into that single connection. Elsa responded in kind, her arms winding around his neck to pull him closer. In that moment, the differences between their worlds seemed insignificant – mere details that couldn't possibly matter in the face of what they had found together.

When they finally broke apart, Victor rested his forehead against hers, his breath coming in visible puffs between them. 'I want you to know that this isn't casual for me,' he said, his voice rough with emotion. 'You aren't just another girlfriend, Elsa. You're – everything.'

Elsa felt tears prick her eyes, instantly freezing in the cold air. 'I was so afraid,' she confessed. 'That this week would show us how different we are, how impossible it would be – '

'And now?' Victor prompted, his eyes searching hers.

'Now I think maybe none of that matters,' Elsa replied. 'Not if we're together.'

Victor's answering smile was like a sunrise – slow, radiant, transforming everything it touched. 'Together,' he echoed, sealing the promise with another kiss.

As they stood there on the mountaintop, wrapped in each other's arms with the vast Arctic wilderness stretching in every direction, Elsa felt something settle inside her – a certainty that whatever challenges lay ahead, they would face them together. It was the happiest moment of her life.

Back at the lodge that evening, they gathered with the others for their final dinner. Elsa found herself watching Victor across the table as he laughed at something Henrik had said, his head thrown back in genuine amusement, his eyes crinkling at the corners. He caught her gaze and winked, a private gesture that sent warmth flooding through her.

Linnea, seated beside Elsa, followed her gaze and smiled knowingly.

'I've never seen him like this before, you know,' she commented quietly.

'Like what?' Elsa asked, taking a sip of her wine.

'Happy,' Linnea replied simply. 'Truly happy, not just the surface charm he shows everyone else. You're good for him, Elsa.'

The sincerity in Linnea's voice touched Elsa deeply.

'He's good for me too,' she admitted. 'Though I never expected it to happen.'

Linnea laughed softly. 'The best things usually come when we least expect them, don't they?'

As the evening progressed, Elsa found herself drawn into the easy camaraderie of the group. The initial awkwardness had faded entirely, replaced by the warmth of new friendships and shared experiences. Even Mikael seemed to have forgotten his initial opposition to Elsa and Victor's relationship. Elsa caught his eye across the table and returned his relaxed smile.

Later, as the others settled in for more drinks by the fire, Victor took Elsa's hand and led her outside onto the deck. The cold was intense, but the sight before them was worth it – ribbons of green and violet light shifting across the vast starry sky, more spectacular than any they'd seen before.

'Our last night,' Victor murmured, his arms around her waist as they watched the ethereal display. 'The lights are putting on quite a show for us.'

'Legend says they're the spirits of the departed,' Elsa said, remembering something she'd read. 'Or caused by a magical fox sweeping its tail across the snow.'

'I think it's all about solar particles and magnetic fields,' Victor said, smiling down at her.

'You with your boring scientific explanations,' Elsa replied. 'I think I prefer the fox.'

Victor laughed, the sound carrying across the silent landscape. 'Of course you do.'

They stood there in comfortable silence, watching nature's most magnificent light show unfold above them. In that moment, with Victor's arms around her and the aurora borealis painting the sky in vibrant hues, Elsa felt a perfect contentment she had never known before.

'What are you thinking?' Victor asked, his voice low against her ear.

Elsa turned in his arms to face him, the Northern Lights creating a halo around his silhouette. 'That I've never been happier than I am right now, here with you.'

The raw honesty in her voice seemed to strike something deep within Victor. His expression softened, his eyes reflecting the dancing lights above them.

'I love you,' Victor murmured, pressing a kiss to her forehead as she nestled against his chest. 'More than I've ever loved anyone or anything.'

'I love you too,' Elsa replied, tracing patterns on his skin with her fingertips. 'Do you think it's mad that I feel like this is – forever?'

Victor's arms tightened around her. 'Not mad at all,' he assured her. 'You're it for me, Elsa Berg. The one.'

That night, as they drifted towards sleep, tangled in each other's arms with the memory of the Northern Lights fresh in their minds, Elsa believed with her whole heart that nothing could ever come between them. Their love, born in the crisp winter air of Helsinki and sealed beneath the dancing lights of Lapland, felt unbreakable, eternal.

She could never have imagined that in less than four years, it would all be over.

Chapter Twenty-Eight

Lapland, Now

Elsa approached Tobias who was still in conversation with Simona. He was leaning in to whisper something in her ear, and she was laughing like a schoolgirl.

The sight of it made Elsa's chest tighten. How many times had she watched Victor do the same thing? How many times had she told herself she was imagining things, that she was being paranoid, that she was overreacting?

'Elsa,' Victor said quietly behind her. She hadn't realised he'd followed her. 'This isn't over.'

She looked at him, seeing the determination in his eyes, and felt a flicker of the old fear. Victor had always been persuasive, always been able to make her doubt her own perceptions. But she was older now, wiser. She wouldn't let him manipulate her again.

'Yes, it is,' she said firmly. 'It's been over for ten years, Victor. And watching him tonight has just reminded me why.' She made a slight gesture with her head, indicating the giggling pair behind them.

'Tobias,' she said, approaching him and Simona with a polite smile.

He looked up, his hand still resting casually on Simona's arm. 'Elsa. There you are.'

'Simona, what a lovely dress,' Elsa said warmly, genuinely admiring Kat's mother's elegant outfit.

'Oh, thank you, dear! And you look absolutely stunning. Doesn't she, Tobias?' Simona beamed, clearly delighted by the compliment.

'Indeed,' Tobias replied smoothly. 'Simona was just telling me about the most marvellous spa treatments they have here at the hotel. Apparently, the reindeer milk facials are quite rejuvenating.'

'How wonderful,' Elsa replied, noting how Tobias's thumb was now tracing small circles on Simona's arm as he spoke.

'You should book one, darling. You've seemed rather tense this evening.' His voice carried that patronising edge she'd grown to recognise, the word 'darling' delivered with calculated emphasis.

'Perhaps it's all this excitement,' Simona said kindly, oblivious to the undercurrents. 'Weddings can be quite overwhelming, can't they?'

'They can indeed,' Elsa agreed, touched by Simona's genuine warmth. 'You must be so proud of Kat. She looks radiant.'

'Oh, she does, doesn't she? I'm absolutely over the moon.' Simona's eyes sparkled with maternal joy.

'Well,' Tobias interjected smoothly, 'we should let you find your table, Simona. Thank you for the – spa recommendations.' He gave her arm a final, lingering squeeze.

As they walked away, Tobias caught Elsa's elbow. 'Everything alright?'

'Perfectly fine. Simona seems lovely.'

'She is very friendly, isn't she?' His tone was carefully neutral, but she caught the satisfied edge beneath it.

Elsa stopped walking and faced him. 'Were you?'

'Was I what?'

'Being friendly. Or were you doing what you always do at parties – flirting with other women whilst making me feel like I'm imagining it.'

Tobias's expression grew cold. 'I don't know what you mean.'

'Don't you?' She kept her voice low, conscious of the other guests around them. 'The way you touched her arm, leant in close, made her laugh. You knew exactly what you were doing.'

'You're being ridiculous, Elsa. This is exactly the sort of paranoid behaviour that – '

'That what? That ruins relationships?' She felt something settle in her chest, a clarity she hadn't experienced in months. 'Because I'm starting to think it's not paranoia when the pattern keeps repeating itself.'

She walked away from Tobias, towards the other guests. But even as she smiled and made conversation, even as she looked for their table, she couldn't shake the familiar feeling of déjà vu.

'Are we there yet?' she had asked from the passenger seat of Victor's Range Rover, seventeen years old and already desperately in love, with no idea that the man she trusted with her heart would one day break it so completely.

The memory made her chest tight with emotion. She'd been so naïve then, so trusting. She'd believed in happy endings and forever love, believed that Victor would never hurt her.

How wrong she'd been.

And now here Victor was, trying to worm his way back into her life with the same charm, the same intensity, the same promises. But she could see through him now. She could see him for what he really was: just another man who couldn't be trusted, just another heartbreak waiting to happen.

She wouldn't make the same mistake twice.

Chapter Twenty-Nine

'The chart says we're at table three. I think it's that one?' Tobias had caught up with her and was acting as if their argument hadn't happened. He turned to face her and placed his hand on her arm. 'We just need to get through the meal and then we can disappear, right?'

But Elsa wasn't looking at him or listening to his words. She was concentrating on the table Tobias had pointed at, her heart sinking. How could Mikael have done this to her? Not only were both Ulla and Erik Andersson seated at the same table, but Victor was standing, grinning, next to an empty seat. When Ulla waved towards them, she wanted to pull Tobias's arm and direct him to another table. But it was too late. Besides, she didn't want to show Victor she was uncomfortable around him or his parents. He had always denied that they didn't approve of her, but she knew better.

The memory of that horrible day in Erik Andersson's office flashed through her mind – his cruel words about her not having the 'necessary pedigree' for his boys, the way he'd dismissed her so casually. She'd been waiting for Victor to get back from a meeting and was planning to go bowling with him. Instead, she'd run from that office in tears, straight into Victor's arms.

'You're not still upset with me about Simona. It was nothing, I swear – ?' Tobias's voice pulled her back to the present.

She moved closer to Tobias and swallowed hard. 'No, I'm fine.'

Elsa decided to take the bull by the horns and give Erik Andersson as good as she got. Walking ahead, she led Tobias to the table where the Andersson clan was sitting.

'Hello,' she said simply and gave Ulla Andersson an air kiss, ignoring her husband and Victor.

'I saw you were at our table. How wonderful!'

Victor's mother leaned towards her and stage whispered, 'You're looking very beautiful. I love that outfit.'

Ulla Andersson's cropped brown bob had grey strands in it, and her face had deep lines that were new. Her eyes were bloodshot as if she'd been crying. Happy tears, Elsa hoped, but was afraid the cause of her misery might be her husband.

'Elsa, how lovely to see you after all these years.'

Erik had got up, and to Elsa's horror, was moving towards her.

Before she could stop him, Erik Andersson was also

hugging her, finishing the unexpected gesture with a kiss on her cheek. Elsa's first instinct was to wipe the wet patch his lips had left with her hand, or better still, a paper tissue she had in her handbag, but she just stayed put, trying to raise a smile to her lips.

'Where did you disappear to all those years ago, you naughty girl? You have no idea what grief you caused. Victor here has been pining after you for years!'

Once again, just as he did in his dark, scary office, Erik Andersson had rendered Elsa speechless.

'This is Tobias – Lundgren,' she stammered.

Erik shook her boyfriend's hand, while Tobias's eyes darted back to her full of questions.

She gave a slight shake of her head.

Not now.

'Let's all sit down,' Victor said, giving an awkward laugh. His eyes didn't meet Elsa's, but when he pulled a chair out for Elsa to sit down, he whispered in her ear.

'I'm sorry about him.'

How long was he going to carry on apologising for his father? And how many times did he have to do it in a day?

Elsa nodded and turned towards Tobias, away from Victor. She no longer needed to worry about Erik Andersson.

Or Victor.

Chapter Thirty

Victor wondered for the thousandth time what he had done to make Elsa leave him – and Finland.

He still remembered that evening when she hadn't answered her phone and had ignored his texts. She'd already finished all her exams, and they'd planned to celebrate the end of her studies the following weekend. Victor hadn't told Elsa, but he had a surprise in store for her. He'd wanted to take her on a trip abroad, perhaps somewhere flashy like Ibiza, or even the Bahamas, but he knew she would hate not having any money of her own to spend, so he'd booked a suite at the Kämp Hotel for one night. He'd ordered champagne for the room and rose petals to be scattered on the bed. They would dine in the room, and afterwards he'd present her with the ring he'd bought at Lindroos on Alexi. He'd been planning the proposal for months, even years, because as soon as he'd realised he was in love with Elsa, he knew she was the girl he was going to marry.

And then, two nights before he was going to pop the question, she disappeared.

The memory of that night taunted him, the hurt still raw. Worried sick, he had driven to Pasila on the outskirts of Helsinki and rung the bell to her student apartment. She had no landline, so this was the only way he could reach her. But when the door opened, it wasn't Elsa standing there. It was her friend, Nina.

'She doesn't want to talk to you,' Nina said, blocking his way in.

Victor swore under his breath. It had to be Nina, the same girl he had drunkenly kissed two years ago while celebrating his own exams. Elsa had seen them, and it had taken him months to convince her that he hadn't known what he was doing that night. Seeing Nina standing in front of him, he realised the truth was staring back at him with accusing eyes.

'She left,' Nina continued, her voice tinged with bitterness. 'She's gone, Victor.'

His heart clenched at her words, a mixture of confusion and desperation swirling inside him. She narrowed her eyes at Victor.

'If you try anything, I'm going to scream.'

'All I want to do is talk to her. I don't know what's going on!'

The brown-haired girl sighed and turned her head towards the inside of the flat behind her.

'What do you want to do?'

Elsa appeared in the doorway. Her face looked puffy as if she'd been crying.

'Go away, Victor. I don't want to see you again, ever.'

With those words, she disappeared inside the flat. The door slammed in Victor's face.

'Elsa, please just talk to me,' Victor had pleaded outside the door, his heart sinking at her words. He had no idea what had caused her sudden change of heart, but he refused to believe that their relationship was over just like that.

The door remained closed, and there was no response from inside the apartment. Victor leaned against the wall, running a hand through his hair in frustration. He didn't want to give up on Elsa, not after all they had been through together.

As he stood outside Elsa's apartment, memories flooded his mind – their first date at the cosy cafe in Helsinki, their skiing and snowmobile escapades on the pristine fells in Lapland, her soft laughter echoing through the quiet mountains. Elsa had become his world, his anchor amidst the chaos of his family.

Facing the closed door that separated him from Elsa, Victor felt a wave of helplessness wash over him. He couldn't understand what had changed between them so suddenly, why she had shut him out without a word of explanation.

Determined not to give up on her, Victor snapped into action. He wasn't going to leave without getting some answers. He took out his phone and dialled Elsa's number, hoping she would pick up.

To his surprise, she answered on the second ring.

'Elsa, please what's going on?'

'I don't want to see you, Victor,' came her cold reply. 'Please, just leave.'

But Victor would not let her off that easily. 'Why? What did I do? Can we please just talk about this?'

'There's nothing left to talk about,' Elsa said with finality before hanging up.

Frustrated and confused, Victor stood in the cold stairway of the Pasila student's accommodation for what seemed like an age. A couple of students, two girls holding hands, glanced at him as they passed, then descended the stairs. He sat down with his back to Elsa's flat, his head in his hands. He wracked his brain for the reason Elsa might be so angry and upset, but he couldn't think of anything.

He finally gave up and walked back towards his car. The familiar streets of Helsinki were a blur as he drove home alone, consumed by thoughts of Elsa. He couldn't understand why she suddenly wanted nothing to do with him.

Was it Nina? Had she told lies about Victor? But even if she had, he couldn't believe Elsa would cut him out of her life without giving him the chance to explain or defend himself. The questions swirled in Victor's mind, a storm of doubt and hurt raging within him.

Days turned into weeks, and Elsa remained resolute. His attempts to reach out to her were met with stony silence or terse rejections. She had blocked him from all her social media accounts and changed her number. Victor felt like he was losing a piece of himself as each day passed without Elsa.

Ending their relationship and the resolute silence, with no explanation of why she had disappeared, had made Victor physically ill. At first, his mother Ulla had plied him with medication and well-meaning advice, but nothing could ease the ache in Victor's heart. It wasn't just the loss of Elsa that tormented him, but the lack of closure, the unanswered questions that gnawed at his soul. He even sought Mikael's advice, despite never having that kind of relationship with his younger brother. But Mikael refused to explain or tell him where Elsa had gone. When Victor visited the flat in Pasila again, he found strangers living there.

It took Victor years to accept that Elsa was gone. And now she was here, celebrating Mikael's marriage, more beautiful than ever. The pain of her sudden disappearance years ago still lingered in his heart, a wound that had never fully healed.

Chapter Thirty-One

Mikael gazed at his parents, who sat together with Victor, Tobias and Elsa. Elsa's smile was somewhat frozen as she picked at the wedding breakfast. How did that happen? He was certain they'd put Elsa and her boyfriend with Kat's family. No guesses who'd swapped the place cards.

To his horror, Mikael saw his father had pushed his untouched plate away and was now rising to his feet, tapping his knife against a glass.

But before Mikael could say a word, Reg jumped up and announced into the microphone, 'Ladies and Gentlemen, Erik Andersson, the father of the groom.'

Mikael tried to catch Reg's eye to stop him, but Reg wasn't looking at him. He took Kat's hand under the table and whispered, 'I'm afraid of what my father's going to say.'

She pressed a kiss on his cheek and replied in a low voice, 'It'll be fine.'

Erik, impeccably dressed in his dark blue suit, straightened his shoulders and began speaking. 'Thank you for the introduction,' he nodded towards Reg. 'I wanted to welcome you, Katherine, to our humble family.'

Before he could continue, Kat's friend Tuija, in traditional Lappish dress with her distinctive pink hair appearing even brighter than usual, shot to her feet. 'No mines in Lapland!'

To Mikael's horror, Kat rose beside him, her fist clenched, eyes blazing. 'No mines in Lapland!'

Several guests repeated the gesture and words. This was a complete disaster.

Kat saw his expression and quickly sat back down, mouthing, 'Sorry.'

Reg stood up calmly. 'Now, now. Let's all settle down. This is a joyous occasion, and the groom's father would like to say a few words.'

There was a shuffling of chairs as the protesters sat down, followed by an ominous silence. Mikael saw his father's dark eyes and feared what might happen next. Ulla placed a warning hand on Erik's arm. He turned towards her and stood there for a long moment, looking at his wife while the room waited.

Then Erik continued, his voice measured. 'We've had our differences with my son, some of which you seem to be well aware of, but we are all the same, family. I haven't had the pleasure of getting to know you, Katherine, yet, but I am certain my clever and brave son would not wish to marry anyone who wasn't a good and smart woman.' He raised his glass. 'I'd like to toast the bride and groom, Mr and Mrs Mikael Andersson!'

Mikael's relief was so overwhelming that he forgot to raise his own glass until Kat nudged him. Everyone was standing, glasses raised, waiting for him.

'To Mr and Mrs Andersson!' the room chorused.

'That wasn't too bad,' Kat whispered. 'I'm sorry; I didn't mean to do that. It was just a gut reaction.'

'It's okay. He deserves to know how the local people feel,' Mikael replied, squeezing her hand.

This was why he loved her so dearly. She was passionate about the things that mattered and stood up for her beliefs. Even his stubborn father couldn't change that about her.

Chapter Thirty-Two

The gentle clink of cutlery against plates began to subside as Reg, once again, stood up, his silver hair catching the candlelight. He tapped his wine glass with a spoon, the delicate chime drawing the attention of the wedding guests.

'Ladies and gentlemen,' Reg announced with his booming voice, 'If I could have your attention, please. It's time for our best man to say a few words.'

Mikael felt his stomach tighten as he watched Victor rise from his seat at the nearby table. His brother's expression was carefully neutral, the polished smile he wore in boardrooms firmly in place. Victor's brown hair fell across his forehead as he stood, and he pushed it back with that familiar flick of his head.

Mikael glanced at Tuija, and shook his head at her, imperceptibly, he hoped. Tuija nodded and smiled a reassurance. At least there wouldn't be a repeat of the previous protest, Mikael hoped.

'Thank you, Reg,' Victor said, his voice carrying the smooth confidence Mikael recognised from countless family gatherings. 'I must admit, when Mikael asked me to be his best man, I wasn't entirely sure what to expect.'

A few polite chuckles rippled through the guests. Victor's gaze swept across the room before settling on the bride and groom.

'My brother and I have always been different,' Victor continued, choosing his words carefully. 'Different interests, different priorities, different ideas about what constitutes success. Mikael always was the idealistic one, even when we were children.'

Mikael detected the slight edge beneath Victor's diplomatic tone. It wasn't overtly critical, but not warm either.

'When he announced he was leaving Helsinki to start a ski school in Lapland, I'll be honest, I thought he'd lost his mind,' Victor said with a self-deprecating laugh that didn't quite reach his eyes. 'A successful future in the family business, guaranteed financial security, and he wanted to trade it all for snow and reindeer.'

The guests laughed, but Mikael caught the subtle barb. Victor was playing to the crowd whilst making his point.

'But then I met Kat,' Victor's tone shifted as he looked towards the bride, 'and I began to understand what drew my brother to this place. Kat, you have a passion and conviction that's quite remarkable. You've clearly found someone who shares your environmental concerns and your commitment to this region.'

It was complimentary, but somehow felt clinical, as if Victor were delivering a business assessment rather than a wedding toast.

'Mikael has always been the brother who follows his heart,' Victor continued, that polished smile never wavering. 'Sometimes that's taken him in directions the rest of us couldn't quite understand, but there's no denying his sincerity. He genuinely believes in what he's doing here.'

Mikael felt an uncomfortable flutter at his brother's tone. The words were supportive, but something underneath felt hollow, as if Victor was merely going through the motions.

'They say that opposites attract, and perhaps that's true for brothers as well,' Victor said, glancing briefly at Mikael. 'While I've stayed in Helsinki, managing the responsibilities that come with the family business, Mikael has carved out his own niche here in the North. We've chosen different paths, but that doesn't mean we can't respect each other's choices.'

The comment about 'managing responsibilities' carried just enough weight to suggest sacrifice without explicitly saying so. Mikael recognised his brother's skill at saying one thing whilst implying another.

'Kat, thank you for making my brother so obviously happy,' Victor said, raising his glass. 'Anyone can see that you two are well-matched in your shared interests. And Mikael, thank you for reminding us all that there are many ways to live a life.'

Victor's smile became marginally more genuine as he concluded. 'So please, join me in raising your glasses to Mikael and Kat. May your marriage be as strong as your convictions and your commitment to each other be as enduring. To the bride and groom!'

The room erupted in polite applause and the clinking of glasses. Victor remained standing for a moment, accepting the guests' appreciation with practised grace, before settling back into his seat beside Elsa.

Mikael felt oddly unsettled by the speech. On the surface, it had been perfectly appropriate. It was complimentary, warm enough, with just the right touches of humour. But underneath, he'd sensed his brother's ongoing frustration, carefully masked but still present. The references to responsibility, to different choices, to his own bewilderment at Mikael's decisions. It all felt like Victor performing the role of supportive brother whilst harbouring deeper resentments.

As the applause died down and conversations resumed, Mikael glanced over at Victor, who was already engaged in quiet conversation with Elsa. His brother's expression had returned to that careful neutrality, the mask firmly back in place.

Kat squeezed his hand. 'That was lovely,' she whispered, though Mikael caught a note of uncertainty in her voice that suggested she, too, had detected the undercurrents in Victor's words.

Mikael nodded, forcing a smile. He suspected that whatever lay beneath Victor's diplomatic exterior would surface soon enough. Probably when they were away from the watching eyes of wedding guests and could speak more honestly about their differences.

Chapter Thirty-Three

After the cake had been cut, Mikael led Kat onto the dance floor for their first dance as husband and wife. The string quartet began playing 'All of Me', a song they'd chosen because it perfectly captured how they felt about each other, loving every part, every flaw, every perfect imperfection. As the familiar melody filled the dining room, Mikael felt the weight of the day's tensions finally lift from his shoulders.

'We did it,' Kat whispered in his ear, her smile radiant despite the exhaustion he could see in her eyes. 'Despite everything, your father's speech, the protesters, my mother's outfit, we actually did it.'

Mikael spun her gently, her vintage dress swirling around her legs. The lyrics, about loving someone completely, flaws and all, floated between them unspoken. They both knew them by heart. 'No regrets?' he asked, though he could see the answer in her face.

'Only that we can't escape to our room right now,' she murmured, making him laugh.

As the song built to its chorus, and other couples began joining them on the floor, Kat pulled back slightly to look into his eyes. 'I love you, Mr Andersson,' she said softly.

'I love you too, Mrs Andersson,' he replied, still getting used to the sound of her new name.

They danced, the music enveloping them. In that moment, only their love, commitment, and future mattered. Other couples circled around them. Elsa and Tobias moving stiffly together, her mum 1980s disco dancing to the rhythm, while laughing with Daniel, guests from London and Lapland mixing and mingling in the warm glow of celebration.

As the final notes faded and applause filled the room, Kat squeezed his hand. 'I should speak to Lily and rescue Daniel from the dance floor. You don't mind, do you?'

Mikael nodded and gave her a kiss. 'Of course not.'

'Why don't you go and talk to your mum and dad?' she added, lifting her eyebrows. 'Maybe now's the time?'

Mikael felt his stomach tighten. He knew Kat wanted him to make peace with his parents, but she didn't understand just how difficult his father could be. Still, after Erik's surprisingly restrained speech, perhaps there was a window of opportunity.

'Maybe,' he said, watching her face light up with hope.

'I love you for trying,' she said, rising on her tiptoes to kiss him once more. 'No matter what happens.'

He watched her walk over to Simona and Daniel, her dress catching the soft lighting as she moved. Around them, the reception was settling into a more relaxed rhythm, ready for the evening. Guests mingled freely, the formal structure of the meal giving way to conversation and laughter. The string quartet had been replaced by softer background music, creating an atmosphere that felt both celebratory and intimate.

Mikael took a deep breath and looked across the room to where his parents sat. It was time to find out if there was any hope of healing the wounds that had divided their family for far too long.

Chapter Thirty-Four

Mikael made his way across the dining room, his heart beating faster with each step. The last time he'd attempted a serious conversation with his father, it had ended with Erik telling him never to darken his door again. But that was over a year ago, before his relationship with Kat had deepened, before he'd built a successful business, before he'd proved he could make his own way in the world.

As he approached their table, Mikael noticed Victor watching him. Elsa sat beside Victor, and an empty chair marked where Tobias had been.

Mikael tapped his brother's shoulder and said, 'Thanks for the speech. It was great.'

'My pleasure,' Victor replied, his voice betraying no emotion whatsoever.

I was right, Mikael thought and wondered if he should return to the top table and forget about family reconciliations. Perhaps today wasn't the right day after all? Mikael glanced back to see Kat talking animatedly with her siblings, and decided to have a go. At least he wouldn't have any regrets after this day was over.

'Erik, Mother,' Mikael began, his voice carefully controlled. 'I wanted to thank you both for being here today. I know it wasn't easy.'

Erik studied his youngest son for a long moment, his pale blue eyes unreadable. 'Your mother insisted we come. She was right to do so.'

The admission surprised Mikael. His father rarely acknowledged being influenced by anyone, even Ulla. He saw his mother's face register amazement, too.

'I appreciate that,' he said, settling into the chair across from them. 'I know we've had our differences, but today – seeing you here, hearing your and Victor's speeches – it means more than you know.'

Ulla reached across the table and placed her hand over his. 'You're our son, Mikael. No matter what's happened between us, that will never change.'

'Your mother's right,' Erik said quietly, his gaze moving to where Kat was laughing with her family. 'Your wife seems like a remarkable woman. Passionate, principled.' He paused, choosing his words carefully. 'I can see why you're happy here.'

Mikael noticed Victor shift uncomfortably beside Elsa, his hands tightening around his wine glass.

'I'm not saying I agree with your choices,' Erik continued, his voice measured. 'The environmental activism, walking away from the company. But I can see that you've built something successful here. Something that matters to you.'

Mikael felt a cautious hope rising in his chest. This was more than he'd dared expect. 'Thank you for saying that.'

Victor's sharp intake of breath was audible. 'Father, surely you're not suggesting that abandoning the family business was the right choice?'

'I'm suggesting,' Erik said carefully, 'that perhaps there's room for more than one definition of success in this family.'

Mikael watched his brother's knuckles whiten as he gripped his glass tighter. 'Success?' Victor's voice was controlled but strained. 'He walked away from everything you built. Everything you taught us mattered.'

'And you stayed,' Erik said, turning to his eldest son. 'You've carried more than your share of responsibility, Victor. I know that.'

'Do you?' The pain in Victor's voice was raw, though he kept it low, mindful of the other guests, and perhaps of Elsa, who was listening quietly beside him. 'Do you have any idea what it's been like? Taking on double responsibilities while being constantly reminded that I'm not the son who had the courage to leave?'

The bitterness in Victor's words made Mikael's chest tighten with familiar guilt.

'I never asked for any of this,' Mikael said quietly. 'I never wanted you to suffer because of my choices.'

Victor looked at him for a long moment, conflict

warring in his dark eyes. Then he set down his glass with careful precision and stood. 'If you'll excuse me,' he said, his voice steady despite the emotion flickering across his features, 'I think I need some air.'

He walked away with dignity intact, though Mikael could see the tension in his shoulders. Elsa watched him go with an expression Mikael couldn't quite read.

Erik observed his eldest son's departure with a troubled expression. 'I've failed him,' he said quietly. 'Failed you both, in different ways.'

'It's not too late,' Ulla said softly, though there was a hint of uncertainty in her voice.

'Isn't it?' Erik's voice carried through the room. Mikael turned around but saw no one had been paying particular attention to the tense discussion between Victor and his father.

He leaned forward, sensing an opening. 'You could start by really listening, Father.'

'You mean to your wife's environmental protests?' Erik's tone carried a familiar edge of dismissal.

'I mean her research into sustainable development,' Mikael corrected carefully. 'Tourism projections, environmental impact assessments, economic modelling that shows long-term viability. It's not idealistic thinking, Father. It's practical business analysis.'

'Pretty theories don't pay wages, Mikael. This community needs real jobs, not academic studies about what might work in an ideal world.'

'But what if those studies show that sustainable tourism could create more jobs than mining? What if the economic projections actually support environmental protection rather than contradicting it?'

'What if they don't?' Erik countered. 'What if the research is simply wishful thinking dressed up in academic language?'

Mikael felt his frustration rising but forced himself to remain calm. 'Then at least you'd know you'd considered all the options before proceeding. Wouldn't the board appreciate due diligence?'

Erik was quiet for a long moment, his fingers drumming against the table. 'I've built this company on proven methods, reliable returns. I can't risk everything on environmental theories, however well-researched they might appear.'

'I'm not asking you to risk everything,' Mikael said. 'I'm asking you to look at the research with an open mind. To consider that there might be a way forward that doesn't require choosing between prosperity and preservation.'

'And if I disagree with those conclusions?'

'Then we'll know where we stand,' Mikael replied honestly. 'But at least we'll have had the conversation based on facts rather than assumptions.'

Erik studied his son's face, clearly weighing his words. 'I make no promises about changing direction,' he said finally. 'The Northern project represents significant investment and planning. But – I suppose examining alternative perspectives isn't entirely unreasonable.'

It was more than he'd expected. His father

remained deeply sceptical, but at least he wasn't dismissing the possibility outright.

'That's all I'm asking for,' Mikael said. 'A fair hearing.'

Mikael felt something shift between them – not a complete reconciliation, but the beginning of one. They were still father and son, still carrying decades of complicated history, but for the first time in over a year, they were also having a conversation instead of an argument.

It was, Mikael thought, a start. Whether it would lead anywhere remained to be seen, but it was more progress than he'd dared hope for.

Chapter Thirty-Five

After Mikael had left the table, there was an awkward silence. Ulla wore a tired smile on her face, but neither husband nor wife had said a word to each other or Elsa for a few moments.

When Victor returned to his seat, between Elsa and Ulla, he nodded to his father and placed his hand on his mother's arm.

'You OK? I'm sorry I lost my temper.'

Ulla patted Victor's hand. 'Don't worry.' She gave a cautious glance to her husband, whose gaze was fixed to his phone.

Elsa felt acute embarrassment witnessing the family feud at its rawest. At the same time, she was glad she didn't have to live through it. How awful for Kat to be right in the middle of such a rift. When she'd been with Victor, she'd known Erik Andersson was a bully – he'd tried to antagonise her – but at the time, the two boys were both destined to join the firm, following their father's wishes.

Sitting at their table, alone now that Tobias had abandoned her, felt wrong. She should leave, but getting up and excusing herself after her boyfriend had already left, seemed bad manners somehow. Besides, Victor would think she wanted to avoid him too.

How had she got into a situation like this? Her boyfriend had embarrassed himself with Kat's mother and had now left her alone with the warring Anderssons. She suspected Tobias would stay in their room for the rest of the day and evening. When he'd told her he was going to make some calls, Elsa had pointed out that it was a Saturday afternoon.

'Criminal law doesn't follow office hours, you know that,' he'd said, giving her a quick peck on her cheek.

She emptied her glass of wine and looked around the beautifully decorated dining room, with its winter flowers and flickering candles. The relaxed conversation and laughter were in sharp contrast with what had been going on at her table.

On the other side of the room Simona, Lily, and Daniel were chatting among themselves. She noticed Kat's sister, Lily, looking at her with curious, friendly eyes. When their gazes met, the young woman with the striking flame-red hair gave her a warm smile and a little wave. Elsa smiled back, genuinely glad for the first time that day.

'I'll just go say hello to Kat's family,' she murmured

to Victor, who nodded with what looked like relief. As she approached their table, Lily immediately brightened. 'You're Elsa, right? Please come sit with us. There's an empty chair right here.'

'Oh, I don't want to intrude,' Elsa began, but Simona was already pulling out the chair beside Lily. 'Nonsense, dear. We'd love to have you join us,' she said warmly. 'Much more fun than sitting with all that serious business talk, I imagine.'

Elsa gratefully settled into the chair, immediately feeling the difference in atmosphere. This table buzzed with warmth and laughter.

'I was hoping we'd have time to chat properly,' Lily said, turning her full attention to Elsa. 'I noticed during the ceremony how intently you were listening to the vows. You seemed really moved by it all.'

Elsa felt herself relax, and she tucked a strand of hair behind her ear. 'It was beautiful, wasn't it? There's something about witnessing genuine love that makes you examine your own life.'

'That's exactly what I was thinking!' Lily exclaimed, her eyes lighting up with delight. 'Are you in academia? You have a thoughtful quality about you.'

'No, I'm a lawyer,' Elsa replied. 'Commercial law mostly. Though I have to admit, watching Mikael and Kat today has made me question whether I'm actually doing meaningful work.'

'I know that feeling,' Lily nodded. 'I'm just finishing my History degree at Edinburgh and everyone keeps asking what's next. But honestly? I'm terrified I'll end up in some career that pays well but feels completely hollow.'

Daniel looked up from his phone. 'Lily's having an existential crisis about her future. Very dramatic.'

'It's not dramatic!' Lily protested. 'It's a legitimate concern, it's about weighing the desire to have a sense of purpose against the need to achieve success.'

'That's not dramatic at all,' Elsa said with genuine sympathy. 'The pressure to succeed can be overwhelming, can't it? I remember being the scholarship student who had to get perfect marks just to belong. Now I'm successful by conventional standards, but – '

'But success and fulfilment aren't the same thing?' Lily finished, leaning forward eagerly.

'Exactly. Sometimes I feel like I'm just shuffling papers to make rich people richer, when what I really wanted was to help people, to make a difference.'

'Kat was always my inspiration,' Lily said, glancing affectionately towards the head table where her sister sat with Mikael. 'She followed her passion for environmental work, even when it wasn't the safe choice.'

'She sounds like a wonderful sister,' Elsa smiled. 'I always wished I had siblings.'

'Well, you're welcome to borrow these two anytime,' Simona said with motherly warmth, earning protests from both Daniel and Lily. Elsa was surprised to see this totally different side to the woman who'd openly flirted with her boyfriend.

'Now then, Elsa, tell us about yourself. Kat mentioned you've known Mikael since childhood?'

'Since we were eleven,' Elsa confirmed. 'We went to the same school. Mikael's like the brother I never had.'

'How lovely,' Simona beamed. 'And you're Finnish? Growing up in Helsinki? I moved away in my twenties, from Rovaniemi.'

'Oh, so you're local!'

'Sort of. Long, long time ago now. But now you live in Stockholm with that lovely boyfriend of yours. But I can't see him anywhere?'

Elsa noticed Lily roll her eyes.

'Oh, he had to take a call. He's a criminal lawyer,' Elsa said, trying to be brief.

'I say!' Simona replied.

'What's your speciality in history?' Elsa asked, trying to move the conversation away from her boyfriend.

'I love stories about second chances, really,' Lily said, though her enthusiasm was more measured than before. 'My dissertation is on romantic correspondence in 18th-century Scotland. Letters between separated lovers, couples navigating arranged marriages, second chances at love. Like Jane Austen's *Persuasion* when Anne Elliot and Captain Wentworth find each other again after years apart. There's something rather romantic about the idea that time and experience can make love deeper, more meaningful.'

Elsa felt a little flutter in her chest.

'That's – that's one of my favourite novels, actually.'

'Really?' Lily's face lit up. 'Isn't it wonderful? I've always believed that the best stories are about people getting second chances at happiness.'

Across the table, Daniel caught Elsa's eye and gave her a knowing look.

'Fair warning. Lily's quite the romantic. She thinks everyone deserves a happy ending.'

'Well, don't they?' Lily asked, then glanced meaningfully towards the table where Victor sat looking increasingly uncomfortable.

'Kat mentioned you used to know Mikael's brother as well?'

Elsa felt her cheeks warm.

'Yes, we – we were close once. A long time ago.'

'How interesting,' Lily said gently, clearly sensing this was delicate territory. 'Old friendships can be complicated, can't they?'

'Well, you may have noticed that I am, was, here with someone else,' Elsa stammered, something she rarely did.

'I'm sorry,' Lily said quickly. 'I don't mean to pry.'

Elsa laughed, suppressing the anger that had flared up at the thought of Tobias. 'You're not prying. I suppose I just – sometimes old connections are more powerful than we expect them to be.'

'That's beautifully put,' Simona said warmly, topping up everyone's wine glasses. She stole a fresh one from the table next to theirs and poured one for Elsa too.

As the conversation flowed more naturally, moving from travel stories to university memories to shared interests in books and films, Elsa found herself genuinely charmed by this family's warmth. Despite their differences, Simona's theatrical tendencies, Lily's academic intensity, Daniel's boyish humour, there was an authenticity about them that felt refreshing after the careful politeness she was used to.

Looking around at their smiling faces, and then glancing over at Victor, who was still trapped in uncomfortable conversation with his father, Elsa felt a shift in her perspective. Perhaps she needed to untie herself from Tobias. This wedding could mark the beginning of something new – not just for Mikael and Kat, but for herself as well.

When there was a brief pause in the conversation, Lily leaned forward slightly, her voice gentle but direct.

'You know, Elsa, I've been watching you and Victor this evening. There's something between you two, isn't there? Something that goes deeper than old friendship.'

'Lily – ' Daniel started to warn, but Lily held up a hand.

'I don't mean to be presumptuous. It's just – well, sometimes the most important conversations are the ones we're most afraid to have.'

Elsa looked across the room at Victor, who at that moment glanced up and met her eyes. For a second, the years seemed to fall away.

'It's complicated,' she said quietly.

'Of course it is,' Lily replied with a small smile. 'But that doesn't mean it's impossible.'

'You know what?' Elsa said, surprising herself with her candour. 'I have a feeling you're going to be trouble, Lily Wootton.'

Lily's grin was radiant but less intense than before. 'The very best kind, I hope.'

Chapter Thirty-Six

Elsa stood with the other wedding guests on the hotel's front steps, watching as Mikael helped Kat into the waiting car. The bride had changed from her flowing wedding gown into a smart cream-coloured trouser suit with a heavy wool overcoat, her short dark hair tucked beneath a matching woollen hat. Even in the bitter cold – it had to be at least minus ten – and the dim light from the hotel's entrance, she was glowing with happiness.

'Ready, Mrs Andersson?' Mikael asked, his voice carrying across the crisp night air as he closed Kat's door and moved round to the driver's side.

'More than ready, Mr Andersson,' came Kat's laughing reply through the open window.

Elsa could hear the gentle tinkling of small bells and what sounded like tin cans tied to the car's rear bumper. Someone had clearly been busy whilst the couple were changing. A few traditional

Sami wooden love spoons hung from ribbons alongside the makeshift noisemakers, adding a distinctly Lappish touch to the send-off. Elsa felt genuinely happy as she watched the couple's obvious joy. Whatever problems she might have with Tobias, whatever complicated feelings Victor's presence had stirred up, this moment was pure and untainted. Here were two people who had found each other and were brave enough to build a life together.

As Mikael started the engine, Kat leaned out of the passenger window one last time. 'Thank you all for being here!' she called out, her voice bright with emotion. 'We love you!'

The car pulled away slowly, the bells and cans creating a cheerful racket that echoed across the snowy landscape. The wooden love spoons swayed gently from their ribbons, catching occasional glints of light from the hotel windows. Elsa watched and listened as the happy noise grew fainter and the red tail lights grew smaller.

As the sound of the engine faded and the other guests began to hurry back inside, seeking warmth, Elsa remained on the steps for a moment longer. The cold was biting at her exposed skin, and her breath formed small clouds in the frigid air, but she wasn't ready to go in yet. She pulled her fur coat tighter around her shoulders and looked up at the star-filled sky, feeling an unexpected pang of longing. When had she last felt the kind of certainty she'd just witnessed? When had she last been sure, absolutely, unquestionably sure, about anything?

Elsa could hear Tobias's sarcasm about what she'd just witnessed ringing in her ears. Sighing, she decided to go and see where he was. It was only just past nine, surely too early to go to bed?

The hotel corridor was quiet, the thick carpet muffling Elsa's footsteps as she approached their room. She paused outside the door, key card in hand, steeling herself for what she knew she'd find inside. The warm glow of the time she'd spent with Kat's family still lingered in her mind. The genuine laughter, the easy conversation, the brutal honesty from Lily. Even if some of what she'd said was romantic nonsense, Elsa had enjoyed herself for the first time in months.

She slipped the key card into the lock and pushed the door open.

Tobias sat propped against the headboard of the king-sized bed, his laptop balanced on his knees, papers scattered across the duvet like fallen leaves. He'd changed out of his suit into a white hotel bathrobe, his hair mussed from running his fingers through it. The bedside lamp cast a harsh circle of light over his work, while the rest of the room remained in shadow.

He glanced up as she entered, his expression mildly irritated at the interruption.

'You're back early,' he said, already turning his attention back to the screen. 'I thought these things went on until dawn.'

'It's just past nine,' Elsa replied, closing the door

behind her. 'The reception is still going on, but I thought I'd check on you.'

'How considerate.' His tone was distracted, professional. The same voice she imagined he used with junior associates who'd interrupted him during important work.

Elsa stood at the foot of the bed, taking in the scene. Legal briefs and case notes were spread across what should have been their shared space. His phone lay beside him, screen up, notifications blinking.

'Important case?' she asked, though she already knew the answer.

'The Akerman case. New evidence has emerged, and the prosecution is scrambling to adjust its strategy.' He typed something, deleted it, typed again. 'Amateur hour, but I need to stay ahead of it.'

'Of course.' Elsa moved to the window, looking out at the snow-covered landscape bathed in moonlight. 'You couldn't have handled this from Stockholm?'

'I needed the quiet. No interruptions.' He saved his document and reached for a highlighted brief. 'You know how it is with these criminal cases. New evidence, urgent motions. People's lives hang in the balance. I can't just switch off because we're in the middle of nowhere.'

The casual dismissal in his voice – the middle of nowhere – made something cold settle in Elsa's chest. This wasn't the middle of nowhere to her. This was home, or as close to home as she'd felt in years.

'You agreed to come,' she said quietly, not turning from the window.

'Yes, I did.' His typing paused. 'And I'm here, aren't I?'

'Are you?' She turned to face him. 'Because it feels like you've been working to avoid every moment of this trip from the second we arrived.'

Tobias looked up then, his expression shifting to the carefully neutral mask he wore in court. 'I've been polite. I've attended the events you wanted me to attend. I've made conversation with your friends.'

'You've been polite?' Elsa's voice rose slightly. 'You spent last night criticising the food, the venue, the environmental message. You made snide comments about Mikael's choices, and you – ' She stopped, not sure how to articulate what had happened with Simona.

'I what?'

'Today you were inappropriate with Kat's mother. You knew she was trying too hard, and you encouraged it. You were making fun of her and made everyone around you uncomfortable.'

Tobias set his laptop aside with deliberate care. 'I was being friendly. If she misinterpreted that, it's hardly my fault.'

'Friendly?' Elsa stared at him. 'You were flirting with a woman who's clearly struggling with getting older, whilst her daughter was right there. It was cruel, Tobias.'

'Come on, you're spiralling over this.'

'Am I?' She moved closer to the bed, her voice dropping to the level they both used during professional negotiations. 'Tell me, what was the point of coming here if you were just going to complain about everything? If you had wanted to spend the weekend working, you should have stayed in Stockholm.'

'I came because you asked me to.' His tone was reasonable, logical. 'I sacrificed my weekend, my time, to support you. I've been patient with the travel, the cold, the rustic accommodation. I've smiled and made small talk with people I have nothing in common with.'

'Sacrificed.' The word hung in the air between them. 'You sacrificed your time.'

'Yes.' He picked up his laptop again, as if the conversation was over. 'And now I'm trying to salvage what's left of it by getting some work done.'

Elsa watched him, this man she'd lived with for two years, and felt something fundamental shift inside her. The way he sat there, so certain in his righteousness, so convinced that his presence alone was a gift she should be grateful for.

'Do you even know why this wedding was important to me?' she asked.

'Mikael is a friend of yours from school. You wanted to maintain the relationship.' He didn't look up from his screen. 'I understand professional networking.'

'Professional networking.' She laughed, but there was no humour in it. 'That's what you think this is?'

'Isn't it? You hadn't spoken to him for years before you ran into him in Helsinki. Now suddenly you're flying to Lapland for his wedding.' He shrugged. 'It's smart career management.'

Elsa felt the last piece of something break inside her.

'Mikael isn't a networking opportunity, Tobias. He's my friend. He was my friend when I had nothing, when I was nobody. He knew me before I became this person who shuffles papers to make rich people richer.'

Now he looked up, eyebrows raised. 'That's a rather cynical view of our profession.'

'Our profession?' She sat down on the edge of the bed, careful not to disturb his papers. 'When did you last take a case that changed someone's life? When did you last help someone who was actually innocent?'

'We help our clients navigate the criminal justice system. We protect people's rights, their freedom – '

'You help guilty rich people escape consequences.' The words came out flat, matter-of-fact. 'You make lots of money making sure justice doesn't interfere with wealth.'

Tobias closed his laptop with a snap. 'At least what I do matters. At least I'm not just shuffling contracts so corporations can make more money.'

The casual dismissal of her work – work he'd never shown any interest in understanding – made Elsa's chest tighten.

'There it is.'

'There what is?'

'The way you really see what I do. The way you see

me.' She stood up, smoothing down her dress. 'I'm going back to the reception.'

'Elsa,' his voice carried a warning, 'don't be childish.'

'Childish?' She turned back to him. 'Is it childish to want to spend time with people who enjoy my company? Is it childish to want to be with someone who doesn't see every moment we spend together as time stolen from more important things?'

'You're being unreasonable.'

'Am I? Or am I finally being reasonable for the first time in months – years?'

She moved towards the door, then stopped.

'For what it's worth, I didn't ask you to come here to network. I asked you to come because I wanted to share something that mattered to me with someone who mattered to me. I wanted you to meet my friends, to see where I come from, to understand why this place is important to me.'

'And I've done that.'

'No,' she said quietly. 'You've endured it. There's a difference.'

She reached for the door handle, then paused again.

'The reception will go on for a few more hours. I'm going to rejoin it, and I'm going to enjoy myself. With or without you.'

'Fine.' He opened his laptop again. 'I have work to do, anyway.'

Elsa left him there, surrounded by his papers and

his righteous certainty, and walked back towards the sound of distant music and laughter.

Chapter Thirty-Seven

Tobias stared at the closed door for a long moment before returning his attention to the Akerman case. The silence in the room felt heavier somehow, but he pushed the feeling aside. He had work to do, proper work that mattered.

He'd sacrificed his entire weekend for this trip. A weekend he could have spent preparing for the case or doing many other productive activities. Instead, he was stuck in a hotel room in the frozen north, surrounded by people who thought saving trees was more important than economic growth.

The prosecution's so-called findings blurred as he read them, and he rubbed his eyes. He was tired, that was all. It had been a long day of forced smiles and polite conversation with people who had nothing interesting to say.

He'd been civil to everyone. If Kat's mother had misunderstood his friendliness, that wasn't his fault.

He'd only been making conversation, showing interest in the only person at the event who seemed to understand that life wasn't all about environmental causes and rustic charm.

Elsa was being dramatic, as usual. She'd always been prone to emotional responses, reading too much into simple social interactions. It was one of her less attractive qualities, though usually she kept it better controlled.

The Akerman brief lay open beside him, but his concentration was fractured. He could hear music drifting up from the reception hall below, faint but persistent. Elsa was down there somewhere, probably telling her friends about their 'argument', painting him as the villain in her story.

He'd given up his weekend for her. He'd flown to this godforsaken place, endured the uncomfortable travel, the basic accommodation, the endless small talk about things that didn't matter. He'd smiled and nodded and played the supportive boyfriend, and this was the thanks he got?

She'd accused him of being cruel to that woman – Simona. It was absurd. He'd been kind to her, engaging, showing more interest in her conversation than anyone else had. If she'd interpreted that as something more, well, that was her problem, not his.

The case files demanded his attention, but his mind kept returning to Elsa's words. She'd even suggested his work was less noble than hers, as if helping corporations shuffle money was more meaningful than defending people's fundamental rights. At least his work had real stakes – freedom, justice, life-changing outcomes. What did commercial law offer? Bigger profits for people who already had everything.

He'd tried to understand her attachment to these people. Mikael seemed pleasant enough, if somewhat idealistic. His new wife was attractive but more interested in saving the planet than building a stable future. The people who would struggle financially while congratulating themselves on their principles.

Tobias preferred a more pragmatic approach to life. Work hard, build security, make smart choices. It had served him well so far.

His phone buzzed. A text from Annabel: *How's the Arctic wedding?*

He smiled, typing back: *As expected. Rural. Earnest. Cold.*

Three dots appeared immediately: *Poor you. Missing you.*

Missing you too. He hesitated, then added: *Looking forward to being home.*

Me too. Monday dinner?

Perfect.

He deleted the conversation and returned to his work, feeling better. At least someone understood him, understood what he'd sacrificed to be here. Someone who didn't expect him to pretend that rustic charm was more important than professional success.

The music from downstairs seemed to grow louder, more insistent. He could imagine Elsa dancing, laughing, playing the part of the carefree friend. She was a master of disguise, always knowing how to please.

It was one thing that had attracted him to her – her chameleon-like ability to fit in anywhere. Useful at work functions, dinner parties, professional events. But sometimes, like tonight, it felt like she forgot who she was underneath all the performance.

She'd come around. She always did. By the time morning arrived, she would feel ashamed, ready to think clearly. They'd fly back to Stockholm, return to their normal routine, and this entire episode would become just another story about the time they went to a wedding in Lapland.

Tobias opened the case file and studied it, the distant sound of music fading into background noise. He had work to do, important work that mattered, that couldn't wait for anyone's hurt feelings or romantic notions about friendship.

After all, someone had to deal with genuine problems.

Chapter Thirty-Eight

Elsa found a quiet corner in the bar, where most of the guests had gathered. One of Kat's friends was dancing with Lily, and she waved. Near the bar, Elsa could see Simona and Daniel laughing, but she didn't want company. She needed a few moments to herself. How had she not noticed how incompatible they were? Not only had Tobias been seeing Annabel behind her back, in itself something she was struggling to forgive, but she now understood that they didn't really like each other – let alone love.

'So what do you think of the new bride?'

Victor plopped himself next to her on the sofa, startling her out of her thoughts. She looked at her old boyfriend. Another cheater.

He was grinning at her.

'Cheer up, it's a bloody wedding!'

Elsa tried to laugh, feeling awkward, but a strange gurgling sound came out of her mouth instead.

'I've just been to see my boyfriend,' she quickly added, trying to regain her composure.

The mention of Tobias had the desired effect, and for a moment, Victor's confidence seemed to crumble. But he soon regained his cool.

'Well, if I were you, I'd leave him be if he makes you so miserable.'

'Funny,' Elsa said.

She let her anger at Tobias wash over her and pulled her mouth into a smile.

'That's better,' Victor said, and for a moment, Elsa gazed into his eyes, so familiar with their dark brown hue.

It *was* nice to see Victor. Elsa felt as if she were seventeen again, madly in love with the rich heir to the Andersson empire. Her girlfriends had been so jealous at first, but once they'd seen how he'd looked at her, they'd simply sighed and said how they wanted to find someone as wonderful as Victor Andersson. For four years she and Victor had been deliriously happy. They'd planned to get a flat together after her graduation and then marry soon after that.

They'd had some good times before –

Before.

'You haven't got a drink? Would you like a glass of champagne?'

Victor got up and was on his way to the bar before Elsa could reply.

Watching him talking to the bar staff, she forced herself to take a few deep breaths. How could the man have such a profound effect on her after all these years? While his back was turned, she adjusted the cleavage of her dress and smoothed down the fabric around her tummy and thighs.

When Victor returned carrying two flutes of champagne, he sat in front of her instead of next to her on the sofa.

'*Kippis*,' Elsa said and sipped her drink.

Victor put his glass down and leaned in closer. She could smell his aftershave. He still used the same citrus scent he had when they were together. Suddenly she had a vivid memory of him in bed next to her. It was early in their relationship, and they hadn't yet had sex. There'd been months of kissing and heavy petting at house parties and in cars, but Elsa hadn't yet felt ready to go all the way. Until the trip to Lapland.

After that, they were inseparable.

Now in the semi-darkness of the hotel bar in Lapland, Victor was staring at her, and she had to once again remind herself that she was supposed to be acting cool, rather than reminiscing about their past romance.

'You didn't answer my question. What do you think of Kat – the Green Goddess?' he said.

'Don't be rude. Kat is lovely.'

'Lovely isn't the word I would have used. She's pretty enough, I guess, if you like that sort of short-haired hippy type, but I think she's a bit uptight? And by the way, I'm starving. That vegan crap just doesn't fill you up, does it?'

Elsa had to laugh. If she were honest, she also felt a

little peckish. She'd been looking forward to a reindeer steak – something she rarely got in Stockholm.

'I know I should be a vegan – for the environment – but I just love meat too much.'

As soon as the words left her mouth, she realised the double entendre.

On cue, Victor said, with a wide grin on his face, 'I remember.'

The comment made them both fall silent.

Elsa lowered her eyes and brushed off an imaginary piece of fluff on her dress.

She remembered the cosy bedroom all those years ago, wooden beams overhead and on the walls, a fur throw at the bottom of the bed, and his naked body. She had turned into a woman during that week in Lapland. The desire she'd found inside herself had surprised and scared her in equal measure. As if she knew the pain the object of her desire would later bring her.

The memory of his cruel deception stirred Elsa out of the rose-tinted thoughts of the past. The man sitting opposite her was a self-centred, unfeeling man. A person who needed to be reminded that he can't treat people exactly as he likes without his actions having some consequences.

But even as she thought this, she found herself drawn to the familiar warmth in his eyes, the way his mouth curved when he smiled at her. The champagne was making her feel lighter, more reckless.

'Dance with me,' Victor said suddenly, extending his hand.

Elsa looked around the bar. The music had shifted to something slower, more intimate. Several couples were swaying together on the small dance floor, lost in their own worlds. The lighting had dimmed further, creating pockets of shadow and warmth.

'I don't think that's a good idea,' she said, but her voice lacked conviction.

'Come on,' he said, his voice softer now. 'It's just a dance. For old times' sake.'

Before she could protest further, he'd taken her hand and was leading her to the dance floor. The music was a haunting Finnish ballad, something she remembered from her childhood. Victor pulled her close, one hand on her waist, the other holding her fingers gently.

They moved together as if no time had passed at all. He'd always been a good dancer, confident and leading, and her body seemed to remember the rhythm of being with him. For a moment, she allowed herself to forget everything – Tobias upstairs with his case files, the years of silence between her and Victor, the betrayal that had torn them apart.

'You're still the most beautiful woman in any room,' Victor murmured against her ear.

The compliment sent a shiver down her spine, but she pulled back slightly to look at him. 'Don't.'

'Don't what?'

'Don't try to charm me. I'm not seventeen anymore, Victor.'

'No,' he agreed, his dark eyes serious for the first

time that evening. 'You're not. You're even more beautiful now.'

The song ended, but neither of them moved to step away. Around them, other couples continued to sway, but Elsa was aware of the space between their bodies, the warmth of his hand on her back.

'We should go back to our table,' she mumbled.

'Should we?' He didn't move, and neither did she.

Another song began, something even slower, and without conscious decision they began to move together again. This time, Victor pulled her closer, until her head was almost resting on his shoulder. She could feel his heartbeat, steady and strong, could smell that familiar citrus scent that brought back so many memories.

'Elsa,' he whispered.

She looked up at him, and for a moment, the years fell away completely. She was seventeen again, in love for the first time, believing in forever. The way he was looking at her now – with such intensity, such tenderness – made her forget to breathe.

'I – ' she said, but the words died in her throat.

The music stopped, breaking the spell. Around them, the bar had emptied. Where there had been dozens of guests, now only a handful remained. Lily was sitting at the bar with a ruggedly handsome guy, deep in conversation. Simona and Daniel had disappeared.

The party was winding down, transforming into something more personal, more real.

'It's getting late,' Elsa said, though she made no move to leave his arms.

'Is it?' Victor leaned towards her ear. 'Late can be the best time of all.'

For the first time all evening, they were alone. With no family watching, no other guests to perform for, no Tobias to consider. Just the two of them, and the weight of everything they'd never said to each other.

'Victor,' she began, but he shook his head.

'Not here,' he breathed. 'Too many ears, even now.'

He was right. Even with the guests dwindling, the bar still felt public, exposed. She needed air, space to think, to process what was happening between them.

'Would you like to go for a walk?' he asked, as if reading her thoughts.

'Isn't it too cold for a walk?'

'They'll have snowsuits and boots in reception. C'mon, it'll be bracing!'

Elsa looked around the bar once more. The staff were clearing glasses, and the remaining guests were settling in for the long haul. No one would miss them.

'Just a walk,' she said, though even as she said it, she knew it wouldn't be just anything.

Victor smiled, and for the first time since she'd arrived in Lapland, it wasn't his practised, charming smile. It was something real, something that reached his eyes and made her remember why she'd once fallen for him.

'Just a walk,' he agreed, though they both knew he was lying too.

He helped her into the snowsuit, his fingers brushing her shoulders as he lifted it around her. The simple touch sent electricity through her, and she had to grip the back of a chair to steady herself.

What was she doing? She was supposed to be mad at him, to act tough and show she didn't care. Instead, she was melting at his touch as if she was seventeen again.

But as they walked towards the exit, passing the few remaining guests who were too absorbed in their own conversations to notice them leaving, Elsa experienced something she hadn't felt in months: anticipation. For the first time in so long, she didn't know what would happen next, and instead of terrifying her, it felt like freedom.

Chapter Thirty-Nine

The frosty night air would clear her head, she told herself. They would talk properly this time about what had happened between them. She would tell him exactly what she thought of his behaviour all those years ago, and then she would walk away, closure finally achieved.

The walk into the centre of the ski resort seemed longer than the five minutes advertised by the hotel. Elsa was wearing a thick beanie, but even with the snowsuit and moon boots, the chill wind crept into every crevice of her body, freezing her cheeks and making the tips of her fingers go numb inside her gloves.

'It's bitter, isn't it?'

She glanced at Victor, who didn't seem even slightly bothered by the cold.

'This is nothing. It was -30C here in January. Now that was cold.'

Elsa didn't reply. Victor had always been arrogant. It was a side of him that Elsa never liked. Especially as she got older and saw how others reacted to him. As a boy from a wealthy family, he should have shown some humility, but that was never Victor. Perhaps, Elsa now wondered, she would have fallen out of love with him if what happened hadn't happened.

Instead of discussing the temperature, Elsa changed the subject.

'You come up here a lot?'

Victor turned his face towards Elsa as they continued to trudge on the snow-covered path towards a set of lights in the distance.

'Yeah, we're doing exploratory work for the mine here, drilling for samples. Some of the local population, including my brother and Kat are against it. Vocally against it. Well, you saw what happened at the wedding, how they tried to interrupt my father's innocent speech to congratulate his son's nuptials. Which is why I have less affection for my new sister-in-law than I might otherwise have.'

'And Mikael?'

Victor paused, his expression hardening. 'The permits are nearly finalised, Elsa. Father's been working on this for three years. The board meets next week to approve the final phase. After that –'

He gestured towards the lights of the village. 'All this environmental romanticism won't matter. The economic benefits will be enormous – hundreds of jobs, millions in revenue.'

'And if the community opposes it?'

Victor's smile was cold. 'They'll adapt. They always do when the alternative is economic stagnation.'

Victor's words stopped Elsa in her tracks.

'You blame Kat for Mikael's refusal to join the family firm?'

'Mikael is my brother, and I respect his passion for this place. But sometimes sentimentality can cloud judgment,' Victor replied coolly, his tone betraying a hint of irritation. 'Obviously Kat has got into his brain, but I'm sure he'll soon see that this environmental nonsense doesn't pay the bills!'

Elsa felt her annoyance simmering. His words echoed what Tobias had said during the pre-wedding dinner.

'That's a very simplistic view. Mikael was never keen on working with your father, was he? He was much more of an outdoorsy person, so I wasn't at all surprised when he told me he'd opened a ski centre here in Ylläs. Besides, I remember he was very much his own man.'

Victor lifted his eyes towards Elsa and grunted. The rift was obviously a lot rawer and more painful than Elsa had thought. Elsa knew that siblings' relationships could often be antagonistic, as she had worked with a few family businesses. And those relationships were critical to their success.

'I don't know enough about the mine and the environment here, but surely you should listen to the locals too. Wouldn't it be better if you had them on your side?

Surely there are some compromises that could be worked out to keep everyone happy?'

'Spoken like a true lawyer,' Victor said and smiled, but something shifted in his expression. He stared out at the snow-covered landscape, and for a moment Elsa saw a flicker of uncertainty cross his features.

'You know,' he said slowly, 'it's not that I don't have any sympathy. I remember a lecture from university. Professor Virtanen was talking about geological time scales – how ecosystems that take millennia to develop can be destroyed in decades.' His voice grew quieter. 'I've always understood the science of it. I suppose I've just never applied it to – to what we do.'

He turned back to her, and Elsa saw something she hadn't expected: genuine conflict in his dark eyes. 'But the jobs, the economic benefits – ' he began, then stopped himself. 'Christ, I sound like my father.'

They had stopped in the middle of the path, and Elsa was shivering. Victor grabbed her arm to propel her forward.

'It's cold, and you look frozen. Standing still will make it worse.'

Victor was right; it was bitterly cold, and she needed to be somewhere warm.

The ski centre was mostly closed for the evening, but a small bar remained open, its windows glowing warmly against the dark landscape. Victor pushed open the door, and Elsa was grateful for the rush of heat that greeted them.

'Two mulled wines, and a reindeer pizza,' Victor

said to the young man behind the counter, then he guided Elsa to a table by the window.

She tugged off her beanie and gloves and pulled the snowsuit down to her waist. She flexed her fingers to get the circulation back. The place was cosy, with wooden tables and chairs, and fairy lights strung along the windows. Only a few other patrons remained – a couple sharing a pizza in the corner, and an elderly man reading a newspaper by the fire.

'Better?' Victor asked as their drinks arrived, steaming and fragrant with cinnamon and cloves.

'Much.' Elsa wrapped her hands around the warm mug, inhaling the spicy scent. The warmth was welcome, but her mind was still churning from their conversation about the mine, about Mikael and Kat. 'I'd forgotten how brutal it can be here at night.'

'You never used to mind the cold.' Victor's voice was quieter now, more thoughtful. 'Remember that first trip we took here? You said the cold made you feel alive.'

Elsa looked up at him, surprised by the shift in his tone. Gone were the arrogant confidence and casual dismissiveness about environmental concerns. He looked almost – uncertain.

'I remember,' she said carefully. 'I was young. Everything felt intense then.'

'Including us.'

The words hung between them, laden with memory and meaning. The young guy brought them the pizza, which also smelled delicious. Elsa took a slice and quickly devoured it in a few of bites.

'I was hungry,' she laughed, wiping her mouth with a paper napkin.

Victor was already having seconds, and with his mouth full, smiled and nodded.

Elsa took a sip of her wine, using the moment to gather her thoughts. The conversation about the mine had shown her a side of Victor she didn't like – dismissive, entitled, uncomfortably similar to Tobias. But now, looking at him in the soft light of the bar, she saw glimpses of the boy she'd fallen in love with.

'Victor,' she said finally, 'why are we really here? Not just in this place, but – why did you ask me to go for a walk?'

He leaned back in his chair, studying her face. 'I could ask you the same thing. You could have stayed at the hotel or gone back to your boyfriend and his case files.'

'Don't deflect. Answer my question.'

For a moment, she saw a flash of the old Victor – the one who hated being challenged, who always had to be in control. But then his expression softened, and when he spoke, his voice was different. Vulnerable.

'Because seeing you again has reminded me of everything I lost,' he said quietly. 'Because I've spent ten years trying to forget you, and five minutes in your presence proved how spectacularly I've failed at that.'

Elsa's breath caught. She'd expected charm, practised lines, the kind of smooth talk that had always come so easily to him. She hadn't expected honesty.

'You lost me?' The words came out sharper than

she'd intended. 'That's an interesting way to put it, considering you're the one who – '

'Who what?' Victor leaned forward, his dark eyes intense. 'What exactly do you think I did, Elsa?'

The question hung in the air between them. Elsa stared at him, suddenly uncertain. There was something in his voice, in his expression, that didn't match the narrative she'd carried for ten years.

'You know what you did,' she said, but her voice lacked its earlier conviction.

'No, I don't think I do.' Victor's voice was urgent now. 'Because if I knew what had driven you away, if I understood why you left without a word of explanation, don't you think I would have tried to fix it?'

'Fix it?' Elsa's words were louder than she'd intended, drawing a glance from the couple in the corner. She lowered her voice to an angry whisper. 'You can't fix betrayal, Victor. You can't fix the fact that I saw you with – '

She stopped abruptly, realising she was about to reveal something she'd never planned to share.

'Saw me with whom?' Victor's voice was very quiet now.

Elsa looked away, staring out at the snow-covered landscape. For ten years, she'd carried the image of that day at Café Strindberg. The blonde girl, the intimate conversation, the way Victor had leaned towards her. It had been the defining moment of her young adult life, the reason she'd fled Helsinki, the reason she'd never fully trusted anyone since.

'The blonde girl,' she said finally, her voice barely audible. 'At Café Strindberg.'

She heard Victor's sharp intake of breath, saw his hands tighten around his mug.

'You were there?' he asked, and there was something in his voice, shock, but also something that might have been understanding.

'I was outside.' The words came out in a rush now, as if saying them quickly would make them hurt less. 'I'd come to surprise you. My meeting with Professor Saarnio had been cancelled, and I thought – I thought we could spend the afternoon together. But when I got there, I saw you through the window. You were sitting by those large windows with a girl I'd never seen before. Blonde, pretty. And the way you were looking at her, the way you leaned towards her –'

Victor was staring at her with an expression she couldn't read. 'Elsa –'

'I couldn't watch you kiss her,' she continued, the words spilling out after years of being held back. 'I couldn't stand there and watch you betray everything we had. So I left. And then I kept leaving until I was as far away from you as I could get.'

Victor sat perfectly still, his face cycling through a series of emotions: shock, understanding, and then something that looked like grief.

'You thought I was having an affair,' he said finally.

'I didn't think it. I saw it.'

'No.' Victor's voice was firm, urgent. 'You saw something, but it wasn't what you think. Elsa, I never cheated on you. I never even came close.'

'Don't lie to me. Not now, not after all these years.'

'I'm not lying.' Victor reached across the table, his fingers brushing hers. 'Her name was Ingrid Larsson. She worked for my father's company, and she was in the worst kind of trouble. I was trying to help her.'

Elsa pulled her hand away. 'Help her? Is that what you call it?'

'Yes.' Victor's voice was passionate now, desperate. He ran his hands through his hair. 'I know how it must have looked. But I swear to you, Elsa, there was nothing romantic between us. Nothing.'

Elsa stared at him, her carefully constructed world-view beginning to crack around the edges. 'You expect me to believe that? After ten years of silence, you want me to believe you have some innocent explanation?'

'It's not just innocent – it's the truth.' Victor's eyes were fierce with conviction. 'If you'd stayed that day, if you'd come inside and asked me, I could have explained everything.'

'Could you? Really? Because you'd been secretive for months before that. All those phone calls you wouldn't explain, the meetings you couldn't talk about. I thought we told each other everything, but you were living a completely separate life.'

'I couldn't tell you.'

Elsa felt a chill that had nothing to do with the weather. 'Tell me what?'

An elderly man by the fire folded his newspaper

and left, the sound of the door closing echoing in the suddenly quiet bar. The couple in the corner were deep in their own conversation, oblivious to the drama unfolding at the window table.

'What did you do?' Elsa asked quietly.

Victor's smile was bitter. 'I tried to do the right thing. And in the process, I lost everything that mattered to me.'

Elsa felt the ground shifting beneath her, ten years of certainty suddenly uncertain. 'Tell me,' she whispered. 'Tell me everything.'

Victor looked out at the snow-covered landscape, then back at her. 'Are you sure? Because once I tell you, you can't unknow it. And it might change everything you've believed about that time in our lives.'

Elsa thought about Tobias and his righteous indignation. She thought about the life she'd built in Stockholm – safe, predictable and emotionally distant. She thought about the girl she'd been at twenty-one, so certain of her love, so devastated by what she'd thought was betrayal.

'Tell me,' she said again.

Victor nodded slowly, then began to speak.

Chapter Forty

Helsinki, Ten Years Earlier

It was early March and snow was falling heavily outside the floor-to-ceiling windows of Erik Andersson's corner office, muffling the sounds of the centre of Helsinki. Victor had been summoned late by his father, told it was urgent family business that couldn't wait.

'We have a situation that needs delicate handling,' Erik said without preamble, sliding a thin file across his mahogany desk.

Victor opened the file, seeing a personnel photo of a young blonde woman. She was pretty, but not in the polished way of the women in their social circle. There was something vulnerable about her face that made him uncomfortable even before his conversation with his father had begun.

'Ingrid Larsson, Administrative Assistant, Legal Department,' he read aloud.

'She's been having an affair with Lars Holmberg,'

Erik said bluntly. 'Our Operational Director. It's become – complicated.'

Victor looked up from the file, already dreading where this was heading. 'How complicated?'

'She's pregnant. And she's started making noises about Lars leaving his wife.' Erik's expression was granite-hard. 'Lars's wife is Margareta, nee Bergström – as in Bergström Industries, our largest private investor. If this scandal breaks, we could lose the Northern expansion contract. That's forty million euros. Besides, she has been privy to a lot of commercially sensitive material.'

Victor felt his stomach turn. He'd known his father was ruthless in business, but this felt different. More personal. 'What exactly are you asking me to do?'

'Clean it up. Quietly. Lars is too emotional to handle this properly. The fool actually feels guilty. I need someone who can be objective, professional.' Erik's eyes were cold as winter steel. 'Make her understand that pursuing this matter further would be – inadvisable for everyone involved.'

'You want me to threaten her?'

'I want you to solve a problem using whatever method you deem appropriate. Offer her money, a new position elsewhere, whatever it takes. Just make her disappear.'

Victor stared at the photograph in the file. Ingrid Larsson had kind eyes and a genuine smile. She looked like someone who might be friends with Elsa. She was young, hopeful, trusting. 'And if she refuses?'

Erik's smile was sharp as a blade. 'She won't refuse. Not once she understands the consequences of crossing the Andersson family. You're good at reading people, Victor. Use that skill.'

As Victor left his father's office with the file tucked under his arm, he told himself it would be simple. A business transaction. He'd offer the girl money, she'd take it and disappear, and everyone could move on. It was his first year working for his father and he needed to prove that he was up to the task. He had no idea he was about to make the biggest mistake of his life.

Victor didn't know what to expect when he arranged to see Ingrid Larsson at a small cafe in Punavuori, far from the business district where someone might recognise either of them. Victim or gold digger? He found her hunched over a barely touched cup of coffee, her eyes red-rimmed and her hands shaking slightly, stirring sugar that she'd already dissolved minutes ago.

'Miss Larsson? I'm Victor Andersson.'

She looked up with desperate hope, and Victor felt his first pang of unease. 'You're here from Lars? He sent you?'

Victor's prepared speech died in his throat. She looked so young, so broken. Nothing like the scheming opportunist he'd feared. 'Not exactly. I'm here on behalf of Andersson Mining regarding your – situation with Mr Holmberg.'

The hope flickered and died in her eyes like a snuffed candle. 'Oh. I see.'

'I understand you're expecting a child.'

Ingrid's hand moved protectively to her still-flat stomach, and Victor noticed how thin she was, how her clothes hung loose on her frame. 'He told you?'

'The company is aware, yes. And we'd like to help you through this difficult time.'

'Help me?' Ingrid's laugh was bitter, hollow. 'Is that what you call it? Let me guess – you want me to sign something saying the baby isn't his, take some money, and disappear quietly so your precious executive doesn't have to face any consequences.'

Victor winced at her accuracy. That was exactly what he'd come to do. 'The situation is complicated –'

'It's not complicated!' Ingrid's voice cracked, drawing stares from other patrons. She lowered her voice to a whisper, but the pain was still raw. 'He told me he loved me. He said he was going to leave his wife. We had plans, dreams – and now he won't even take my calls.'

Her composure crumbled then, tears spilling over her cheeks as she tried to muffle her sobs with a napkin. Victor looked around the cafe, aware of the curious glances being cast their way. This wasn't going at all according to plan.

'He was going to take me to Paris this spring,' Ingrid continued, her voice barely audible. 'We were going to announce our engagement once his divorce was final. I even started looking at wedding dresses –'

As he looked at this broken young woman, Victor made his first deviation from his father's instructions.

Instead of presenting the non-disclosure agreement Erik had prepared, he said, 'Tell me what happened. All of it.'

For the next two hours, Ingrid told him everything. How Lars had pursued her when she'd started working at the company fresh out of secretarial school. How he'd convinced her that his marriage was already over, that his wife was cold and unloving.

He'd promised her a future together, painted pictures of the life they'd build once he was free.

'I should have known better,' Ingrid said as her story wound down. 'My mother always said, "If a man will cheat with you, he'll cheat on you", but I thought – I thought what we had was different.'

Victor found himself moved. This wasn't a woman trying to destroy a marriage for money or status. She believed in love, and a man with more power and experience had manipulated her.

'What will you do now?' he asked.

'I don't know,' Ingrid admitted. 'I can't afford to raise a child on my own, but I can't – I can't just pretend this baby doesn't exist. It's his child too. Doesn't that mean anything?'

Victor left that meeting with the confidentiality agreement still unsigned in his briefcase and a problem much more complex than his father had led him to believe.

Chapter Forty-One

'She's not what you think,' Victor said, standing in front of his father's desk while Erik poured himself a whisky. The evening shadows were long across the office, and the building was mostly empty except for the cleaning staff.

'I don't care what she is,' Erik replied coldly. 'Did you get her signature on the confidentiality agreement?'

Victor hesitated, and that moment of silence told Erik everything he needed to know.

'Victor.' His father's voice carried a warning that had intimidated him since childhood. 'I gave you a simple task.'

'She will not be bought off easily. Ingrid genuinely believed Holmberg was going to marry her. She's talking about going to Mrs Holmberg directly, telling her everything.'

Erik's glass stopped halfway to his lips. 'She threatened that?'

'She's desperate, Father. And desperate people do unpredictable things.'

'Then make her less desperate. Double the offer.'

'Money isn't what she wants. She wants acknowledgment, responsibility. She wants Holmberg to step up and be a father to his child.'

Erik's laugh was harsh and grating. 'Absolutely not. Lars has a family, a reputation to maintain. This girl is a temporary inconvenience, nothing more.'

'She's a human being carrying his child,' Victor said, the words slipping out before he could stop them.

The temperature in the room seemed to drop ten degrees. Erik set down his glass and fixed Victor with a stare that had made grown men reconsider their career choices.

'She's a liability,' Erik said, his voice brooking no argument. 'A potential threat to this company's reputation and our most valuable business relationships. Handle it, Victor. However you see fit. But handle it. And don't let your emotions cloud your judgment the way Lars did.'

Victor realised he was caught between two impossible positions as he left his father's office. Elsa was waiting for him at her apartment, probably wondering why he'd been so distracted lately. How could he explain he was being asked to destroy a young woman's life to protect a company's reputation?

He couldn't tell Elsa – this was confidential business, and she wouldn't understand the complexities involved. She'd see it in black and white terms, right and wrong, good and evil. But the real world wasn't that simple.

At least, that's what Victor told himself.

'I've been thinking about what you could do instead,' Victor said as he and Ingrid walked along the tree-lined paths of Esplanadi Park during her lunch break. It was April and the air was still crisp, but the first hints of spring were emerging – tiny buds on the branches, the promise of life returning after the long winter.

Ingrid looked at him with cautious hope. She'd lost more weight, and there were dark circles under her eyes that suggested sleepless nights. 'Instead of what?'

'Instead of fighting a battle you can't win against people who have all the power.' Victor stopped walking, turning to face her. 'What if I could get you a position at another company? A desirable position, with benefits that would help you raise your child.'

'You mean run away.'

'I mean a fresh start. Away from Lars, away from the gossip, away from a situation that's only going to get uglier.'

Ingrid was quiet for a long moment, her hand resting on her stomach where the first slight curve of pregnancy was showing. 'He won't leave his wife, will he?'

'No,' Victor said gently. 'He won't.'

The tears came then, quiet and heartbroken. Without thinking, Victor put a comforting arm around her shoulders, the way he might comfort Mikael or any friend in pain. 'I'm sorry, Ingrid. You deserved so much better than this.'

'I feel so stupid,' she whispered. 'If they knew, everyone at the office would think I'm just some pathetic girl who threw herself at her boss.'

'I don't think that. And anyone who matters wouldn't either.'

That was when Victor noticed the man with the camera across the park, too far away to identify but close enough to capture the image of Victor comforting a crying blonde woman. His blood ran cold as he realised what this meant – his father's insurance policy, no doubt. Erik Andersson never left anything to chance.

'Ingrid,' Victor said, 'I need you to listen to me very carefully –'

The call came at eleven o'clock on a Thursday night. Victor was in his apartment, trying to read documents his father had told him to study on the company structure, with complicated financial reports going back five years, but thoughts of Elsa distracted him. They'd had dinner earlier, and she'd seemed distant, asking questions about why he'd been so preoccupied lately. He'd deflected her questions with kisses and promises to explain later, but 'later' never seemed to come.

'Victor?' Ingrid's voice was barely recognisable,

thick with tears and something that might have been panic. 'Something terrible has happened.'

'Where are you?' Victor was already reaching for his jacket.

'I don't know. Near the office. I think – I think I've ruined everything.'

Victor found her twenty minutes later, wandering the streets near the Andersson Mining building in the cold spring rain. She was completely soaked, her hair stuck to her head, and she shivered in a thin coat that didn't protect her from the weather.

'Get in,' Victor said, pulling his car to the curb. 'You'll catch pneumonia.'

She climbed into the passenger seat. Her makeup had streaked down her cheeks, her eyes were swollen, and she shook, though he couldn't tell if it was from cold or shock.

'What happened?'

'I went to see him,' Ingrid said, her voice hollow. 'I couldn't stand it anymore, the wondering, the hoping. I thought if I could just talk to him face to face, make him understand –'

Victor felt dread settling in his stomach. 'You went to his office?'

'I waited in the lobby. I knew he always worked late on Thursdays. When he came down to leave, I called his name.' She laughed bitterly. 'You should have seen his face. Like I was a ghost, come back to haunt him.'

'What did you say to him?'

'I told him I wasn't going away. That he had responsibilities. That his wife deserved to know what kind of man she had married.' Ingrid turned to Victor with desperate, haunted eyes. 'He called security, Victor. Told them I was a disturbed employee making false accusations against him.'

Victor felt a hot rage burn in his chest.

'He what?'

'I've been fired. My contract has been terminated for inappropriate conduct towards senior management.' They escorted me out as if I were a criminal, with everyone watching.' Her voice broke completely. 'They made me clean out my desk while security stood over me. Thank God the office was empty by then. I don't know what I would have done if my colleagues had seen it.'

Victor pulled her into his arms as she sobbed against his shoulder, her whole body shaking with the force of her grief and humiliation. She felt so small, so fragile, and a protective fury he'd never experienced before overwhelmed him.

'What am I going to do?' Ingrid whispered. 'I have no job, no references, and a baby coming. Lars has destroyed my reputation – no one in this industry will hire me now.'

In that moment, Victor made a decision that would change the course of both their lives. 'I'm going to fix this.'

'How?'

'I don't know yet. But I'm not going to let him destroy you.'

Ingrid pulled back to look at him, her eyes wide with something like wonder. 'Why? Why would you do that for me? You barely know me.'

Victor thought of Elsa, of how she'd looked at him earlier that evening with growing suspicion and hurt. He thought of his father's cold calculations, of Lars Holmberg's cowardice, of the pregnant young woman shivering in his arms.

'Because someone should,' he said simply. 'Because you matter, and what's happening to you is wrong.'

Chapter Forty-Two

'I've arranged everything,' Victor said, sliding an envelope across the table at Café Strindberg. The May sunshine streamed through the large windows, making the moment feel deceptively cheerful.

It had taken him weeks to set up what he considered a fair solution – weeks of careful negotiation, veiled threats, and calling in favours he'd been saving for his own future. But looking at Ingrid now, seeing the hope returning to her eyes, he knew it had been worth every sleepless night.

Ingrid opened the envelope with trembling fingers, scanning the documents inside. 'This is – this is a good job. Better than what I had.'

'You deserve it. Nordström Industries thinks you're being transferred due to your excellent work record, not because you're running from a scandal.' Victor had been very careful about that part. 'And Tampere is far enough from Helsinki for you to start afresh, but close enough for you not to be completely alone.'

'What about child support? Will Lars –? '

'He'll contribute anonymously through a trust fund I've set up. Enough to ensure you and the baby are comfortable.' Victor's jaw tightened as he remembered that particular confrontation. 'He doesn't know the details yet, but he understands that supporting his child quietly is preferable to having his affair become public knowledge.'

Tears spilled over Ingrid's cheeks, but for the first time in months, they seemed to be tears of relief rather than despair. 'I can't believe you've done all this for me – '

Victor was quiet for a moment, thinking of all the things he couldn't say. How helping her had made him realise he didn't want to become the kind of man his father was. How her situation had shown him that behind every 'business problem' was a real person with real feelings. How defending her had cost him more than she would ever know.

'I should thank you. You've reminded me that behind every 'situation' that needs 'handling,' there's a real person with real feelings,' he said finally. 'My father sees problems to be solved, obstacles to be removed. But you're not a problem, Ingrid. You're someone who deserved better than what you got.'

Ingrid reached across the table to cup his face, her

touch gentle and grateful. To anyone watching from outside, it would have looked intimate, romantic. But Victor knew it was simply a gesture of profound thankfulness from someone who had been drowning and suddenly found herself saved.

'I don't know what I would have done without you,' she whispered. 'You've saved my life.'

'You saved your own life,' Victor replied. 'I just helped clear the path.'

She leaned forward and kissed his cheek; the way a sister might kiss a brother, full of gratitude and affection and goodbye. 'I'll never forget what you've done for me. If there's ever anything I can do to repay you – '

'Just be happy,' Victor said. 'Raise your child well. That's all the repayment I need.'

As Ingrid gathered her things to leave, clutching the envelope that represented her new future, Victor felt a mixture of satisfaction and hopelessness. How could he carry on working with his father now? He respected him even less than he had before.

His father barely spoke to him anymore, furious about the 'complications' Victor had introduced to a simple business matter. What's more, Elsa had grown distant and suspicious, sensing that something was wrong but unable to get him to explain.

He'd tried to tell her, had started the conversation a dozen times. But how could he explain that he'd been meeting secretly with another woman for months? How could he make her understand that it wasn't what it looked like when he couldn't reveal the details that would prove his innocence? Even if he could tell her everything, how would his future in the family firm look to her now? How could he justify working with a monster like his father?

Chapter Forty-Three

Lapland, Now

Victor's voice was rough when he finished the story. 'Three days later, you were gone. I tried to find you, tried to explain, but by then Ingrid had already left for Tampere. I couldn't break her confidentiality, couldn't expose what she'd been through just to clear my name.'

Elsa stared at him, her world shifting on its axis.

'All those months of meetings, the secrecy, the phone calls – '

'Were about helping a vulnerable young woman who'd been used and discarded by a powerful man. I fell in love with you, Elsa, not her. She was never anything more than someone who needed help.' Victor's eyes were intense, pleading. 'But I can see how it looked. How it must have destroyed you to think I was betraying you.'

'I thought – ' Elsa's voice was barely a whisper. 'I

thought you'd found someone better. Someone who fitted your world.'

'There is no one better than you. There never was.' Victor reached for her hands. 'I chose to protect her secret. You have no idea how much I regret that now. I should have found a way to make you understand. I should have trusted you with the truth.'

As they sat in the quiet of the now almost deserted bar, a sense of finality settled over them, mingled with a lingering connection that time and distance couldn't erase. The weight of their shared history hung heavy in the air, a tapestry of love and loss woven with threads of regret and forgiveness.

Elsa felt ten years of anger and hurt beginning to crumble, replaced by a profound sadness for all the time they'd lost. The truth about Ingrid had shifted everything – not just the past, but the present moment stretching between them like a bridge neither dared to cross.

'We were both so young,' she whispered. 'So scared.'

'Too young to know what mattered the most,' Victor agreed, his voice rough with emotion. 'But we're not young anymore, Elsa. And I'm not going to make the same mistake twice.'

The words hung between them, heavy with implication. Victor leaned forward, his eyes intense, searching her face. 'Tell me there's still something here. Tell me I'm not imagining what I felt when we danced tonight.'

Elsa's breath caught. She could feel the pull of him,

the same magnetic force that had drawn her to him all those years ago. For a moment, she was twenty-one again, believing in forever love and happy endings.

'Victor – ' she began, but her voice faltered.

He reached across the small table, his fingers brushing against hers. The touch sent electricity shooting through her, and she didn't pull away.

'I know you're with someone else. I know you've built a life in Stockholm. But before you walk away from this, from us, I need to know if you feel it too.'

The moment stretched between them like a taut wire. The bar around them had emptied save for the soft murmur of the cleaning staff in the background. Stars covered the sky outside the windows, creating a cocoon of intimacy around their small table.

Victor's hand covered hers, warm and familiar. She could see the rapid pulse at his throat, could feel the tremor in his fingers. He was as affected as she was, as torn between the past and the impossible present.

'I shouldn't,' she whispered, but she didn't move away.

'But you want to?' he asked, his voice barely audible.

He was leaning closer now, and she found herself meeting him halfway. The years collapsed around them. Ten years of silence, of building separate lives, of trying to forget what they had been to each other. None of it mattered in this moment.

Her eyes fluttered closed as she felt his breath against her lips. Just another centimetre, another heartbeat, and they would cross a line that would change everything. The kiss that would unravel her carefully constructed life, that would force her to choose between the safe love she had built with Tobias and this dangerous, all-consuming fire that had never truly died.

Her phone buzzed.

The sound cut through the moment like a blade. Elsa's eyes snapped open, and she saw her own shock reflected in Victor's face. They were frozen, lips almost touching, the weight of what had almost happened settling around them.

With shaking hands, she picked up her phone. A text from Tobias: *Where are you? It's nearly midnight.*

Reality crashed back in a cold wave. Tobias. Her life in Stockholm. The man in her hotel room, who had betrayed her, but still trusted her, who had no idea that his girlfriend was sitting in a late-night bar about to betray him as he had betrayed her. No, she would not stoop that low.

She pulled back sharply, the spell broken. Victor's hand fell away from hers as if burnt.

'I can't,' she said, her voice barely a whisper. 'I can't do this to him. To us. To anyone.'

Victor nodded slowly, devastated but also under-standing. 'I know,' he said quietly. 'I wouldn't want you to be the kind of person who could.'

The almost-kiss hung between them like a ghost, more powerful for what it represented than what it had been. They had come to the very edge of destroying everything – and pulled back.

But the damage was done. They both knew now that the connection between them was still there, still dangerous, still capable of consuming everything in its path.

'I should go,' Elsa said, getting back inside the snowsuit with unsteady hands.

'Elsa, wait.' Victor's voice stopped her. 'I won't ask you to choose. I won't put you in that position. But I need you to know – what we almost had just now? That wasn't about the past. That was about right now, about who we are today.'

She looked at him, memorising his face in the soft lighting, knowing this might be the last time she saw him this way.

'I know,' she said. 'That's what makes it so impossible.' Elsa spoke, her voice soft yet laced with emotion.

'I want to believe you, Victor. I want to believe that there's still hope for us. But I've moved on, Victor. I'm not sure I can just turn around and start again with you. My life is in Stockholm.' She didn't add, "With Tobias", because she didn't know what would happen between them. But that had nothing to do with Victor.

'I understand, Elsa,' Victor murmured, his voice heavy. 'I never wanted to cause you pain or stand in the way of your happiness. You deserve all the love and joy in the world, even if it's not with me.'

Elsa met his gaze, seeing the turmoil etched on his features, the regret that mirrored her own. Despite the hurt lingering between them, there was a flicker of something unspoken that passed between them; a shared history that neither could fully let go.

'I'm sorry, Victor,' Elsa whispered. 'I wish things could have been different for us, but we've both changed too much. Maybe it's time for us to find our own paths to heal the wounds of the past.' There was a bittersweet smile playing on her lips.

Victor nodded, a mixture of acceptance and grief in his eyes. 'I'll always cherish what we had, Elsa. Thank you for being honest with me, for giving me closure.'

Elsa zipped up her suit, stood up and said, 'I'm glad we finally managed to speak properly. I'm sorry I left you like I did, but perhaps it was for the best.'

'Yeah,' Victor agreed, getting up.

'It's time to get back to the hotel, I think?' Elsa said, not looking at him.

Victor nodded. 'OK, let me order a cab.'

Chapter Forty-Four

Lily had been enjoying the quieter atmosphere of the hotel bar when she heard raised voice coming from the enclosed terrace outside. Through the glass doors, she could see a small group of smokers gathered around someone who was speaking with obvious passion, their gestures animated against the backdrop of the snow-covered landscape.

Curiosity drew her outside, where she discovered the speaker was a lean, dark-haired man in his early thirties, wearing a wool jumper that had seen better days and jeans that were clean but clearly not bought for the occasion. She recognised him vaguely from the protest during Erik Andersson's speech – one of Kat's environmental activist friends.

' – and meanwhile, we're sitting here celebrating whilst the government fast-tracks mining permits that will destroy this ecosystem permanently,' he was saying in English, his Finnish accent thick with emotion. 'The hypocrisy is staggering.'

'Oh, come off it, Joak,' said one of the other guests, an English woman Lily didn't recognise. 'It's a wedding. Can't we have one evening without discussing the end of the world?'

'The world doesn't stop ending because we're having champagne,' Joak replied sharply, taking a deep drag on his hand-rolled cigarette. 'That's exactly the kind of privileged thinking that got us into this mess.'

'Privileged thinking?' Lily spoke before she'd consciously joined the conversation. 'Or human thinking? People have been celebrating love and commitment for thousands of years, through wars and plagues and every kind of crisis. Maybe that's because personal connections give us the strength to face larger challenges, rather than being a distraction from them.'

Joak turned to look at Lily properly for the first time, his dark eyes assessing her. He was handsome in a fierce, uncompromising way, with an intensity that came from deeply held convictions. 'And you are?'

'Lily Wootton. Kat's sister.' She stepped closer to the group, feeling the bite of the Arctic air on her cheeks. 'And you're clearly someone who thinks caring about individual happiness is selfish when there are bigger problems to solve.'

'Joak Lindström,' he replied, extending his right hand, while stubbing his cigarette in a sand-filled plant pot with his left. There was a slight mocking formality to his actions.

'And yes, I think that worrying about wedding flowers whilst the Arctic ice caps melt is a spectacular example of misplaced priorities.'

His handshake was firm, calloused from outdoor work, and lasted a fraction longer than necessary. Despite herself, Lily felt a spark of awareness that had nothing to do with their philosophical disagreement.

'That's remarkably reductive thinking for someone who presumably cares about human welfare,' she said, not stepping back from him. 'Love isn't the enemy of environmental action. If anything, it's the foundation. People fight to protect what they love – their families, their children's futures, the places that matter to them.'

'Pretty words from someone who's probably never had to choose between heating her flat and buying groceries,' Joak replied, but there was less venom in his voice now, more curiosity.

'You know nothing about my background,' Lily shot back, her cheeks flushing with anger. 'And even if you did, dismissing someone's perspective based on their economic status is just intellectual laziness disguised as moral superiority.'

The other guests had drifted away, worried where the tension between them might lead, but neither Lily nor Joak seemed to notice. They stood facing each other on the terrace, their breath forming clouds in the cold air, locked in a battle of wills that was becoming something else entirely.

'Besides, that's a filthy habit, surely not good for the environment.' Lily gazed at the pot of cigarette stubs.

'Intellectual laziness?' Joak ignored the jibe about his smoking and his voice dropped to a more dangerous register. 'That's rich, coming from someone who studies dead people's love letters while the living world burns around her.'

'How do you – ' Lily began, then stopped. 'Kat told you about my research?'

'She mentioned her sister was doing some sort of romantic history project. Very fitting for someone who thinks personal feelings matter more than collective action.'

'I think,' Lily said, stepping even closer, so that she had to tilt her head back to meet his eyes, 'that you're terrified of personal feelings because they complicate your neat little worldview where everyone can be sorted into heroes and villains based on their politics.'

Joak stared down at her, his jaw tight with frustration. 'And I think you're a privileged romantic who's never had to face the reality of the world's indifference.'

'Then we're at an impasse, aren't we?' Lily's voice was breathless now, though whether from anger or the unexpected charge in the air between them, she couldn't say.

'Apparently so.'

They stood there in the silence. Lily noticed the star-filled sky, but she was too angry to have time to admire the display. Neither of them moved away, though every rational part of Lily's mind was telling her to end this conversation and return to the warmth of the bar.

'You know what's fascinating?' she said finally, her voice softer now but no less challenging. 'For someone who claims not to believe in the power of personal connection, you're remarkably good at creating it.'

Joak's eyes narrowed. 'What's that supposed to mean?'

'It means you've had my complete attention for the past ten minutes, made me more angry and more engaged than I've been all evening, and somehow convinced me to stand out here in subzero temperatures arguing with a complete stranger.' Lily's smile was small but genuine. 'If that's not seduction, I don't know what is.'

Something shifted in Joak's expression. There was surprise, perhaps, or recognition. 'You think I'm trying to seduce you?'

'I think you're passionate about everything you believe in, and passion is inherently seductive, even when it's wrapped up in moral outrage and environmental statistics.' Lily tilted her head, studying his face. 'The question is whether you're brave enough to admit that human connection, even the inconvenient, complicated kind, might actually be worth something.'

Joak was quiet for a long moment, his gaze moving between her eyes and her mouth in a way that made her pulse quicken. 'You're not what I expected,' he said finally.

'What did you expect?'

'Someone easier to dismiss.' His voice was rough, honest. 'Someone who'd back down when challenged or get offended and storm off. Not someone who'd fight back with equal conviction.'

'Disappointed?'

'Terrified,' he admitted, and the honesty in his voice sent a thrill through her that had nothing to do with the cold. He took a step closer to her. She could smell the tobacco on him but found it strangely attractive. Perhaps she'd had more champagne than was wise.

'Dance with me,' Joak said quietly.

She should have said no. Should have recognised the dangerous territory they were entering and chosen the safe path back to her room alone. Instead, she nodded and followed him towards the dance floor.

The music was 80s ska, which Lily adored, and the two of them danced until they both collapsed onto one of the sofas around the bar.

'I owe you an apology,' Joak said finally, out of breath.

'For what?'

'For making assumptions about you based on your family's circumstances. That was unfair and, as you pointed out, intellectually lazy.' He sat up, turning to face her. 'I've spent so long fighting against systems of privilege that sometimes I forget that individuals within those systems can still think for themselves.'

'And I owe you an apology for suggesting that your convictions were less valid because they make you uncomfortable with emotional displays,' Lily replied. 'That wasn't fair either.'

They sat facing each other in the slowly emptying bar.

'Can I tell you something?' she said impulsively. 'Something that might surprise you?'

'Please.'

'I think you're wrong about love being a luxury. I think it's actually a necessity, not the fairy-tale kind, but the genuine kind. The kind that makes people willing to make sacrifices for something bigger than themselves.' She moved closer, emboldened by the honesty in his expression. 'I think people who've never loved deeply are the ones who can't understand why others would fight to protect what they cherish. Love doesn't make people selfish. It makes them fierce.'

Joak reached out to touch her face, his fingers tracing the line of her cheek. 'You're trying to convert me to your romantic worldview.'

'Is it working?'

'More than I care to admit,' he said, and kissed her.

The kiss was nothing like the gentle, exploratory kisses Lily had experienced with previous boyfriends. This was urgent, filled with all the tension and conflict and unexpected desire that had been building between them. When they broke apart, both were panting, their faces flushed with more than just the effort of jumping up and down on the dance floor.

'This is a terrible idea,' Joak said, his forehead resting against hers.

'Terrible,' Lily agreed, and kissed him again.

Later, Lily would blame the champagne, the star-filled sky, the intoxicating atmosphere of the wedding, and the most intellectually stimulating argument she'd had in years. But in that moment, walking back to his room with Joak's hand in hers, she felt only the exhilarating terror of someone who'd just jumped off a cliff and was hoping that she'd land somewhere soft.

Chapter Forty-Five

Elsa stood outside their hotel room, staring at the number on the door, without seeing it. The rollercoaster of emotions she had felt in the last 24 hours had left her exhausted and deflated.

She wondered why she hadn't told Victor about Tobias and his affair with Annabel. Instead, she had pretended that she was happy with her life in Stockholm. Victor didn't bring up Tobias's awful flirting with Simona at the reception, nor did he mention his behaviour in general, which surprised her. Tobias had been bad-tempered, condescending, and rude about Kat's very admirable environmental beliefs.

Elsa glanced down at her phone, in two minds about what to do. She didn't want to go inside, to be in the same room as Tobias. She bitterly regretted bringing him with her to Lapland. He had spoiled it all for her. She'd been a fool to think that there could be any reconciliation.

Suddenly the door opened, and Tobias, clad in a white robe engraved with the hotel logo, stood facing her.

'Where the hell have you been?'

Tobias sounded and looked angry, and Elsa swore under her breath as guilt crept up her spine and settled in her chest. She had been with another man, but not in that way. And what right did Tobias have to question her?

'You have no right – '

Elsa didn't continue, because she suddenly understood there was no point in arguing with the man. The realisation that she would not stay with him after this trip hit her like a flash of lightning. He would understand very well why. Then there would be a fresh case, and he'd forget all about her, she was certain of that.

'Right,' Tobias said.

He had the sense to look a little sheepish for a fraction of a second until his expression changed to one of irritation.

'Come in, I was worried about you.'

'Oh yeah?' Elsa said, hoping her voice was as sarcastic as she felt.

Tobias placed his hand on his hips.

'Last time I looked, we were in a relationship. The least you could do is let me know what you are doing. Or answer my text. Especially as we are in a foreign country, in the middle of bloody nowhere!'

'This is not a foreign country to me! And we are in a five-star hotel, so it's unlikely wolves would have mauled me. Besides, you have no right to question my whereabouts after what you've been up to.'

As soon as the words left her mouth, Elsa regretted saying them. She should have kept her cool and not risen to Tobias's bait. An argument like this was exactly what she had wanted to avoid. But before she could try to diffuse the situation, Tobias's eyes narrowed, and he took a step closer to Elsa.

'What? This is your revenge. Is that what all this with your old flame is about? Did you use him to make me jealous? I am surprised. Didn't think you'd stoop that low, Elsa Berg!'

Elsa took a breath, trying to steady her feelings. This was preposterous! How absurd that Tobias would act all jealous after his own infidelity back in Stockholm, and his behaviour with Simona. He had absolutely no right to question her. But Elsa was tired, and she didn't want to argue with Tobias. What was the point?

'I'm so sorry. We went for a drink in the village, and then there were no cabs – '

'We? Who were you with?'

Elsa's breath caught in her throat.

'What do you mean?'

She was buying time.

'You said, "We went for a drink"?'

Elsa now gave a little laugh. She tried to sound casual by controlling her breath.

'Oh, I forgot my boyfriend is a celebrated lawyer.'

She made herself stop there, deciding not to

explain too much. A thought occurred to her. This was the first time Tobias had shown any kind of jealousy. What was it about Victor that was different? Every time Hugo, for example, had tried to flirt with her, Tobias had just laughed. But surely, if he'd been worried about Elsa being here with Victor, he would not have left early? It was his choice to leave the wedding reception when he did. And he'd more or less told her to go back to the party while he worked on his case.

There was silence.

Tobias was glaring at her. Was he expecting more from her? Elsa tried to control herself. She had learned from experience in her own profession as a lawyer that the less you said, the better. It was what she always advised her clients.

But this was not a legal battle. She wasn't in court being cross-examined by Tobias, she reminded herself. And she had done nothing wrong. She might have wanted to, but she had controlled herself because she despised and abhorred cheating and disloyalty of any kind. A small voice in her head asked if she had been disloyal by cosying up to Victor, allowing him to almost seduce her. It had felt so good to hear that he'd suffered and yearned for her after she'd left him that day in Helsinki.

If that were true.

Was Victor playing a game too?

Elsa had wanted to confront Tobias about Annabel, and all that she had found out before their trip up here, but she now decided it didn't matter. She would not stay with him anyway, so why make it into an argument?

'OK,' Tobias said drily. 'I just wanted to know you are OK. Did the rest of the evening go well?'

Now he's trying to catch me with a different tack, Elsa thought, but she brushed away those thoughts. Why would Tobias suspect anything had happened? This is not a criminal court, she reminded herself again. It was all in her head. But she did feel guilty.

'Yeah, it was very nice,' Elsa added. 'It's a shame you had to leave early. Did you get all your work done?'

Tobias gave Elsa a knowing look, one that she recognised from watching him in court. It was to acknowledge the opponent's skill in deflecting their guilt, or an opposing counsel changing the path of the questioning with a valid argument.

'Yeah,' he said simply.

Chapter Forty-Six

Elsa gave him a look that Tobias couldn't interpret and began to undress. Wearing a bathrobe over her bra and knickers, which she'd kept on, he noticed, she grabbed a brush from the bedside table and began brushing her hair with methodical strokes.

'You're very quiet tonight,' he said, sitting beside her on the bed.

'Just tired. It's been a long day.'

'Has it? I thought you seemed to enjoy yourself.' He couldn't keep the edge out of his voice.

Elsa's hand stilled on the brush. 'What do you mean?'

'I mean, Victor Andersson seemed very interested in reminiscing about old times.'

'We're old friends, Tobias. I told you that.'

Did he detect a quiver in her voice?

'Friends.' He laughed, but there was no humour in it. 'Is that what they're calling it?'

Elsa turned to face him, her eyes flashing with anger. 'Are you jealous? Of a conversation about university?'

'I'm not jealous,' he said, and realised it was true. He was annoyed, not jealous. Annoyed that his carefully arranged life was being disrupted by inconvenient emotions and complicated histories. 'I'm practical. I don't like the way he looks at you.'

'How does he look at me?'

'Like he wants to devour you.'

The words hung between them, and Tobias saw something shift in Elsa's expression. Not anger anymore, but something else. Something that looked almost like longing.

'Maybe,' she said, 'that's not such a terrible thing.'

With those words, she disappeared into the bathroom.

Tobias sat up in bed, watching the dark night sky, littered with bright stars, through the floor to ceiling windows of the room. Something had changed in Elsa. Not only had she been evasive since coming back, due no doubt to Victor Andersson, but she also had a certain determination in her eyes and in the set of her mouth that he hadn't seen for a long time. She had been guarded when they first dated, and he had needed all his powers of persuasion to make her believe he was a good guy and that he wanted to be with her. He'd known then she had trust issues, but he hadn't delved deeper into why she found it so difficult to enter a relationship. Whatever it could be was in her past and had nothing to do with him.

When she'd agreed to take things further, to move in with him, Tobias had felt a sense of triumph. Wasn't it always more satisfying to make a complicated woman happy?

But things changed when they began living together. Elsa became needy, wanting constant reassurance, which he couldn't provide.

And then they went to that wedding in Provence, and he saw Annabel again. He couldn't resist her. Their fling at university had been short but it had set a bar for him that he had since found difficult to find. Why had he not pursued her after they graduated? He'd got busy with his own career, and one important case after another, and Annabel had gone over to the US to take a postgrad degree at Stanford. She was now a financial whizz, on the board of one of the largest forestry companies in Sweden. She possessed self-assurance, drive, a great sense of humour, and they had an undeniable physical chemistry. Like two pieces of a puzzle.

That was all there was to it. Tobias had to have her, to share his life with her.

But he didn't want to be that man. The man who cheats on his girlfriend. Every morning as he woke up to Elsa, wishing it was Annabel, it tore him apart. He couldn't tell Elsa the truth, so they were in limbo, making each other unhappy. Perhaps now was the time for change.

Chapter Forty-Seven

Elsa walked into the bathroom and closed the door. What was happening to her? She remembered Lily's words about choosing love and was surprised to see a smile settle on her face. She straightened her lips and felt ashamed. Her life was not a romantic novel. This was about real people and their real emotions.

As she removed her make-up, she thought back to what Victor had told her about Ingrid. She knew in her heart that the story was right, but could she really trust him? And could she really go back to a relationship she'd had when she was young? When they'd first started dating, she was only a teenager and not much older when it all ended. She'd thought she had long buried that period in her life. Now it had all been brought back to the surface again.

Ten years was a long time. She had changed, as must Victor, although tonight he didn't seem any different from how he had been then. The connection between them was the same too. Or was the occasion of Kat and Mikael's wedding playing into her state of mind? Was she imagining – or embellishing – how she really felt?

Her eye caught the sauna at one end of the large bathroom. Why shouldn't she heat it up and relax a little? She couldn't imagine settling down and going to bed yet.

In the sauna, as the intense heat enveloped her, she decided she'd draw a line under both Victor and Tobias for good. She'd refuse to see either of them, however much they'd plead with her. She would not reply to any communication; she would block both men's numbers from her phone. She thanked her stars that she was on an early flight, making it unlikely she'd bump into Victor in the lobby tomorrow.

She would have to travel with Tobias, but he'd be engrossed in his oh-so-important case, so it wouldn't be a great strain on her.

As she was gazing out of the little window of the sauna, checking if she could see those stars shining on her, she was amazed by what she saw. In the far horizon, above the little houses with snow-covered roofs, and the Ylläs mountain beyond, the clear ink-blue sky had come alive. Streaks of vivid green, pale yellow, and bright purple flickered across the vista. This display of the aurora borealis was different from the lights they'd seen with Victor in Lapland all those years ago. This was somehow brighter, as if some better filter had been applied to the colours. Elsa wanted to tell Victor to look out of his window. She was about to climb out of the sauna to retrieve her phone when she remembered she wasn't going to speak to him ever again. Hadn't she just decided that Victor was history?

Elsa stepped into the shower cubicle and set the temperature to cold. She wanted to wash away all remainders of Victor, his smile and the familiar feeling of his body against hers while they had waited for her cab earlier. It was as if all the years had fallen off by the snowy pavement. She needed to forget how right it had felt to be close to him, to talk to him about the past and to admire the stunning landscape around them. The memories they both shared. Elsa had forgotten how well they knew each other.

After the sauna and shower, and wrapped in a towel, she told herself she would stop thinking about Victor as soon as she was on board the flight to Stockholm. Before then, she could still wallow in self-pity for what might have been and reflect on the wonderful evening they'd had. Come morning, however, Victor would forever be dead to her. She would return to Stockholm and begin to unravel her life with Tobias. She'd need all her strength to do that. For the past 24 hours, she'd had enough emotional upheaval to last a lifetime!

Chapter Forty-Eight

Tobias looked up from his papers as Elsa appeared in the doorway to the bathroom. Without makeup, she looked young and vulnerable, and for a moment he felt a flicker of the affection that had once drawn him to her.

But it wasn't love. It had never been love, not really. It had been convenience, compatibility, the path of least resistance. But he'd thought Elsa had been happy.

Clearly he'd been wrong. Elsa had never looked at him the way she did at Victor Andersson. Like he was the only man in the room.

The hotel room felt colder than the Arctic air outside. Tobias sat on the edge of the bed, his case papers next to him, watching Elsa move quietly around the room. She'd returned an hour ago, her cheeks flushed from the cold, her eyes bright with something he couldn't quite name. She'd been with Victor, he guessed that much. The question was what had transpired between them.

'We need to talk,' he said finally, his voice cutting through the silence.

Elsa paused, a hotel towel clutched in her hands. 'Yes,' she agreed quietly. 'We do.'

She sat down in the chair by the window, the one that overlooked the snow-covered fells. In the lamplight, she looked smaller somehow, more fragile than he'd ever seen her. But there was something else in her posture. There was a kind of resolve that made his chest tighten.

'I know this has been difficult,' he began, choosing his words carefully. 'Coming here, seeing Victor again –
'

'It's not about Victor,' she interrupted, her voice steady. 'Not really. It's about us, Tobias. About what we've become.'

He felt the familiar urge to deflect, to turn the conversation to safer ground. But something in her tone stopped him. This wasn't the Elsa who'd confronted him in Stockholm a week ago, hurt and angry and desperate for answers. This was someone who'd already found her truth.

'I've been thinking,' she continued, 'about everything. About Stockholm, about Annabel, about why we're both so unhappy.'

The shame hit him like a physical blow. He'd been dreading this conversation since Hugo's revelation had forced the truth into the open. But sitting here, in this remote hotel room with dark skies peppered with streaks of blue and green outside their window, he realised something had shifted. The lies had become too heavy to carry.

'Elsa,' he said, his voice barely above a whisper. 'I need to tell you something. About Provence.'

She looked at him then, her green eyes calm. 'I already know.'

'No, you don't. Not everything.' He ran his hands through his hair, feeling the weight of months of deception. 'That night in Provence, when you'd gone to sleep early – I went down to the bar. Annabel was on the balcony, and she was upset about something. We talked, and then –'

'You slept with her,' Elsa finished quietly.

He nodded, unable to meet her eyes. 'I told myself it was the wine, the setting with the lavender fields, the moonlight, the romance of it all. But that's not true. I wanted her. I've wanted her since university, and I was too much of a coward to admit it – to you or to myself.'

'And since then?'

'We've been seeing each other. Meeting for dinner, talking for hours. We haven't – we haven't slept together since that night. We both felt too guilty, too ashamed. But that doesn't make it any less of a betrayal.'

Elsa was quiet for a long moment, her fingers tracing patterns on the arm of the chair. 'Do you love her?'

The question hung in the air between them. He could lie, try to salvage what was left of their relationship. But they were both past the point of comfortable deceptions.

'Yes,' he said simply. 'I now know I do.'

She nodded slowly, as if confirming something she'd already suspected. 'I thought so. The way you looked at her in Provence – I told myself I was imagining it, but I wasn't, was I?'

'No,' he admitted. 'Even if I didn't know it myself then. You weren't imagining it.'

'And tonight,' she continued, 'when you accused me of being with Victor – You were angry because you thought I was doing what you'd already done.'

The observation stung because it was true. He'd been projecting his own guilt onto her, looking for absolution in her own betrayal.

'I'm sorry,' he said, and meant it. 'I'm sorry for lying to you, for betraying you, for making you doubt yourself. I'm sorry for being such a bloody coward.'

'I know you are,' she said gently. 'And I understand why you did it. We've been living a lie for a long time, haven't we? Both of us.'

'What do you mean?'

She stood up, walked to the window, and looked out at the aurora borealis lighting up the sky. 'We've been trying to be something we're not. You've been trying to love me the way I needed to be loved, and I've been trying to be the kind of woman you actually wanted. But we're not those people, are we?'

He thought about it – really thought about it – and realised she was right. They'd been playing roles, trying to fit into each other's lives like pieces from different puzzles.

'I don't think we ever were,' he said finally.

'No,' she agreed. 'We weren't. We were convenient for each other, comfortable. But that's not enough, is it? Not for either of us.'

'What are you saying?'

She turned back to face him, and he saw tears in her eyes, but they weren't tears of anger or betrayal. They were tears of sadness, of mourning for something that had never really existed.

'I'm saying I think we both know this is over,' she said quietly. 'We've known it for months. We've just been too scared to admit it.'

The relief was immediate and overwhelming. He'd been carrying the weight of their failing relationship for so long that he'd forgotten what it felt like to breathe freely.

'Victor?' he asked.

'Victor is my past,' she said firmly. 'What happened with him happened years ago. We talked tonight, and we both agreed too much time has passed. We've both changed too much. Some things can't be reclaimed.'

'So what now?'

'Now we stop lying to ourselves,' she said. 'We stop pretending we're something we're not. We let each other go.'

He stood up, crossed the room to where she was standing. For a moment, they looked at each other and he saw the woman he'd been living with for two years, the woman he'd tried so hard to love properly, the woman who deserved so much better than what he'd given her.

'I'm sorry,' he said again. 'For all of it. For the lies, for the affair, for wasting your time. You deserve someone who loves you completely, without reservation.'

'And you deserve someone who makes you feel alive,' she replied. 'Someone who challenges you, who makes you want to be better. Someone like Annabel.'

They stood there in the silence, the weight of their shared failure settling between them. But it didn't feel heavy anymore – it felt like liberation.

'Will you be all right?' he asked.

'I will,' she said, and he believed her. 'Will you?'

'I don't know,' he admitted. 'I've made such a mess of things. I don't know if Annabel wants a relationship.'

'She will,' Elsa said with surprising certainty. 'She loves you. That was obvious even in Provence.'

'And you? What will you do?'

'I'll figure it out,' she said. 'I always do.'

He kissed her forehead gently. 'Thank you,' he whispered. 'For being so gracious about this. For being better than I deserved.'

'We both deserved better,' she said. 'But we're both going to be fine.'

As they moved around the room, packing their things for the early morning flight, Tobias felt the shame of his actions settling into his bones. He'd handled everything wrong: the affair, the lies, the cowardice. He'd hurt someone who'd trusted him, who'd done nothing to deserve his betrayal.

But he'd also learned something about himself in the process. He'd learned that he was capable of passion, of the kind of love that made him reckless. He'd learned that safety and compatibility weren't enough, that he needed someone who saw through his careful composure to the man underneath.

He'd learned that he didn't want to be the kind of person who settled for less than everything.

The guilt would stay with him, he knew that. The knowledge that he'd been weak when he should have been strong, that he'd chosen deception over honesty, that he'd hurt someone who'd deserved better. But perhaps that was the price of finally being truthful about what he wanted.

As he closed his suitcase, Tobias made a silent promise to himself. Whatever happened next, he would be honest. With Annabel, with himself, with everyone. No more lies, no more cowardice, no more living half a life.

He owed that much to Elsa. But more than that, he owed it to himself.

Chapter Forty-Nine

Elsa lay in the darkness, listening to Tobias's steady breathing beside her. The conversation they'd just had echoed in her mind. It had been brutal in its honesty, but somehow liberating. The weight of their failing relationship had finally been acknowledged, lifted from both their shoulders like a heavy cloak they'd been carrying for too long.

She stared at the ceiling, watching the occasional faint flash of light. How strange it had been that neither Tobias nor she had mentioned the nature's light show happening outside while they'd been deciding on their separate futures. It was the perfect backdrop to the drama of the occasion. So why did she feel calmer and happier than she had in years? And how had she got it so wrong? For months, she'd been clinging to a relationship that had been slowly suffocating them both. She'd convinced herself that Tobias's emotional distance was just his way, that his increasing coldness was due to work stress, that his lack of physical affection was simply a phase they'd work through together.

But tonight, as they'd finally spoken truthfully to each other, she'd seen the relief in his eyes when she'd suggested their relationship was over. The same relief she'd felt, if she were being honest with herself.

She'd been trying to be the woman she thought he wanted. A polished, undemanding, professionally successful person who didn't threaten his achievements. She'd moulded herself into someone who fitted neatly into his world, someone who asked for nothing more than he was willing to give.

But that wasn't love, was it? That was a performance.

Real love was what she'd felt at seventeen, when Victor had looked at her like she was the most fascinating person in the world. When he'd encouraged her passion for justice, when he'd made her feel brilliant and beautiful and completely herself. She'd trusted him with her whole heart before fear and misunderstanding had torn them apart.

Victor.

The conversation in the bar had changed everything. Not just her understanding of the past, but her perception of herself. For ten years, she'd built her identity around being the woman who'd been betrayed, who'd been strong enough to walk away from love that had disappointed her.

She'd run. Not just from Victor, but from the possibility of being hurt again. She'd chosen safety over passion, predictability over the terrifying vulnerability of real love.

And where had that got her? Lying next to a man who'd been having an affair for months, in a relationship so hollow that they'd both been relieved to end it.

The irony wasn't lost on her. She'd been so afraid of being betrayed that she'd chosen a man who'd actually betrayed her. She'd been so determined to avoid the pain of loving completely that she'd settled for loving not at all.

What if Victor was right? The thought crept into her mind like dawn breaking over the Arctic landscape. *What if what we felt tonight wasn't about the past, but about who we are now?*

She turned onto her side, facing away from Tobias. She allowed herself to think about Victor for the first time in years. Not the Victor of her nightmares – the phantom betrayer who'd haunted her relationships – but the real Victor she'd spent time with today.

He'd grown up, certainly. The arrogant edge of youth had been tempered by experience, by what looked like genuine regret for the choices he'd made. But underneath, he was still the man who'd fallen in love with her mind as much as her body, who'd seen her potential when she'd barely seen it herself.

The connection between them had been immediate and undeniable. Not nostalgia, not the ghost of what they'd once been. Instead, it had been something alive and present and achingly real.

When they'd danced, when they'd walked in the snow, when they'd sat in that bar as he'd told her the truth about Ingrid, she'd felt more like herself than she had in years. Not the controlled, careful woman she'd become, but the passionate, trusting girl who'd believed in love's possibility.

Could we really try again?

The question terrified her. She'd spent so long building walls around her heart, so long convincing herself that she was better off alone than risking the kind of devastating heartbreak she'd experienced in her early twenties. Starting over with Victor would mean dismantling all of that protection, making herself vulnerable again to the one person who'd already had the power to destroy her.

But maybe, she thought, vulnerability wasn't weakness. Maybe it was the only way to experience real love. She thought about what Lily had said about taking risks. *Life's too short and too precious to waste on careful.*

She thought about Mikael and Kat, the way they'd looked at each other during the ceremony. They'd both been hurt before. Kat by her celebrity chef, Mikael by his family's rejection of his choices. But they'd found the courage to risk their hearts again, to believe that love was worth the potential for pain.

What if Victor and I could have that?

The thought sent a thrill of possibility through her

chest, immediately followed by a wave of terror. She was thirty-two next birthday, not twenty-one. She had a career, a life, and responsibilities. She couldn't just throw everything away for a man who'd once broken her heart, could she?

But then she remembered the way Victor had looked at her in the bar, the raw honesty in his voice when he'd told her about Ingrid. The way he'd pulled back from kissing her, respecting her relationship with Tobias even when they both knew it was over.

He'd changed too. He was more measured, a little less flashy. He'd apparently never stopped loving her, never stopped hoping for a second chance.

Some things can't be reclaimed, she'd told him. But what if she'd been wrong about that too?

Elsa closed her eyes, letting herself imagine what it might be like. Moving back to Finland, perhaps. Finding work in Helsinki, starting afresh in a place that held both her worst memories and her best. Rebuilding a relationship with someone who knew her completely, who'd loved her before she'd become successful, who'd seen her potential when she'd been nothing more than a scholarship girl with big dreams.

It wouldn't be easy. They'd both been shaped by their years apart. The choices they'd made had changed them. Victor still carried the weight of his father's expectations and his complicated relationship with his family's business. She'd grown cautious, careful, afraid to trust anyone completely.

But maybe that was why it could work now, when

it couldn't have worked then. They were both old enough to know that love wasn't just about passion. It was about choosing each other, every day, even when it was difficult.

Especially when it was difficult.

In a few hours, she'd fly back to Stockholm. She'd have to face the practical realities of ending her relationship with Tobias. She needed to untangle two years of shared life. She didn't yet know what she wanted to do about her career, an apartment, and her carefully constructed existence.

But tonight, in this moment between ending and beginning, she allowed herself to hope. To believe that maybe, just maybe, some things could be reclaimed. Some love could be redeemed.

Some hearts could learn to trust – and to love again.

Victor, she thought, and this time his name didn't carry the weight of old pain. It carried the promise of new beginnings.

The steady rhythm of Tobias's breathing continued beside her, peaceful and untroubled. He'd slept well, relieved that they would finally be free from the burden of pretending to be something they weren't.

As Elsa drifted towards sleep, her last conscious thought was of Victor's smile in the bar, the way he'd looked at her with such hope and tenderness. The way he'd always looked at her, even when she'd been too hurt to see it.

Tomorrow would bring difficult conversations and

painful decisions. She would start the messy work of rebuilding her life. But tonight, she felt something she hadn't experienced in years. The thrilling, terrifying possibility of falling in love again. Could she do it? Could she really take that chance?

Chapter Fifty

Ulla Andersson stood at the floor-to-ceiling windows of the family chalet, her wedding outfit replaced by a simple cashmere jumper and trousers, her makeup washed away to reveal the face Erik had fallen in love with thirty-five years ago. The reception had ended hours ago, but she couldn't bring herself to go to bed. Being back in Lapland always made sleep elusive – not from discomfort, but from a deep, almost spiritual restlessness that called her to witness the night.

Behind her, she could hear Erik moving through the familiar rooms, the soft sounds of a man trying to unwind from a day that had challenged everything he thought he knew about his family. They'd barely spoken during the drive back from the hotel, both lost in their own thoughts about Mikael's radiant happiness, the protest that had interrupted Erik's speech, and the encouraging conversation between father and son that had unfolded at the reception table.

'You should get some rest,' Erik said quietly, appearing beside her at the window. He'd changed into casual clothes, as well, and looked more relaxed than she'd seen him all weekend. 'It's been a long day.'

'I'm not tired,' Ulla replied softly, though that wasn't entirely true. The emotional weight of the weekend had exhausted her, but something else kept her awake. It was the same restless ache that had accompanied her through decades of marriage, the feeling of words unspoken and truths carefully avoided.

'The view is spectacular tonight,' Erik observed, settling into the chair beside the window. 'I'd forgotten how clear the sky gets here in winter.'

Ulla glanced at her husband, noting the way his shoulders had finally lost some of their rigid tension. After years of watching him, reading the signs of his displeasure or approval, she'd learned to navigate the unpredictable waters of his moods.

'I never forgot,' she said quietly, her voice barely above a whisper. 'This landscape is in my blood, Erik. It always has been.'

Erik was quiet for a moment, and Ulla found herself holding her breath slightly, waiting to see if he would dismiss her sentiment as he so often did. Instead, he nodded slowly.

'I know,' he said finally. 'I've always known how much this place means to you.'

The acknowledgment was so unexpected that Ulla

felt tears prick her eyes. How long had it been since he'd validated something that mattered to her without making her feel foolish for caring?

'Have you?' she asked, then immediately regretted the question. It sounded too much like a challenge, and she'd learned long ago that challenging Erik rarely led anywhere good.

But tonight, perhaps softened by the day's events, Erik didn't bristle. Instead, his expression grew thoughtful, almost remorseful.

'I know I haven't always – appreciated your connection to this place,' he said carefully. 'I suppose I saw it as something from your past that you'd moved beyond.'

Ulla felt the familiar sting of dismissal, gentler now but still painful. She'd spent decades learning to make herself smaller, trying to fit into the life Erik had built for them in Helsinki. 'I see,' she said, her voice neutral in the way she'd perfected over the years.

'No, that's not – ' Erik stopped himself, running a hand through his silver hair. 'I was wrong to think that. Tonight, listening to Mikael talk about this place, about what it means to him and Kat – I realised he has inherited something from you that I never fully understood.'

Before Ulla could respond, movement outside the window caught their attention. The aurora borealis was beginning its sublime dance across the star-filled sky, ribbons of green and purple light pulsing and shifting in patterns that seemed to follow some cosmic choreography beyond human understanding.

'Oh,' Ulla breathed, her hand flying to her throat in

automatic wonder. Even after a lifetime in Lapland, the Northern Lights never failed to move her. 'Look at that.'

Erik followed her gaze, and she saw his expression shift to something approaching awe. For a moment, they sat in comfortable silence, watching the lights move above them.

'Your conversation with Mikael tonight,' Ulla ventured carefully. 'It was good.'

She'd been beside him at the table, watching the tentative reconnection between father and son, hardly daring to breathe lest she somehow interrupt the fragile progress being made.

'Better than I expected,' Erik admitted. 'He's not the foolish idealist I thought he was. His ideas about sustainable development – they're quite sophisticated.'

Ulla felt a surge of protective pride for her younger son, mixed with the familiar anxiety that came whenever the family dynamics shifted. 'Mikael has always been thoughtful about the things that matter to him.'

'Yes,' Erik said quietly. 'Like his mother, but I have always protected this family. You need to be strong to do that.'

Without quite realising what he was doing, Erik reached for her hand. Their fingers intertwined, and Ulla felt some of the day's tension beginning to ease, though she remained watchful, uncertain how long this gentler mood would last.

'Being stubborn isn't the same as being strong,' Ulla said, her voice steady in spite of the turmoil churning inside her. She didn't often venture her opinions about the business to Erik but tonight seemed like an unmissable opportunity to try to heal the rift between father and son.

Erik turned to look at his wife, his brow creased. Ulla held her breath, meeting his gaze. Finally, he turned back to admire nature's magnificent display above.

'You may be right. I have been stubborn. I guess I was hurt by my youngest son's rejection of my life's work.' Erik's voice was unusually hesitant, 'I've been thinking about the things Mikael said. About working with the community rather than against it.'

Ulla squeezed his hand gently, encouraging but not wanting to say too much. She'd learned that Erik's moments of openness were fragile things, easily shattered by the wrong word or tone.

'It's a different approach,' she offered carefully.

'Yes. Different.' Erik was quiet for a long moment, his thumb tracing circles on the back of her hand. 'Perhaps it's time I considered different approaches to – to many things.'

Something in his tone made Ulla look at him more closely. There was a quality to his voice she didn't recognise. It was something that might have been the hurt he'd just admitted, or perhaps shame. The expression on his face was complex, layered with emotions she couldn't quite decipher.

'Erik?' she said softly, not quite daring to ask what he meant.

He was staring out at the aurora, but she sensed he

wasn't really seeing it. Instead, he seemed to be looking inward, examining something that caused him pain.

'I haven't always been the husband you deserved, Ulla,' he said quietly, the words so unexpected that she felt her heart skip a beat.

The admission hung between them, heavy with implication. Ulla felt a familiar tightness in her chest. It was the same feeling she'd carried for years whenever she'd glimpsed Erik in deep conversation with an attractive colleague, whenever he'd returned from a business trip with the scent of unfamiliar perfume on his clothes, whenever he'd been unusually attentive after periods of distance.

She'd never spoken of her suspicions aloud. The few times she'd gathered the courage to ask gentle questions, Erik's responses had been so dismissive, so coldly certain, that she'd retreated into silence. Over the years, she'd learned it was easier to pretend not to notice than to risk the explosive anger that came when she challenged him.

'We've had a good life together,' she said carefully, the diplomatic response she'd perfected over decades of marriage.

'Have we?' Erik turned to look at her, and she saw something raw in his eyes that she'd never seen before. 'Or have you simply made the best of the life I imposed upon you?'

The question was so direct, so vulnerably honest, that Ulla felt tears well. She'd spent so many years being the peacemaker, smoothing over conflicts, adapting herself to Erik's needs and moods, that she'd almost forgotten there had once been other possibilities.

'I love you,' she said simply, because it was true, even if it wasn't the whole truth.

'And I love you,' Erik replied, his voice thick with emotion. 'But I know I haven't always shown it in ways that – that honoured what you deserved.'

Ulla felt something crack open in her chest after years of careful silence, of swallowed hurt, of making herself smaller. 'Erik – '

'I want to do better,' he said urgently. 'I want to be better. Tonight, watching Mikael with Kat, seeing how they speak to each other as equals, as partners – I admitted to myself how much I've failed you.'

The words should have felt like vindication, but Ulla found herself thinking of the phone calls that had interrupted their morning, and the board meeting Erik had rescheduled around the wedding.

'The Northern project,' she said quietly. 'You're still planning to proceed?'

Erik's hands stilled on hers.

'The board meets on Monday. I have been thinking that we may need a new direction.'

'You have doubts?'

'Perhaps I owe it to our family, to both our sons, to find another way forward. Even if it costs us everything we've built.'

As they sat together watching the Northern Lights fade into the approaching dawn, Ulla felt both hope and exhaustion settling in her bones. The conversation had opened doors that had been closed for decades, but she couldn't shake the feeling that they were still only at the beginning of a much longer, more difficult journey.

Erik's acknowledgment of his failures felt genuine, but she knew him well enough to recognise that this was not the same as him making changes. And buried beneath his apparent remorse was still the same fundamental inequality that had always shaped their marriage: his assumption that he would decide when and how they moved forward, that she would adapt herself to his timeline and his terms.

But for tonight, in the beautiful light of the aurora borealis, it felt like enough to have been seen, to have had her sacrifices acknowledged, to have glimpsed the possibility that their marriage might become better.

Whether Erik would have the courage to sustain this vulnerability once they returned to their ordinary life remained to be seen.

Chapter Fifty-One

Lily found Daniel in the hotel restaurant the next morning, slumped over a cup of coffee with the unmistakable pallor of someone who'd discovered that Arctic air and champagne were a punishing combination. His usually perfect hair was sticking up at odd angles, and he was wearing a crumpled shirt.

'You look like death,' she said, sliding into the seat across from him, though she suspected she didn't look any better. Her own head was pounding with a combination of too little sleep, too much alcohol, and the kind of emotional hangover that came from making spectacularly poor decisions.

'Feel worse than death,' Daniel mumbled without looking up. 'How are you so bloody chipper?'

'I'm not chipper. I'm terrified and mortified and in need of caffeine.' Lily signalled to the waitress carrying the coffee pot, her hands trembling slightly. 'Daniel, I need to tell you something. About last night. I did something stupid.'

Daniel raised his head, squinting at her through bloodshot eyes. 'Define stupid. Because if it's worse than me attempting to serenade that Finnish photographer with what I thought was a traditional folk song but turned out to be the theme tune for a children's TV show, I'm impressed.'

'It's worse,' Lily said grimly. 'Much worse. I –'

'Good morning, darlings!' Simona's cheerful voice cut through Lily's confession. Their mother looked impossibly fresh and elegant despite the early hour. She was wearing a cream cashmere jumper and perfectly pressed trousers, her makeup flawless, and her hair looking as if she'd just stepped from a salon rather than a hotel room in the Arctic wilderness.

'How are you both feeling this morning? You left the reception so early, Lily. I was hoping to chat with you about that lovely man Tobias. Such a distinguished man, and quite successful. Elsa is so lucky to have found someone so established.'

Lily shot a desperate look at Daniel, who was staring at their mother with the glazed expression of someone whose hangover had just intensified exponentially.

'Mum,' Lily began, 'we're both feeling rough this morning. Maybe we could –'

'Oh, nonsense! Fresh air and a good breakfast will

sort you right out. I've already been for a walk around the hotel grounds. There was an absolutely gorgeous sunrise over the fell. And I ran into that environmental activist friend of Kat's. Joak, I think his name was? Terribly serious young man, but appealing.'

Lily felt her stomach drop. 'You spoke to Joak?'

'Just briefly. He was loading his car. Heading back to Helsinki this morning and he seemed in rather a hurry. Barely stopped to chat.' Simona settled into her chair, signalling for coffee with the practised ease of someone accustomed to being waited on. 'Though I must say, there was something about his manner – almost guilty, if you can imagine that. Very distracted.'

'Guilty?' Daniel echoed, finally showing interest in the conversation.

'Well, perhaps that's too strong a word. But definitely uncomfortable. Kept glancing towards the hotel as if he was worried about something.' Simona's eyes narrowed slightly as she studied Lily's face. 'You didn't have any sort of disagreement with him, did you, darling? I know how you can be about everything. So passionate sometimes that you forget not everyone shares your views.'

Lily felt heat flood her cheeks. 'We may have had a discussion about different perspectives on activism versus individual action.'

'Ah, that explains it then. Men don't like to be challenged intellectually by women, especially younger women. Threatens their sense of authority.' Simona's tone was matter-of-fact, as if she'd just explained a basic law of physics. 'I'm sure he'll get over it once his ego recovers.'

The restaurant door opened, and Lily looked up to see Joak himself entering. He was carrying a small backpack and wearing the same clothes from the night before, his dark hair dishevelled in a way that suggested he hadn't slept much either.

His eyes swept the room briefly, landing on their table for just a moment. Lily felt her breath catch, but instead of the complete dismissal she'd feared, she saw something flicker across his features – uncertainty, perhaps even regret – before he quickly looked away and headed towards one of the servers.

She watched as he collected a takeaway coffee, his movements efficient but somehow reluctant. As he turned towards the exit, their eyes met again across the room. This time, he held her gaze for a heartbeat longer than politeness required, and in that moment, Lily saw something that looked remarkably like an apology.

Then he was gone, the restaurant door closing behind him with quiet finality.

The dismissal still stung, but it felt different now, a little less cruel, more complicated. As if he were running from something he couldn't handle rather than something he didn't want.

'Well,' Simona said brightly, apparently oblivious to the silent exchange. 'He certainly seemed to be in a rush. Probably eager to get back to whatever important environmental work awaits him in the city.'

Daniel was studying his sister's face with the sharp attention that their shared childhood had taught him to employ. Despite his hangover, he could read the signs of Lily's distress.

'Lily,' he said quietly, 'what exactly did you want to tell me?'

Lily was quiet for a moment, watching through the window as Joak's car pulled away from the hotel. Just before it disappeared around the bend, she thought she saw him glance back at the building one last time.

'I thought I'd met someone last night who might understand me,' she said finally. 'Someone who challenged me and made me think and made me feel more alive than I have in months. But it turns out some people aren't ready for that kind of connection, no matter how strong it feels.'

'And that's it?' Daniel pressed gently. 'You're just going to accept that?'

Lily managed a rueful smile. 'What choice do I have? I can't force someone to see what I see or feel what I feel. If he's not interested, he's not interested. I'd rather preserve what dignity I have left.'

'That's very mature of you,' Simona said approvingly. 'Men like that, all passion and politics and no stability, they're exciting for a conversation, but they're not the sort you want to get seriously involved with. Much better to learn that now rather than later.'

'Right,' Lily agreed, though something in her chest ached as she said it. 'From a distance.'

As they ordered breakfast and the conversation

moved on to lighter topics, Lily found herself oddly at peace with the situation. Yes, she'd made a mistake. Yes, she'd misread the connection between them. But she'd also learned something important about herself: she could take risks, put herself out there, be brave enough to reach for something extraordinary.

The fact that this particular risk hadn't paid off didn't diminish the courage it had taken to try.

'You know what?' she said suddenly, interrupting Daniel's story about his Finnish photographer. 'I'm actually glad I did it. Made a fool of myself, I mean.'

'Are you having some sort of breakdown?' Daniel teased.

'No, I'm having a breakthrough. For the first time in my life, I acted on impulse instead of analysing every-thing to death. I took a chance on something that felt important, even though it was terrifying. It didn't work out the way I hoped, but at least I tried.'

'Good for you, darling,' Simona said warmly. 'That's exactly the kind of confidence you'll need when you meet the right person.'

As they finished breakfast and went to pack for their journey home, Lily felt lighter than she had all morning. She'd learned something valuable about her own capacity for courage, even if the outcome hadn't been what she'd hoped for.

And if sometimes she found herself wondering what might have happened if Joak had been brave enough to take the same kind of risk she had – well, that was a question that would have to remain unanswered.

Some stories, she reflected, were meant to be complete in themselves, even if they felt unfinished. The important thing was that she'd been authentic to herself, had acted from her heart rather than her head.

For now, that would have to be enough.

Chapter Fifty-Two

Victor sat alone at the breakfast table, watching the pale morning light filter through the hotel's dining room windows. The events of the previous night played through his mind on repeat: Elsa's face when he'd told her the truth about Ingrid. The way she'd almost kissed him in the bar, and then her careful withdrawal when reality had reasserted itself.

He'd barely slept, his mind churning with everything they'd said to each other. For ten long years, he'd carried the weight of losing her without understanding why. Now that he knew the truth, that she'd seen him with Ingrid and misunderstood everything, he felt both vindicated and devastated. Vindicated because she knew he hadn't betrayed her trust, devastated because a misunderstanding he could have prevented had destroyed their entire relationship.

Victor had also been thinking about the mine. He

couldn't shake Elsa's words about listening to local communities. Back in his room last night, when the regrets of what could have been between him and Elsa were threatening to send him over the edge, he'd pulled out his laptop. Without thinking, he'd started researching sustainable mining practices. What he found surprised him. Companies in Australia and Canada were successfully implementing community-partnership models, creating long-term employment whilst protecting traditional land use. The profit margins weren't dramatically different – sometimes they were better, due to reduced conflict and regulatory compliance. Why hadn't his father explored these approaches? Victor scrolled through case studies, using his geological training to help him understand the solutions. Selective extraction, ecosystem restoration, partnership with indigenous communities. It wasn't the impossible idealism he'd assumed. He thought of Elsa's calm confidence when she'd suggested there were always alternatives if people were willing to listen to each other. For the first time, he wondered if she might be right.

'You're up early.' Erik Andersson's voice cut through his thoughts as his father approached the table, already impeccably dressed despite the early hour.

'Couldn't sleep,' Victor replied, not looking up from his untouched coffee. 'I thought you and Mother would have breakfast at the chalet.'

'Your mother's having a lie-in. And I wanted to speak with the hotel manager about some arrangements.' Erik settled into the chair across from him, his expression more thoughtful than Victor had seen it in months. 'Good wedding, all things considered. Your brother looked happy enough.'

Victor noted that his father didn't mention the protest, didn't dismiss it as an 'unfortunate outburst'. Something seemed to have shifted in Erik's perspective since yesterday.

'He did look happy,' Victor agreed. 'They both did. They've built something good together.'

Erik was quiet for a moment, studying his eldest son's face. He paused, choosing his words carefully.

'I think I may have been too quick to dismiss alternative strategies for the Northern project without properly examining them.'

Victor's chin nearly hit the floor, but he tried to keep his composure.

'Alternative strategies?'

'I think I may have been wrong to dismiss Mikael and Kat's ideas so quickly. Your mother helped me understand that being stubborn isn't the same as being strong.' Erik looked out the window at the snow-covered landscape. 'Perhaps we should consider whether our current approach is the right one.'

Victor thought about his conversation with Elsa the night before, and the surprising facts he'd learned last night while scrolling on his computer. They'd challenged his assumptions about environmental concerns being merely 'woolly thinking'. For the first time, he'd understood that opposition to the mine wasn't just emotional. Such arguments were based on genuine expertise and legitimate concerns about the future.

'I've been thinking about that too,' Victor said carefully. 'Until recently, I'll admit I saw environmental opposition as – well, as impractical idealism. But talking to people here this weekend – ' He paused, remembering Elsa's words about community consultation. 'I've started to wonder if we're missing something important.'

Erik's eyebrows rose. 'Such as?'

'Such as whether there might be an approach that satisfies both economic and environmental concerns. I know it sounds simplistic, but some of the research I've been looking at suggests – ' Victor stopped, feeling suddenly exposed. 'I mean, the geological principles I learned at university support the idea that sustainable extraction is possible. We've just never seriously explored it.'

'You've been researching this?' Erik's tone was neutral, but Victor caught the flicker of interest.

'Only briefly. But Father, what if the opposition isn't just emotional? What if they have valid technical concerns we haven't addressed?'

Victor felt his confidence growing as he spoke.

'As a geologist, I can see merit in their arguments about long-term ecosystem impact. And as your son, I can see that working with communities rather than against them might actually be better for business.'

Before Erik could respond, a movement near the dining room entrance caught their attention. Elsa had just walked in, looking pale but determined. She was alone, there was no sign of Tobias. As their eyes met across the room, Victor felt his heart skip a beat.

She looked different this morning. Her blonde hair was captured in a low ponytail resting neatly on one shoulder. She wore minimal makeup. The careful composure of yesterday was gone, replaced by something more raw, more real. She hesitated for a moment when she saw them, then walked purposefully towards their table.

'Good morning,' she said politely, though her eyes never left Victor's face.

'Elsa,' Erik said, rising to his feet with practised courtesy. 'How lovely to see you this morning. Please join us. I hope you enjoyed the rest of the evening?'

'It was very illuminating,' she replied, and Victor caught the double meaning in her words.

'Tobias not up yet?' Victor asked, his heart beating harder in his chest.

'He caught an earlier flight. We thought it best.' She paused, meeting his eyes. 'And I decided to change mine.' Elsa sat down next to him, and he had to resist the temptation to turn fully to face her.

'You stayed.'

'I stayed,' she confirmed quietly.

Victor noticed the attention Erik was paying to their exchange and said, 'I was just telling my father about some of the conversations from last night. About the possibility of approaching the mining project differently.'

Something shifted in Elsa's expression. There was surprise, then what might have been approval.

'It's encouraging to hear that's being considered,' she said carefully. 'Community consultation often reveals solutions that benefit everyone.'

'That's what I'm beginning to understand,' Erik said.

Victor was astonished at the genuine interest in his father's tone. 'Though I'll admit I'm not entirely sure how to begin such a process after years of – more traditional approaches,' his father added.

'The real expertise would come from people like your son and daughter-in-law,' Elsa suggested. 'People who understand both the environmental concerns and the local economy. They could help bridge the gap between what the company needs and what the community values.'

Victor felt something click into place: a possible path forward that might heal more than just the rift over the mine.

'Father,' he said, his voice growing stronger as the idea took shape, 'what if we postponed the current timeline? What if we organised a proper consultation process that included Mikael and Kat as advisors?'

Erik's eyebrows rose, but there was consideration rather than dismissal in his expression.

'You want to bring your brother back into company discussions?'

'I want us to listen to people who might have better solutions than the ones we've been pursuing,' Victor said firmly. 'I want us to consider that there might be a way to move forward that doesn't alienate our family or destroy this place.'

For a long moment, Erik studied both their faces. Victor could see him weighing options, calculating not just costs and benefits but relationships and legacies.

'It would be a significant change in direction,' Erik said finally. 'The board meets tomorrow to approve the final phase. I've already changed it once. The investors are getting nervous, asking questions.'

'But you'd consider it?' Victor pressed.

Erik looked out the window at the snow-covered landscape, then back at his son. 'I'd consider postponing the vote two weeks at the most. But only if Mikael can present a compelling alternative immediately. The shareholders won't tolerate indefinite delays, especially with environmental groups already mobilising.'

'They're mobilising?'

'Three separate legal challenges filed last week. International environmental organisations taking interest. Your brother's wife and her friends have been busy.' Erik's tone was neutral, but Victor caught the underlying tension. 'This consultation idea might be our last chance to control the narrative before it spirals into something uglier.'

'So you'll consider it?' Victor pressed.

'After last night's conversations with your mother and Mikael, and now hearing your perspective, yes, I'll consider it. More than consider it – I think it might be necessary.'

Victor felt a surge of something he hadn't experienced in years when talking to his father: partnership rather than conflict.

'Thank you,' he said quietly. 'For being willing to listen.'

'Thank you for finally speaking up,' Erik replied. 'I've been waiting years for you to show this kind of initiative about the company's direction.'

As Erik excused himself to speak with the hotel manager, Victor felt a profound shift. Not just a change of view about the mining project, but about himself. For years, he'd compartmentalised his geological knowledge and his role in the family business, as if they existed in separate worlds. But Elsa's questions had forced him to see the connections. He'd forgotten that the landscape around him wasn't just a resource to be extracted. It was a complex system that had taken millennia to develop. The communities opposing the mine weren't just obstacles to profit; they were stakeholders with legitimate concerns based on generations of local knowledge.

Victor turned to face Elsa fully.

'I couldn't have done that without you. Your support just now – I'm grateful for your help in finally finding the courage to challenge him.

Elsa's expression softened. 'You found that courage yourself, Victor. I just reminded you that it was there.'

There was a silence which Victor was afraid to break. But he needed to know what she was thinking.

'What happened between us last night – '

'Was enlightening,' she said. 'Learning the truth about Ingrid, understanding what really happened between us – it changes things.'

'Does it?' Victor leaned forward, hope evident in his voice. 'Because I meant what I said last night. Every word.'

Elsa was quiet for a moment, her fingers tracing patterns on the tablecloth. 'I don't know, Victor. Ten years is a long time. We're different people now, with different lives, different obligations – '

'But not different hearts,' Victor said softly. 'I saw it last night, Elsa. In the bar, when we danced, when we almost – ' He stopped himself, glancing around the dining room. 'Tell me you didn't feel it too.'

'Feeling something and acting on it are two different things,' Elsa replied, though her voice lacked conviction. 'I need time to think. To figure out what any of this means.'

'It doesn't have to be complicated,' Victor said urgently. 'We're not children anymore. We know what we want, what we've both been missing. I'm going to fight for us this time, Elsa. I'm not going to let pride or fear or misunderstanding destroy what we have again.'

'I don't know – ' Elsa put her head in her hands.

Victor moved closer to her and gently pulled her hands away. 'Is it Tobias? Do you love him?'

Elsa looked directly at him. 'We ended things last night. We both realised we weren't right for each other.'

Victor exhaled softly. 'Then this changes everything,' he said, hope evident in his voice. 'You deserve to be happy, Elsa. We both do. And I know – I know – that we could be happy together.'

Elsa looked down at her hands. 'I need time, Victor. Time to sort through everything that's happened, everything I'm feeling. This weekend has been – '

'Overwhelming,' Victor finished for her. 'I understand. But promise me you'll think about what I said. Promise me you won't dismiss the possibility of us without really considering it.'

Before she could respond, other guests began filtering into the dining room. The moment of privacy was ending, but Victor had said what he needed to say.

'I'm flying back to Helsinki this morning,' he said, standing. 'But this isn't over, Elsa. I'm not giving up on us again.'

As he walked away, leaving her sitting alone at the table, Victor felt something he hadn't experienced in years: hope. Real, terrifying, exhilarating hope.

For the first time in his adult life, he'd stood up to his father not in anger or rebellion, but in partnership. He'd found his voice, his courage, his sense of purpose. And he'd done it with Elsa watching, supporting him, believing in him.

This time, he was going to fight for what mattered most. This time, he wasn't going to let fear win.

Chapter Fifty-Three

Elsa sat frozen at the breakfast table, Victor's words echoing in her mind. *This isn't over, Elsa. I'm not giving up on us again.*

Her coffee had gone cold, but she barely noticed. The dining room bustled around her with the quiet efficiency of a five-star hotel. The guests were murmuring over their phones, there was a gentle clink of cutlery against china, a soft whoosh of coffee machines. Yet she felt utterly alone, suspended between the life she'd known and the terrifying possibility of something entirely different.

Victor's confrontation with his father had surprised her. She'd watched him transform before her eyes from the careful, diplomatic son she remembered into someone willing to challenge the very foundations of his family's empire. And all because of a conversation they'd had about listening to local communities.

He's changed, she realised. The Victor she'd known

at university had been passionate but ultimately deferential to his father's authority. This morning, she'd seen glimpses of the man he could become; someone willing to fight for his principles, not just his desires.

She was still sitting there, lost in thought, when a familiar voice broke through her reverie.

'Mind if I join you? You look about as miserable as I feel.'

Elsa looked up to see Lily, though she looked rather different from the confident young woman who'd been dispensing romantic wisdom the night before. Her copper curls were dishevelled, her eyes slightly red-rimmed, and she was wearing jeans and an oversized jumper that came nearly to her knees. She looked like someone who'd had a complicated night of her own.

'Please,' Elsa gestured to the chair across from her. 'Though I'm not sure either of us will be very good company this morning.'

'Rough night?' Lily asked, settling into the seat with a rueful smile. 'Because mine was spectacularly stupid.'

Heat crept up Elsa's neck. 'You could say that. What happened to you?'

'I made the kind of romantic mistake that I usually lecture people about,' Lily said with bitter self-awareness. 'Turns out it's much easier to give advice about love than it is to follow it yourself.'

There was something in Lily's tone that made Elsa study her more carefully. The young woman, who'd been so confident about second chances and taking risks, looked genuinely shaken.

'Do you want to talk about it?' Elsa asked gently.

'Not particularly. I'd rather pretend it never happened and focus on someone else's love life.' Lily managed a weak smile. 'So please distract me. I saw you dancing with Victor last night, and you both disappeared after that. Did something happen?'

Elsa found herself oddly comforted by Lily's obvious distress. It made her feel less alone in her own confusion. 'We talked. About the past, about why we broke up all those years ago.'

'And?'

'And it turns out everything I believed about our breakup was wrong.' The words spilled out, perhaps because Lily looked like she needed the distraction as much as Elsa needed to voice her thoughts. 'I thought he'd been having an affair, but he was actually helping a young woman who was being exploited by one of his father's executives.'

Lily's eyes widened, some of her own troubles momentarily forgotten. 'So you left him for something he didn't even do?'

'I never gave him the chance to explain. I saw what I thought was evidence of betrayal and just – ran.' Elsa paused, studying Lily's face. 'Rather like you're probably wanting to run from whatever happened to you last night.'

'Touché,' Lily said with a grimace. 'Though at least you had a valid reason for running. I just made a spectacularly poor decision and got exactly what I deserved.'

'Which was?'

'A reminder that passion and compatibility aren't the same thing. And that sometimes when someone shows you who they are, you should believe them the first time.' Lily's voice was heavy with regret. 'But we're not talking about my mistakes. What are you going to do about Victor?'

'I don't know,' Elsa admitted. 'He says he's going to fight for us this time. And part of me wants to let him, but – '

'But you're terrified,' Lily finished, her voice carrying the weight of recent experience. 'Because loving someone completely means risking everything, and sometimes people aren't worth that risk.'

'Yes, exactly.' Elsa was surprised by how well Lily understood. 'How do I know if Victor is worth it? How do I know if what we felt last night was real or just – nostalgia and wedding magic?'

Lily was quiet for a moment, her fingers tracing patterns on the tablecloth. When she spoke, her voice was softer, more vulnerable than Elsa had heard it before.

'I think,' Lily said slowly, 'that the difference between a mistake and a risk worth taking is whether the person makes you feel like a better version of yourself, or just a more reckless one.' She looked up at Elsa with tired but earnest eyes. 'When you were with Victor last night, when you were talking to him – did you feel like yourself? Your best self?'

Elsa considered the question, remembering the way

Victor had listened to her thoughts about community consultation, how he'd valued her perspective, how natural it had felt to be beside him.

'Yes,' she said quietly. 'For the first time in years, I felt like myself.'

'Then maybe that's your answer,' Lily said, mustering a genuine smile despite her own obvious pain. 'Maybe the question isn't whether you're brave enough to risk getting hurt again. Maybe it's whether you're brave enough to risk being happy.'

'What about you?' Elsa asked gently. 'Are you going to take your own advice?'

Lily's laugh was hollow. 'My situation is different. Sometimes people show you exactly who they are, and the smart thing is to listen. But Victor – ' She paused, glancing towards the dining room entrance where Joak had appeared that morning. 'Victor looked at you like you were the answer to a question he'd been asking for years. That's not something you walk away from lightly.'

As if summoned by their conversation, Elsa's phone buzzed with a text message. Her heart jumped when she saw Victor's name on the screen.

In the taxi to the airport. Thank you for listening last night and this morning. Whatever you decide, know that these two days have been the best I've had in ten years. V

She stared at the message, reading it twice before showing it to Lily.

'Well,' Lily said after a moment, her smile becoming

more genuine. 'That's rather lovely, isn't it? No pressure, no demands. Just gratitude and honesty.'

'Very different from – ' Elsa gestured vaguely, not wanting to pry into Lily's obviously painful situation.

'Very different from someone who makes you feel stupid for caring,' Lily agreed quietly. 'Elsa, I may have made a terrible mistake last night, but that doesn't mean you have to. Sometimes the risk is worth taking. Sometimes, the person is worth fighting for.'

'And sometimes they're not?'

'And sometimes they're not,' Lily confirmed with rueful wisdom. 'But you won't know until you try. And regret for what you didn't do weighs a lot heavier than regret for what you did.'

Elsa looked around the dining room one more time, taking in the peaceful scene. In a few hours, she'd be on a plane back to Stockholm, back to her carefully ordered life. Or not. Detangling herself from Tobias and his life would be change enough. But she knew she'd return to her work routine, and perhaps to dating safe, professional men introduced to her by friends and colleagues. But for the first time in years that life felt like a chrysalis she'd outgrown – safe and protective but ultimately limiting.

Maybe it was time to risk everything again. Maybe it was time to see what kind of woman she could become when she stopped hiding from the possibility of being hurt.

Maybe it was time to love again.

'I think,' she said slowly, 'I'm going to need to make some phone calls.'

Lily raised her coffee cup in a mock toast, though her smile was tinged with her own sadness. 'To new beginnings, then. For both of us.'

'To new beginnings,' Elsa agreed, and meant it.

Outside the dining room windows, the Lapland sun was rising higher, turning the snow-covered landscape into a glittering wonderland. Somewhere above those mountains, Victor was soon to fly south, carrying her heart with him whether he knew it or not.

The thought should have terrified her. Instead, for the first time in ten years, it felt like coming home.

Chapter Fifty-Four

Elsa stared at her phone for the tenth time in as many minutes, Victor's message still glowing on the screen. *These two days have been the best I've had in ten years.* The words seemed to pulse with possibility, with hope, with everything she'd been too afraid to reach for.

She was supposed to be packing. Her flight to Stockholm left in three hours, and she'd barely touched her suitcase. Instead, she'd been sitting on the edge of the hotel bed, paralysed by indecision and the terrifying realisation that she didn't want to go back to her old life.

The conversation with Lily had crystallised something inside her. For ten years, she'd been living in careful, measured steps – never taking risks, never allowing herself to want something so desperately that losing it would devastate her. But sitting here now, she understood that the safe life she'd built was actually the most dangerous choice of all. It was slowly suffocating her, turning her into someone she barely recognised.

Her laptop was open beside her, her work emails already piling up despite the fact that she'd only been gone two days. Three urgent messages from her boss about the Lindqvist merger, and four about various projects demanding immediate attention. The old Elsa would have been frantically responding to each one, ensuring that her brief absence wouldn't be noticed or criticised. The old Elsa would have been on that early plane to Stockholm, back at her desk by Monday morning, pretending that nothing significant had happened in Lapland.

But the old Elsa had never had the courage to fight for what she really wanted.

Before she could lose her nerve, Elsa grabbed her phone and dialled her assistant's number.

'Emma? It's Elsa. I know it's Sunday, but I need you to do something for me.'

'Of course. Is everything alright? You sound different.'

Different? Yes, she supposed she did.

'I need you to clear my calendar for next week. Move everything that can be moved, delegate what you can to Nilsson – no, wait, not him. To Blomberg. Tell them I've had a family emergency.'

The silence on the other end was long enough for Elsa to wonder if the call had dropped.

'Emma? Are you there?'

'I'm here,' her assistant said carefully. 'Elsa, in the

five years I've worked for you, you've never taken an unplanned day off. Are you sure you're alright?'

Was she alright? Elsa looked at herself in the hotel room mirror – hair neatly tied back, but eyes bright with something that might have been fear or excitement or both. She looked like a woman on the verge of making a spectacular mistake. Or the best decision of her life.

'I'm better than alright,' she said, and realised it was true. 'I'm finally awake.'

After she hung up, Elsa opened her laptop and began typing the most impulsive email of her professional career:

Lars,

I'm taking emergency leave for the next week. Emma has the details about rescheduling my appointments. I know this is unprecedented, and I know it will cause complications, but for the first time in my adult life, I'm choosing something other than work.

I'll be back next Monday, and I'll work twice as hard to make up for any inconvenience.

Best regards, Elsa

She hit send before she could second-guess herself, then immediately opened a new browser window and searched for flights to Helsinki.

Ten years ago, you ran away, she told herself. You saw something that frightened you, and you disappeared without a word, without giving him a chance to explain. You chose fear over trust, safety over love.

The memory of her nineteen-year-old self, standing

outside Café Strindberg, watching Victor with Ingrid, still made her chest ache. But now she understood what she'd been too young and too scared to see then – that real love meant staying and fighting for the truth, not running away from difficult conversations.

This time, you're running towards something instead of away from it.

This wasn't the desperate flight of a heartbroken teenager. This was the conscious choice of a woman who finally understood the difference between self-protection and self-sabotage, between reasonable caution and paralysing fear.

For ten years, she'd let that moment outside the café define her capacity for love. She'd chosen safe men, safe choices, safe emotions that could never devastate her the way Victor had. But safety, she realised now, was just another word for settling for less than she deserved.

There was a plane leaving in two hours. One seat left in business class, probably vacated by someone with more sense than she had. Her finger hovered over the 'book now' button.

This was insane. She was a (almost) thirty-two-year-old lawyer with responsibilities, not some lovesick teenager following her heart. She had a career and a reputation to maintain. She couldn't just drop everything and chase after a man who'd already broken her heart once.

But then she thought about Victor's face when he'd told her about Ingrid, the raw honesty in his voice when he'd explained why he couldn't confide in her ten years ago. She thought about the way he'd stood up to his father that morning, finally finding the courage to fight for his principles. She thought about the electricity between them when they'd danced, the way her body had remembered his touch as if no time had passed at all.

Some chances only came once in a lifetime. Some mistakes were worth making.

Elsa clicked 'book now' and felt her heart rate double as she entered her credit card details. There was no backing out now. In less than two hours, she'd be on a plane to Helsinki with no plan beyond finding Victor and telling him that she was ready to take the risk.

Her phone rang just as she was closing the laptop. Victor's name flashed on the screen, and for a moment she considered not answering. What if he'd changed his mind?

'Hello,' she said, trying to keep her voice steady.

'Elsa.' His voice was warm, relieved. 'I wasn't sure you'd answer.'

'I almost didn't.' She took a deep breath. 'Victor, about what you said this morning – '

'I meant every word,' he interrupted. 'I know I'm asking a lot. I know I have no right to expect you to upend your life for someone who let you down before. But I had to try. I couldn't live with myself if I didn't at least try.'

The vulnerability in his voice nearly undid her. 'Where are you?'

'Helsinki airport. I've just landed. I sat on that plane thinking about everything that's happened. About how I felt when I saw you again, about how it felt to tell you the truth about Ingrid. About how empty my life has felt without you in it.'

Elsa could hear the boarding announcements in the background, the bustle of a busy airport.

'Victor,' she said, her voice steadier now. 'I need to ask you something, and I need you to be completely honest with me.'

'Anything.'

'If I came to Helsinki – not permanently, not with any promises, but just to see if what we felt in Lapland was real – would you want that? Would you want me there?'

The silence stretched so long that Elsa began to panic. Had she misread everything? Had his declaration this morning been nothing more than wedding emotion and nostalgia?

'Elsa,' Victor said finally, his voice thick with emotion. 'There's nothing I want more in this world than for you to be with me. Nothing.'

Relief flooded through her so powerfully that she had to sit down. 'Good,' she said, trying to sound calmer than she felt. 'Because I've just booked a flight to Helsinki. I land at two-thirty this afternoon.'

The silence this time was different: shocked, hopeful, disbelieving.

'You what?'

'I changed my flight, and I've taken an unplanned

week off work. I've never done this in my entire career. I have no plans beyond seeing you again and figuring out if we can build something real together.' She laughed, hearing the hysteria creeping into her voice. 'I think I might be losing my mind.'

'You're not losing your mind,' Victor said, and she could hear the smile in his voice. 'You're in your right mind. Christ, Elsa, I can't believe you're really coming.'

'Neither can I. This is so unlike me, Victor. I plan everything, I think everything through twice, and I never make impulsive decisions. And here I am, throwing my life into chaos for a man I haven't seen in ten years.'

'For us,' he corrected gently. 'You're doing this for us.'

'Yes,' she agreed, the truth of it settling into her bones. 'For us.'

'I'll pick you up at the airport. We'll figure everything else out as we go.'

After they hung up, Elsa sat in the sudden silence of the hotel room, the magnitude of what she'd just done washing over her. She'd upended her carefully ordered life in the space of thirty minutes, made decisions that would have been unthinkable yesterday morning.

But instead of panic, she felt something she hadn't experienced in years: pure, exhilarating freedom.

She looked around the room one last time, then began throwing clothes into her suitcase with uncharacteristic haste. She had a plane to catch, a life to change, and a love to reclaim.

As she zipped up her suitcase, Elsa caught sight of herself in the mirror again. The woman looking back at her was someone she barely recognised. Her face was flushed, excited, alive with possibility. It was the face of someone brave enough to risk everything for the chance at something extraordinary.

Someone ready to love again.

The taxi ride to the airport passed in a blur of snowy landscape and racing thoughts. Part of her couldn't believe what she was doing. The responsible part of her brain kept listing all the ways this could go wrong: the career implications of her sudden absence, the practical difficulties of a long-distance relationship, the very real possibility that ten years of separation might have changed them both too much.

But the louder part, the part that had been sleeping for far too long, whispered that some risks were worth taking. That she'd rather fail spectacularly while trying for something wonderful than succeed safely at something that left her empty.

At the airport, as she checked in for her flight to Helsinki, the airline agent looked at her with barely concealed confusion.

'You're sure you want to change your destination, Ms Berg? You were originally booked for Stockholm.'

'I'm sure,' Elsa said, and meant it completely.

As she walked towards the departure gate, her phone buzzed with text messages. Her assistant had confirmed the calendar changes, her boss expressed concern about her sudden absence, and colleagues wondered if she was alright.

She typed quick reassurances, promised to explain everything later, then turned off her phone. For the next few hours, she wanted to exist purely in this moment of possibility, suspended between her old life and whatever came next.

The flight to Helsinki was smooth and, mercifully, short. As the plane descended through the clouds towards Vantaa Airport, Elsa pressed her face to the window and watched the familiar landscape of her home city come into view. The same forests and lakes that had shaped her childhood, the same winter light that had illuminated her first love.

She was coming home.

Victor was waiting for her as she emerged from arrivals, and the sight of him nearly stopped her in her tracks. He looked different from this morning – more relaxed, more hopeful, more like the boy she'd fallen in love with all those years ago.

When he saw her, his face transformed with a smile so radiant it made her chest ache. He crossed the distance between them in quick strides, sweeping her into his arms before she could say a word.

'I can't believe you're here,' he murmured against her hair. 'I can't believe you actually came.'

'Neither can I,' she laughed, breathing in the familiar scent of him. 'This is completely mad, isn't it?'

'Completely,' he agreed, pulling back to look at her. 'And absolutely perfect.'

Standing there in the arrivals hall, surrounded by the chaos of travellers and reunions, Elsa felt something click into place. This was what she'd been missing all these years: this feeling of being exactly where she belonged, with exactly the right person.

It was terrifying and wonderful and entirely uncertain. But for the first time in ten years, she was where her heart wanted to be.

'So,' Victor said, taking her hand as they walked towards the exit. 'What happens now?'

Elsa smiled, feeling lighter than she had in years. 'Now we find out if we're brave enough to fall in love all over again.'

'I think,' Victor said, squeezing her hand gently, 'we already have.'

Next in The Anderssons series

To Risk It All

A Lapland Romance
(*The Anderssons, Book 3*)

When Lily Wootton's academic career is wrecked by a mentor's betrayal, she escapes to Finnish Lapland to regroup under the blaze of autumn Ruska. Äkäslompolo offers silence, wide skies, and a chance to heal — until she's pulled into organising the village's Autumn Fair and comes face-to-face with the last man she expected to see again.

Joak Lindström is the uncompromising local organiser Lily shared one electric night with at her sister's wedding... a night he dismissed as a mistake before shutting her out completely. Now he's back in her orbit, all guarded intensity and icy professionalism, and working together means reliving everything neither of them has managed to forget.

As they fight to save the fair after a devastating loss of funding, the village's bitter battle over Andersson Mining flares hot again — and Lily finds herself on the wrong side of Joak's assumptions. To him, she's "an Andersson by marriage," a symbol of everything he's resisting. To her, he's a man who wants her close but won't let her in.

Forced into close quarters, Lily and Joak begin to see past the labels and the walls. But with loyalties fracturing, old wounds reopening, and a shock from Joak's past threatening to upend what little trust they've built, they must decide what's worth risking — their hearts included.

Set beneath Lapland's golden forests and the first hint of snow, *To Risk It All* is a slow-burn, second-chance autumn romance filled with small-town drama, family fault lines, and the kind of love that asks you to be brave enough to begin again.

**Turn over to read the first chapter of
To Risk It All now!**

To Risk It All

Chapter One

The mahogany door to Professor Whitmore's office on Edinburgh University's George Square had always been imposing, but today it felt like the entrance to an execution chamber. Lily Wootton smoothed her red hair behind her ears and knocked, her first-class degree certificate still warm in her bag alongside the essay she'd spent months perfecting.

'Come in.'

Margaret Whitmore sat behind her desk like a queen holding court, her silver hair pulled into its usual severe chignon. The office overlooked the cobbled square where golden leaves drifted down from the ancient trees, their quiet beauty a stark contrast to the gravity Lily sensed in the room.

'Lily, dear. Do sit down.' The professor's smile was the sort reserved for delivering bad news gently. 'I'm afraid I have some rather disappointing information about the Research Assistant position you've applied for.'

Lily perched on the edge of the uncomfortable chair, her heart already sinking. 'Has the decision been delayed?'

'Oh no, the decision has been made.' The older woman steepled her fingers. 'I'm afraid it's gone to young Sebastian Whitmore-Hayes. Brilliant boy, really. His essay on "Economic Structures in Regency England" was simply inspired.'

The surname hit Lily like a slap. Whitmore-Hayes. He was in the same year as her. An arrogant boy with a crop of unruly blond hair and a nonchalant manner. He'd struggled through his undergraduate degree, often asking for Lily's help with feminist terminology used by Professor Whitmore herself.

'I see.' Lily's voice sounded remarkably steady. 'Your nephew.'

'Well, yes, but that's entirely irrelevant. Academic decisions are made purely on merit.' Professor Whitmore's tone suggested the conversation was over. 'Sebastian's work simply demonstrated the kind of rigorous analysis this project requires.'

'May I ask what made his application stronger than mine?'

Something flickered in the professor's eyes. 'Well, your work on love and social mobility was... charming, Lily. But perhaps a bit lightweight for such a prestigious appointment. Academic rigour requires moving beyond emotional interpretations to examine harder evidence.'

Lightweight. Charming.

The words that had followed Lily throughout her academic career, no matter how many modules she'd passed with over 70% grades or how many professors praised her original thinking.

'I'm curious,' Lily said, her voice still unnaturally calm, 'did Sebastian's essay include any analysis of marriage patterns as instigators of social change?'

'Why, yes, actually. Quite insightful of him to make those connections.'

Lily opened her bag and pulled out her own essay, flipping to page twelve. 'Connections like this one?' She read aloud: "Marriage becomes the ultimate promoter of social fluidity, where individual choice challenges inherited privilege." That's my exact wording, Professor Whitmore. From the draft I submitted to you three months ago.'

The silence stretched until it became unbearable. Professor Whitmore's composure never wavered, but her expression grew cold.

'I'm sure any similarities are coincidental, Lily. These ideas aren't particularly original – many scholars have examined marriage in historical contexts.'

'Of course they have.' Lily closed the proposal and slipped it back into her bag. 'How silly of me to think I'd had an original thought.'

She stood, legs steadier than they had any right to be.

'Thank you for your time, Professor Whitmore. And your... mentorship.'

The autumn wind cut through her coat as she emerged onto George Square, but Lily barely noticed. She walked without direction through Edinburgh's Old Town, where couples wandered hand-in-hand, her mind replaying every encouraging comment, every piece of guidance, every moment she'd believed Professor Whitmore valued her work.

Stupid.

That's what she'd been. Too trusting to think merit mattered more than family connections. Naive to believe her passion for her subject would be seen as strength rather than weakness. Foolish to trust someone who'd been feeding her ideas to her own nephew while dismissing Lily's intelligence as 'charming'.

The night train to London was a retreat, though she had to make it in an uncomfortable seat rather than a luxurious – and expensive – sleeper cabin. She watched Edinburgh's spires disappear behind her as she fled south to lick her wounds. By the time she reached her mother's cramped one-bedroom flat in Camden, Lily was hollowed out, like a rare first edition with all the pages torn out and just the fragile covers left intact.

'Darling!' Simona appeared in the tiny hallway wearing a silk dressing gown, her reading glasses pushed up onto her head and a stack of German legal documents in her hand. The flat was even smaller than

Lily remembered, every surface cluttered with her mother's translation work. 'How did it go? Are we celebrating?'

Lily peered at her mother's expectant face, acutely aware of the sofa bed that would be her home for the foreseeable future, and the last of her composure gave way.

'Not exactly.'

'Oh, sweetheart.' Simona set down the papers on the kitchen counter of the open-plan living space, her expression shifting to professional sympathy.

'Well, these things happen for a reason. Perhaps it's time to consider something more... practical? My friend Caroline has a son, James, who has been made partner at his law firm. A lovely boy, terribly successful. I could arrange...'

Lily's jaw tightened. Things didn't 'happen for a reason'. They happened because people like Professor Whitmore chose nepotism over merit, because systems protected the privileged while dismissing hard work as 'charming'. She'd earned that research assistant position. Sebastian Whitmore-Hayes had stolen it.

'Mum, please. Not now.'

'I'm only trying to help, darling. You can't live in romantic fantasies forever. James is very down-to-earth, good prospects, and Caroline says he's ready to settle down with someone special.'

Someone special – code for someone who wouldn't embarrass him at work functions, someone who'd given up foolish academic dreams for something sensible.

Not the sort who thought studying love stories constituted serious academic work, presumably. And certainly not the sort who had recently lost a promising role in academia and was now facing months of sleeping on her mother's sofa while job-hunting.

Lily perched on the edge of the sofa, surveying the cramped space that would be her world for the foreseeable future. Through the thin walls, she could hear her mother's voice on the phone, probably discussing translation rates with a client in rapid German. The constant hum of Simona's work-from-home life – the phone calls, video conferences, the printer churning out documents at all hours – had been suffocating enough in a larger flat when Lily was eighteen. The thought of enduring it now in this tiny space, while job-hunting and pretending she wasn't devastated, felt unbearable.

Her phone buzzed with a WhatsApp message, and Lily's heart lifted slightly when she saw Kat's name. Her sister had an uncanny ability to message at exactly the right moment.

Lily! Hope you're not drowning in job applications and being terribly sensible about your future, because I have a proposal that's completely mad and absolutely perfect for you...

Lily curled up on the sofa that would be her bed for months to come, Professor Whitmore's betrayal still burning in her chest. But for the first time in hours, something that might have been hope flickered alongside the hurt.

Sometimes, she thought, the universe knew exactly when you needed an escape route.

Get your copy of *To Risk It All* now! Just go to HelenaHalmeBooks, or your favorite retailer to learn more.

A Note from the Author

I hope you enjoyed *To Love Again!*

You may have heard authors talk about reviews and the effect they have on the success of the title.

Having a bunch of good reviews attached to a book has been likened to a scene in a new town when you're looking for somewhere to eat. The restaurant you've read about has a queue outside. You notice another place opposite with the same kind of food on offer. But this restaurant is nearly empty, with only a couple of tables occupied, and no queue outside. Which place do you choose? Most people join the queue, because why wouldn't you go for a restaurant that is so popular that people are willing to *wait* to eat there? The other place opposite must serve really bad food if only a handful of diners are inside, right? Perhaps it's had a case of food poisoning or something.

So please form a virtual queue outside my book in your favorite online store and write a review.

Thank you.

Also by Helena Halme

<u>The Nordic Heart Series:</u>

The Young Heart (Prequel)

The English Heart (Book 1)

The Faithful Heart (Book 2)

The Good Heart (Book 3)

The True Heart (Book 4)

The Nordic Heart Books 1-4 Box Set

The Christmas Heart (Book 5)

<u>Love on the Island Series:</u>

The Island Affair (Book 1)

An Island Christmas (Book 2)

The Island Daughter (Book 3)

An Island Summer (Book 4)

The Island Child (Book 5)

An Island Heatwave (Book 6)

Love on the Island Books 1-6 Box Set

<u>The Anderssons Series</u>

To Melt A Frozen Heart (Book 1)

To Love Again (Book 2)

To Risk It All (Book 3)

To Choose Love (Book 4)

To Believe in Christmas Love (Prequel novella)

<u>Other novels:</u>

Coffee and Vodka: A Nordic family drama

The Red King in Helsinki: A Cold War Spy Novel

About the Author

Helena Halme grew up in Finland and moved to the UK via Stockholm and Helsinki at a very tender and impressionable age. She's a former BBC journalist and has also worked as a magazine editor, a bookseller and ran a Finnish/British cultural association in London.

Since gaining an MA in Creative Writing at Bath Spa University, Helena has published 18 fiction titles, including three in her latest series, *The Anderssons*, set in Finnish Lapland.

Helena lives in North London with her ex-Navy husband. She loves Nordic Noir and sings along to Abba when no one is around.

Find Helena Halme online
www.helenahalmebooks.com
hello@helenahalme.com

www.ingramcontent.com/pod-product-compliance
Lightning Source LLC
Chambersburg PA
CBHW030524190726

48283CB00006B/1760